DYING TO BE FRENCH

AN AMERICAN IN PARIS MYSTERY BOOK 3

SUSAN KIERNAN-LEWIS

SAN MARCO PRESS

Books by Susan Kiernan-Lewis

The Maggie Newberry Mysteries
Murder in the South of France
Murder à la Carte
Murder in Provence
Murder in Paris
Murder in Aix
Murder in Nice
Murder in the Latin Quarter
Murder in the Abbey
Murder in the Bistro
Murder in Cannes
Murder in Grenoble
Murder in the Vineyard
Murder in Arles
Murder in Marseille
Murder in St-Rémy
Murder à la Mode
Murder in Avignon
Murder in the Lavender
A Provençal Christmas: A Short Story
A Thanksgiving in Provence
Laurent's Kitchen

An American in Paris Mysteries
Déjà Dead
Death by Cliché
Dying to be French
Ménage à Murder
Killing it in Paris

Ella Out of Time
Swept Away
Carried Away
Stolen Away

The French Women's Diet

1

Have you ever had one of those moments when you could actually *see* your life jump the tracks?

That's how I felt when I opened the door of my Paris apartment and the woman my husband had been sleeping with for a year stepped across my threshold jostling a cranky baby in her arms..

"I've been standing out here forever," Courtney said as she looked around my living room. "Wow, this is nice."

My French bulldog Izzy followed Courtney to the couch where my visitor deposited her now squalling infant onto the silk cushions.

I stood there leaning against the door, overwhelmed by a sudden sense of vertigo.

"What...what are you doing here?" I asked as Courtney dropped her shoulder bag onto my coffee table and began to root around in it.

"I know I've got at least one more diaper left in here somewhere. God, what a nightmare! Hey, puppy."

Courtney turned to give Izzy a pat on the head. Even the

baby seemed momentarily distracted by Izzy. He had stopped crying as the dog sniffed him.

Courtney pulled out a diaper from her bag.

"Thank God," she said. "We were nearly down to airport napkins, Bubbie," she said to the baby.

I watched in bewilderment as Courtney quickly cleaned and changed the baby. She turned to me with the soiled diaper.

"Got a place for this?" she asked handing it to me.

Then she turned and sat down on the couch, nearly causing the baby to roll off in the process. Her eyes scanned the room.

I held the disposable diaper and stared at her.

"What are you doing here?" I said again. A knot was forming in my stomach.

"This is really nice," Courtney said, still looking around my living room. "Two bedrooms, right? God. I haven't slept a wink in forever. Mister Wiggins here just never settled down the whole flight."

She stretched, closed her eyes and leaned back into the couch. That's when my eye went to the baby.

So this was Robbie, my husband's child with Courtney Purdue. The child I had no idea existed until three weeks ago.

Robbie was about five months old but he seemed alert and observant as he scanned the room. Izzy licked his hand and made him giggle. I turned my attention back to Courtney.

"You can't stay here," I said.

I'd sent her five thousand dollars two weeks ago because I'd been told she had no family and no job. My family lawyer back in Atlanta warned me not to do it. How could I have been so stupid?

"Well, I don't have the money to stay anywhere else," Courtney said. "I spent most of what you sent me to pay a few bills and then flying here. I had to fly First Class because of the baby. I have no idea how people do it in Economy."

I couldn't believe what I was hearing.

This idiot had spent the money I'd given her on a First Class transatlantic airplane flight? To a city where she knew no one and couldn't afford to live?

"Why did you do that?" I asked, still holding Robbie's dirty diaper in my hands. "Why in the world would you do that?"

"What else was I going to do?" Courtney asked. "Wait. Are you sorry I'm here?" She waved a hand in the direction of the baby. "I brought Robbie for you to see."

"Why in the world?" I said.

"I didn't think you'd be like this," she said with a frown. "Robbie is Bob's baby."

I was speechless. I glanced at the baby again who was now lying very close to the edge of the couch. Courtney stood up and walked to the window.

"I've never been to Paris," she said. "Bob always said he'd take me but then, you know, he died."

I felt lightheaded for a moment.

"Do you even remember who you're talking to?" I said in disbelief.

Courtney turned and folded her arms across her chest to face me. She was tall and very blonde. Her blue eyes snapped dangerously.

"I have no other place to go," she said.

"You don't have *here* to go. I don't know you. We are not related."

She pointed to the baby. "Uh, *duh!*"

"He's no relation to *me*," I said, fighting the impulse to throw the dirty diaper at her.

"I can't believe you're saying this. How heartless can you be?"

"Heartless? I sent you five thousand dollars!"

"Because Robbie is Bob's baby!"

"No, in spite of that!"

"Well, what am I supposed to do now?"

I was at a loss for words for how truly stupid this woman must be to take the one bit of money she'd lucked into and use it to fly to a foreign city to try and move in with the woman she'd wronged!

It went beyond the boundaries of stupid. I literally had never met anyone like her.

What had Bob seen in her?

I went to the kitchen and put the diaper in the trash, then pulled the bag out and set it by the front door.

"You can stay the night," I said. "Tomorrow, you'll go to the US Embassy."

"Will they give me a place to stay?"

"Probably not. But they'll help you get back home."

"Why would I go back home? I just got here!"

"You have no place to live in France!"

I knew I was raising my voice and out of the corner of my eye I could see Robbie begin to fuss.

Courtney and I stood staring at each other and in a flash I got a picture of me trying to explain to my daughter Catherine that her new baby half-brother—who she still had no idea existed—was living with me.

I had a sour taste in my mouth.

I'd put off telling her about Robbie up to now, but that little illusion was clearly about to come to an end. My eyes went again to the baby—*Bob's baby.* He seemed to be watching me, his little face serious until he very slowly smiled at me.

Dear God, how did my life get so complicated?

2

Jean-Marc LaRue stood before the murder board in the debriefing room at the *Préfecture* of Police of Paris on the Île de la Cité. He felt an insistent tightening sensation in his chest. There were a few other detectives in the room. They milled around drinking coffee, talking, laughing, coming and going.

The room housed eight detectives and was used for training classes, an emergency command post and as a place to strategize investigations. A dry erase board was set up at the entrance to the room. There were check marks on it indicating people's schedules and rotations.

This was a passthrough which served sometimes as an ad hoc bullpen where detectives could brainstorm on cases. There were no other murder boards in the room and occasionally the other detectives glanced over at Jean-Marc with curiosity.

Even in the jaded ranks of a major metropolitan police force like Paris, a murder in the expat community was big news.

Jean-Marc pulled himself up to his full height of over six feet and ran a frustrated hand through his dark close-cropped hair as he studied the board.

A photograph of a blonde teen girl was pinned to a map of Paris. The girl, Cecily Danvers, was a student at Le World School de Paris in the fifteenth arrondissement. The map identified the location of Cecily's apartment building, also in the fifteenth arrondissement and just eight blocks from the Eiffel Tower. The map also showed the section of the Seine in the fourth arrondissement where—thirty hours after going missing —Cecily's body was discovered floating face down in the river. She'd been raped and strangled.

Jean-Marc drew a finger from rue St-Charles where Cecily was presumed to have been taken—a main but quiet street on the way home from her school—to where she ended up in the river near Pont Alexandre III.

Did this mean the killer lived somewhere between those sections?

Cecily had left school at fourteen hundred hours on a Friday afternoon and never made it home. Her American parents were separated. Her mother lived with her in Paris and her father in Florida.

When Jean-Marc had first been handed the case as a missing persons case, he'd had some initial thoughts that solving it and finding the girl would finally end his superiors' lingering doubts about him.

Since Cecily Danvers had been fished out of the Seine at twenty hundred hours yesterday, Jean-Marc saw the imagined trajectory of his career path alter significantly.

And not for the better.

Ideally his professional career would benefit from keeping a calm and preferably low profile for awhile. Months at least.

The horrific murder of a young American girl on his watch was the last thing he needed.

"Chief?"

Jean-Marc turned to see that his two sergeants Pierre Caron and Jean Dartre were waiting for him. Both had been teamed with him in the spring on their last homicide case. They had no reason to trust or respect him. He had single-handedly attempted to ruin an illustrious twenty-five-year police career last summer when he'd deliberately hindered the investigation into the murder of an American businessman. Nevertheless both Caron and Dartre had been responsible for helping Jean-Marc get some of his former position and prestige in the department restored.

He owed them.

A big man in his late forties, Sergeant Caron stood beside him before the murder board.

"You think it could be someone who hates Americans?" Caron asked. "Or just a predator?"

Forensics had come back inconclusive. Yes, there was evidence of rape but it was oddly done. Yes, there was DNA left behind but no match on the international criminal database. Yes, the victim was American but there had been no recent evidence of anti-American sentiment in the Paris expat community.

Still the crime was unusual. Not the fact of the murder itself. This was a major metropolitan city after all. But it had been done in the tourist section of Paris, and that rarely happened.

It's almost like the guy is trying to call attention to himself.

And most murderers don't like to do that.

Jean-Marc knew that if he wanted to keep any semblance of his reputation or indeed his career itself, he would need to find her killer soon.

He felt his phone vibrate in his jacket pocket. When he tore his eyes away from the murder board to see who it was, he saw it was an incoming call from his wife. He pushed *Decline* and was about to put his phone away when another call came in.

This time it was from Police Dispatch.

Jean-Marc tensed when he saw the Interdepartmental ID. There were only two reasons why Dispatch would be calling him.

There'd been another murder.

Or another person was missing.

3

The next morning I was up early. As usual.

So, unfortunately, was Robbie. While I was gratified to see that he was already sleeping through the night, it seemed that mornings didn't rate the same courtesy.

After several long minutes of listening to him fuss, I tiptoed into the guest bedroom where Courtney slept with a pile of pillows on her head to ensure the baby's noise wouldn't disrupt her slumber. Robbie had spent the night in a clothes basket full of towels in the corner of the room. As soon as he saw me he began kicking his feet and waving his little fists as if he knew rescue was near.

I only intended to change him, but by the time I'd done that, Izzy was nagging me to be let out and I didn't have the heart to put Robbie back in the clothes basket.

I attached Izzy to her leash and, with Robbie securely in one arm, crept down the slick stairwell to the lobby below.

The apartment building I lived in had been created in the classic Haussmann style and featured massive double doors off a narrow street. The doors hid a charming little courtyard framed with raised stone flowerbeds of geraniums and roses.

It was unusually chilly this morning especially for June. I let Izzy attend to her business in the one small strip of grass near where the building garbage cans were kept.

Robbie clutched at the front of my cardigan and craned his neck as if to try to look at everything at once. I had to admit he seemed a happy baby. Alert too. I looked into his face and easily saw evidence of his father there. Immediately I felt a sharp stab of sorrow. Not just for me, although Bob had betrayed me in the making of this little dear, but also for Robbie who would never know his father.

I wouldn't wish that loss on anyone.

Once back upstairs, I rummaged through Courtney's diaper bag in the living room for the box of formula I'd seen her use yesterday.

I mixed up the formula and fed Robbie while periodically checking on Courtney to make sure she was still alive.

I was torn between indignation and outrage at her boldness by coming to me in Paris, but I knew she was desperate and alone. I wasn't sure what my responsibility was in relation to that. I looked at the baby as he drank his bottle. But what I did know was that this child was Catherine's brother. So I was pretty sure I was supposed to do something.

As Robbie was finishing up his breakfast, my phone dinged and I saw that I'd received a text from my friend Adele Coté. We had arranged to meet for coffee this morning with Geneviève, my downstairs neighbor.

<We still on for today?>

I texted her back. <Yep. Cafe l'Unix>

I glanced at the baby in my arms.

"Sorry, Charlie. This is a girls-only party."

The café at the end of Malsherbes is just a block and a half from my apartment building. It looks like any other café in Paris. There's a serviceable terrace with a view of the busy street and a constant stream of strong coffee by day and wine, beer and Kir by night.

Because it wasn't far from Adele's apartment, the two of us had taken to meeting here more often than not. The place also made a fantastic *croque monsieur*.

It had warmed up so I wore my favorite peasant skirt, a sleeveless tunic and espadrilles. I wear my hair shoulder-length and today I had it tied back and off my neck so I could feel the sun on my face.

My companions Adele Coté and Geneviève Rousseau were thirty and eighty-years old respectively. They were my closest friends in Paris.

Adele sat across from me at our terrace table and stretched out her long legs. She held Robbie on her knees.

"Such a cute little man," she said leaning in to kiss his cheek.

I had tried to wake Courtney up but eventually decided that even if I succeeded I wasn't confident she was awake enough to be responsible for a five-month old baby. Not without a crib, a highchair or any way to secure him while she showered and dressed.

In the end, I decided little Bub could probably use the fresh air.

"Maybe it's time to have one of your own?" I said to Adele.

"Oh, you are *très droll, chérie*," Adele said to me.

A forensic tech thirty years my junior, Adele and I met last summer when the simultaneous tragedies of her brother's and my husband's murders coincided. Because the DNA laboratory she worked for was often called in to relieve the workload in the forensics department of the Paris homicide division, Adele frequently had proprietary information on various criminal cases.

Just as she had when we'd first met and worked together.

Knowing someone who is a forensic tech is a lucky break for me since I make my living as a private investigator here in Paris, working exclusively for the expat community. Although my relationship with the Paris police has improved in the last few months, I still find it helpful to have an outside source willing to provide me with inside forensic intel.

I hadn't seen Adele recently since she'd spent the spring with a new love interest that in the end hadn't made it to summer. I hadn't witnessed any unhappiness on Adele's part as a result of her amorous crash and burn but she didn't tend to be particularly emotional. If she was sorry to see the back of her beau, she didn't show it.

"No babies for me," she said firmly. "I can't even keep a ficus tree alive."

"Babies tend to be a little more demanding than plants," Geneviève said. "Potted plants don't generally scream until they turn blue if you don't water them."

My downstairs neighbor in my apartment building, Geneviève Rousseau, was in her eighties, and probably my closest friend in Paris. And, since I was set to turn sixty-one in less than two months, also my wiser older friend. I watched her now as she observed Adele fawn over little Robbie.

I knew Geneviève had two grown sons somewhere in the world but she never talked about them and I didn't pry. That is seriously unusual for me since, as a private investigator, prying is literally what I do for a living. I talk a lot about my own daughter Catherine and my grandson Cameron so I knew Geneviève's reticence wasn't for fear of boring me. There was a story there. Someday I hoped she'd trust me enough to tell it to me.

"I'm sure I'd be a much better gardener if they did," Adele said, tickling Robbie under his chin.

"How long is his mother going to stay, do you think?" Geneviève asked me.

"Not long if I have anything to say about it."

"Surely you *do* have something to say about it?" Geneviève said.

"You need to be firm, Claire," Adele said, positioning the baby in the crook of her arm so she could reach her demitasse cup. "She will take advantage of you otherwise."

"I'm going to personally escort her to the American embassy," I said, "just as soon as she wakes up."

"That's good," Adele said. "Isn't it, *ma petite*?" she said to the baby.

"Are you sure you don't want to have kids?" I said. "Like this month?"

Adele laughed. "I love *les bébés*. When the time is right I will be ready!"

"Children are a serious responsibility," Geneviève said, sipping her coffee. Again, I sensed there was something more to her words.

"Do you want to hold him?" Adele said to Geneviève. "I feel like I'm hogging him."

"I am fine, *chérie*," Geneviève said.

"Oh, I've been meaning to ask you about the body they fished out of the Seine," I said to Adele. "I don't suppose you worked that?"

Even in a city as large as Paris, the murder had gotten major press. A young girl had gone missing and then quickly ended up murdered and dumped in the Seine.

"No," Adele said, making a face as if sorry she hadn't worked the case. "But I know she was American."

"Really?"

I hadn't heard that. The fact that an American had been killed inside the heartbeat of the most famous tourist city in the world was a big deal. It was tantamount to a stabbing inside Cinderella's Castle at Disney World.

I'm not saying it couldn't happen. But I'm pretty sure the world would never hear about it if it did.

The other interesting thing about this particular crime was the fact that, because of my profession and language proficiency, I tended to be involved in any and all unfortunate situations affecting the non-French community. At least those affecting the UK and the US expatriates who made Paris their home.

If the victim really had been American, I wondered why I hadn't been informed through my usual expat sources?

"Was she a tourist?" I asked.

Adele shook her head. "No. Her family lives in Paris."

"How did she die?"

"Strangled."

I literally felt a physical reaction to Adele's words. First, because a murder in the expat community was bad enough, but a teen girl? I wondered again why I hadn't heard about it before now.

"How long had she been missing?" I asked. "Was there a ransom request?"

"I don't know," Adele said.

I tapped my nails against the table. If the girl *had* gone missing first, it would have been odd if Laura Murphy, the head of the expat community in Paris had not reached out to me for help in finding her. Finding missing people was ninety-nine percent of the work I did as a private investigator.

It also occurred to me that Jean-Marc must be working the case. He was the police department's acting *Inspecteur principal* for all homicides and major crimes in Paris.

My phone began to vibrate and I looked at the screen and felt a shiver of apprehension when I saw the number there.

It was from Laura Murphy.

"Hey, Laura. What's up?" I said, answering the call.

"I've got a job for you," Laura said, her voice low, as if she was afraid of being overheard. "Can you meet?"

I glanced at Adele and Geneviève who were both looking at me and frowning as if they could tell the call was a serious one.

"What's the case?" I asked.

Laura hesitated before speaking.

"Missing person," she said. "A young girl."

4

"I need to go," I said, standing up.

"What is it, *chérie*?" Geneviève said.

"It's a missing-persons," I said, tossing down five euros to cover our drinks. I stopped when I saw Robbie in Adele's arms. "Crap."

"Do not worry, *chérie*," Geneviève said before turning to Adele. "Can you carry him to my apartment?" She turned back to me. "You can pick him and Izzy up when you are done."

"Thank you," I said, feeling ashamed about making Geneviève take Robbie when she clearly wanted nothing to do with him. "I won't be long."

"Call me later and fill me in on the details," Adele said.

I promised then leaned over and kissed both her and Geneviève before turning and hurrying down the sidewalk in the direction of Laura's office.

My mind was buzzing as I walked down the boulevard Haussmann. Laura had stressed that the media knew nothing about the new abduction and with a body recently recovered from the Seine, it was important that they didn't.

. . .

Laura's office building was probably erected sometime in the fourteen hundreds. Like so much of Paris, it was ancient but still going strong.

Sounds like my new tagline.

The office building was a classic Haussmann complete with cream-colored exterior, a hidden courtyard, black shutters, wrought-iron Juliette balconies on the façade, and a mansard roof.

Once past the building's impressive marbled foyer and rocketing ceiling, there was a contemporary feel to the interior. After all, lawyers and architects and other high-flying professionals had to do business and see their clients here. They could hardly do it with an ambience of flickering gas lamps.

As I rode up to Laura's office in the building elevator, I felt a tiny flutter of guilt. I wondered when that sensation would leave me. I'd felt it for weeks now whenever I had dealings with Laura.

The fact is Laura had every reason to hate me. Earlier this spring I'd made her life miserable during what had already been an extremely bad week for her. Since then she'd surprised me by acting as if nothing had happened. Perhaps it was as a result of what we'd endured together that she was now more impressed with my tenacity and investigative skills than with her grievance against me. I don't know. I do know that a real friendship between us is probably impossible. But I also know she'd given me the bulk of my business since I'd move to Paris.

Laura answered the door with a business-like smile, She was in her late forties, petite and blonde. I imagined that she was also the sort of person who didn't miss a single Botox, hair or nail appointment. I had to admit she looked fabulous. But it sometimes made me tired just thinking of how much effort it took.

She gave me a perfunctory kiss on both cheeks and then turned and led me to her desk.

"The girl's name is Haley Johnson," she said. "She's seventeen. Her parents are Cindy and William Johnson. They're divorced and the father lives in the States. Haley was seen leaving school at two o'clock yesterday afternoon but didn't arrive home. She had a piano lesson at four o'clock so her mother was immediately aware that something was wrong."

"She's been missing nearly twenty-four hours," I said.

I preferred being informed earlier but parents often didn't know their child was missing for several hours.

"Yes, well, the police were informed immediately of course and are following whatever leads they have. But Cindy—I know her from Pilates class—knew I knew someone who specialized in expat missing persons."

"How is Haley connected to the girl whose body was found in the Seine yesterday?" I asked bluntly.

Laura looked instantly guarded.

"They went to the same school. Le World School de Paris."

My heart sank when she said that. Any hope of this being a coincidence extinguished like a match being blown out.

"I can't do it, Laura," I said.

It wasn't the thought of a missing teen case. I've done more than a few of those over the last year. But a runaway kid is one thing. A girl who went missing on her way home from school was another. And a girl who went missing three days after another girl was found face-down in the Seine was something else altogether. I didn't want to even breathe the words *serial killing*. But even without going down that road the one thing I had which *normally* made me an excellent finder of children was a mother's instinct.

And that was precisely the thing that told me today I was out of my depth.

"What?" Laura blinked in surprise.

I could see I'd thrown her. I don't think I've ever turned

down a single case she's offered me. I'm sure she was thinking the same thing.

"I'm sorry," I said, trying to think of a good excuse that would make sense to her.

"The detective assigned to the case is Detective Inspector LaRue," Laura said as if that might encourage me to rethink my answer.

Laura knew that Jean-Marc LaRue was a friend of mine. But if she thought that would change my mind, she was mistaken.

"Look," I said, "I'm horrified that this has happened to this family. Truly horrified. But I can't do it."

Laura studied my face for a moment before nodding.

"I understand," she said. "As you know, I never had children but I understand. It would help me if you would at least meet with Cindy." She held up a hand to stop me from speaking. "Don't take the case. That's fine. But there might be something you can say to her that will help."

My shoulders sagged.

The last thing I wanted to do was talk with a woman experiencing the worst thing that any mother can experience.

"Sure. Okay," I said. I felt a wave of foreboding sweep over me.

"I've set up a meeting with her—and her husband Bill via Zoom—in my apartment for seven this evening."

"Okay."

"And Claire?"

I was half-standing on my way out the door.

"I'm almost positive you're stronger than you think you are," she said.

Spoken like a woman who has never had children.

But I smiled as if her words had helped.

5

I took my time on the way home, skipping the Métro in favor of a long walk. A text from Geneviève assured me that Robbie was asleep, curled up with Izzy in her dog basket on Geneviève's living room floor.

I hadn't gotten any messages from Courtney.

It's true I'd left Courtney a note before I went to meet Adele and Geneviève for coffee, but it was still odd that she hadn't reached out to me.

Wasn't it?

Forcing myself not to think of "the Courtney Problem," I paused in front of the French household and grocery super-store Monoprix before deciding I needed to go in and pick up diapers, more formula, and baby wipes. While there I also loaded up on pastries and a few ready-made meals. While it was true I didn't know how long Courtney would be with me, I didn't want to be constantly running out for Nutella crepes and Parisienne sandwiches for as long as she was.

I'd forgotten how bulky disposable diapers were. They took up three-fourths of the space in my shopping bag as I trudged out of the store in the direction of my apartment building.

It was inconceivable to me that Courtney would stay for long—if for no other reason than she wouldn't want to. What kind of life was it living in your dead boyfriend's widow's guest room? In a country where you didn't speak the language?

No, whatever harebrained motivation had made Courtney think it had been a good idea get on that plane, she would soon see—if she hadn't already—what a mistake it was.

I glanced at my phone. It was nearly two in the afternoon, meaning it was eight in the morning Atlanta time. Catherine would have just gotten little Cameron up for school and was probably rushing around like mad getting ready for her day.

Not the best time to call and tell her about Robbie.

As I turned down my street, rue de Laborde, an image flashed in my head reminding me of the time not long ago when this narrow lane was clogged with three police cars and the loud bray of an obstreperous, overbearing detective determined to arrest me for a crime she had every reason to know I hadn't committed.

It was amazing to me that that whole terrible experience had ended only a month ago.

And it ended definitively with Detective Superintendent Millicent Elicé's suspicious death by a drug overdose in Nice just a week later.

I still couldn't believe Elicé killed herself.

Which is just another way of saying I'm not sure she wasn't murdered.

The fact was, murder or not, Elicé died under suspicious circumstances. But every time I tried to discuss it with Jean-Marc, he shut down and refused to talk about it.

Which only made my imagination go into hyperdrive.

When I think of Elicé and her determination to put me in prison for life I inevitably think of my stepmother Joelle Lapin.

And that's because Joelle was supposedly the reason Elicé had developed her psychotic enmity against me.

Or so I'd been led to believe.

That part was all a little muddy. Elicé's murky connection to Joelle was weirdly coincidental all by itself but making it even weirder was the fact of who Joelle was to me. She was the wife of the man I'd always thought was my father but who turned out not to be. Unfortunately for Joelle, legal or not, she still lost her inheritance to me.

So yes, Joelle hates me. And Joelle is connected either by accident or deliberation to the unseen force I blame for my husband's murder.

Phillipe Moreau. My biological father.

Once I found out that Claude Lapin, Joelle's husband, was not in fact my real father–which was a huge shock, let me tell you—I immediately began to connect the dots.

First, my husband Bob was murdered and the one who killed him vanished just before I received a mysterious text message that seemed to take credit for his murder.

As if the writer of the text felt he'd done me a big favor by having Bob killed.

So far my efforts to track down Phillipe Moreau have failed. Because I'm so good at what I do, that in itself tells me Moreau is wily and two steps ahead.

Not the sorts of traits you normally think of when describing a good person.

I can't draw a straight line from my biological father to Bob's murder or even Millicent Elicé's attempts to railroad me last spring but that doesn't mean I think the connection isn't there because I do—even without evidence or proof.

Call it a daughter's intuition.

In any case, I could do nothing about any of that at the moment. I had my hands plenty full just trying to figure out what I was going to do with the fact that I had my deceased husband's girlfriend and her baby living on my couch for the foreseeable future.

6

The cool morning breeze had withered away leaving the day still and hot.

Jean-Marc had originally only stepped out to get some badly needed air and a change of scenery. He and Caron and Dartre had gone in circles for the last several hours with the new missing girl and the forensic details attached to Cecily Danvers' murder.

He needed to clear his head. But when he left the *préfecture* he found himself walking to his car and heading to the eighth arrondissement.

With the news of the latest missing girl—another student snatched on her way home from the same school Cecily Danvers had attended— Jean-Marc and his team had begun sleeping at the department. What few leads they had—either for Cecily's murder or Haley Johnson's kidnapping—were being systematically and relentlessly pursued.

His team had talked to every teacher—male and female—at the two girls' school. They'd taken the headmaster's statement and had already logged countless hours with the parents of both girls. Well, at least with the mothers. Each of the girls—

both American—lived only with their mothers while their fathers lived offshore.

Are the murders connected? Jean-Marc wondered as he found a parking spot near Claire's apartment. How could they not be? Both American, both from the same school, both nabbed from a public street.

He felt a chisel of dread deep in his gut.

Am I looking at a serial killer?

He shook the thought from his mind. He needed to focus on the facts, not suppositions. His brain just needed a brief respite from the grind, the constant conversations with Dartre and Caron about the cases—from the irresistible, irrefutable fact that the two cases couldn't conceivably *not* be connected.

He just needed a moment to see the woman whose smile brightened his day and soothed his troubled soul.

When she wasn't the one troubling it.

He walked to the corner of rue de Laborde, expecting to make his way to her apartment, when he recognized her familiar form striding down the sidewalk.

So American, he thought as he watched her. *She walks with determination as if she owns the sidewalk. It's not feminine particularly but it is resolutely sexy.*

As much as he tended to pull apart every aspect, every concept and insinuation pertaining to his job, he deliberately worked just as hard not to indulge in those propensities when it came to Claire.

Or frankly Chloe, for that matter.

It was complicated, yes. And dangerous. That was all he needed to know for now. Except perhaps for the awareness that seeing Claire and being her friend—*if that's what we are*—was worth the danger.

He raised a hand in greeting and was pleased to see her stop when she spotted him. A smile spread across her face that warmed him from deep inside. She held in her arms a large bag of groceries and he went to her and kissed her in greeting on both cheeks and took the bag from her.

"I didn't expect to see you!" she said, her beautiful face flushed with delight.

It was all Jean-Marc could do not to kiss her again and this time with meaning.

"I had a free moment," he said. "And I wanted to let you know that I'm going to be hard to reach for the foreseeable future."

"It's about the girl's body in the Seine, isn't it? Do you have any leads? Can you stop long enough for a coffee?"

He glanced at his watch and then nodded toward a café down the block.

As soon as they were settled at a table, Jean-Marc noticed he already felt better, less tense. He pushed the details of the case further to the back of his mind, telling himself that by taking a break like this he was actually helping the possibility that a dormant fact might leap up from the depths of his brain.

"You're not going to believe my news," Claire said.

"Shall I guess?"

"You couldn't in a thousand years. My husband's girlfriend showed up on my doorstep last night." Claire said.

She wore a pale blue V-neck sweater. It was perfect against her golden complexion. If he didn't know for sure that she was from the American South, he would have sworn she was the epitome of the California girl.

"I am impressed, *chérie,*" he said. "Even the French don't tend to raise their mistresses' children—or ask their wives to do it. You have taken the *laissez-faire* French attitude toward affairs too far. Typical of Americans."

She crinkled up her eyes and laughed.

He'd have given anything to have had the right to take her hand or kiss that beautiful mouth.

But he did not have the right.

"What else have you been up to?" he asked as the waiter brought their coffees. "Aside from breaking all the rules of betrayed wives everywhere?"

"Ha ha," she said wryly. "But I'd rather talk about what *you've* been up to. Are you working on the Haley Johnson case?"

He looked at her in surprise. "How the hell did you know that?"

"Laura Murphy told me. She's in contact with Haley's parents."

Jean-Marc ran a hand through his hair.

"I've been with them all morning," he said. "Or at least the mother. The father resides in Texas."

"I'm supposed to meet with them this evening."

"Don't do it, *chérie*. This is a bad one."

"Is it like the other girl?"

Her question included the unspoken phrase: *the one found dead in the river.*

"You know I can't tell you that. Promise me you won't take this as a case."

"I told you, I have no intention of taking it."

"Which is not a promise."

"I promise I won't take it."

"*Bon.* I must go."

He sighed. He wanted to reach out and take her in his arms but he could count on one hand the number of times he'd done that. And in every situation something terrible had happened to justify it. This was a public street. As much as he might want to, he wouldn't.

"I just can't imagine the horror," Claire said, shaking her head, clearly still thinking about the parents.

"I mean it, *chérie*," he said, as he stood up and tossed a few euros on the table. "You cannot solve this one and it will break you if you try."

7

It helped seeing Jean-Marc. If even for just a few minutes. I grant that ours must be the strangest relationship in the history of dalliances, but I can't deny that seeing him even briefly made me feel better and more grounded. I don't know if that's love since I'm not sure those emotions have ever been the byproducts of any romantic endeavor I've ever experienced. But whatever it is, it's very nice.

My first stop was Geneviève's apartment where I collected Izzy and Robbie and brought them and my bag of groceries up to my apartment.

When I crossed my threshold I saw my kitchen was piled high with dirty dishes and empty soft drink bottles but no pans. Courtney had clearly only eaten what was ready to eat.

"There you are!" she called from the living room where she sat with my laptop. "I wondered where you all got to!"

"I would ask if you've eaten," I said, depositing Robbie in her arms, "but I can see you have."

"Hello, Mister McGoo-Goo," Courtney said to the baby. "Oh! He needs changing."

I fished the packet of disposable diapers out of the grocery bag and set it on the couch beside her.

"Don't change him on the couch, please," I said.

"I'll just spread down a towel," she said, unsnapping his onesie. "Do you have a towel I can use?"

I felt a vein throbbing in my forehead.

"Please don't change him on the couch," I repeated. "It's too late to visit the embassy today so you'll need to go first thing in the morning."

"I was just so jet-lagged!" Courtney said. "And I couldn't figure out how to work your stupid French cable TV. And what's your Wi-Fi password?"

I bit my tongue and counted to ten. I heard her take Robbie into the bedroom.

"I'll prepare the sink in the bathroom," I said, "if you want to give him a bath."

"No, he had one last week," Courtney said. "He's good."

I washed my hands before turning to go into the guest room where she had him stripped and laying on a cardigan sweater on the guest bed. He waved his arms and legs playfully.

"Give him to me," I said. "I'll do it."

"I can tell he really likes you," Courtney said hurrying back to the living room and her laptop. "Did you bring any snacks?"

I put my hand on Robbie to ensure he wasn't about to roll off the bed, and he smiled at me. I swear Courtney acted like she was doing me a favor by allowing me to bathe Robbie or change him or feed him. Like these were all things a woman of my age must be longing to do.

"Your mama is very silly woman," I said to Robbie and then felt instantly guilty. Silly or not, she was who he was stuck with. I very nearly said *But you have me,* but stopped myself in time. He did *not* have me. I'm sure he will someday have all kinds of wonderful influences in his life—teachers and what not—but I could not be a part of that group.

As I carried him into the bathroom to prepare the bathroom sink for his bath, it occurred to me that Catherine might be one of those loving influences in his life.

I looked at him and imagined how much he would adore my daughter. How in his life he would look to Catherine as the aunt to his children and perhaps even as a sort of mother. I felt glad for Robbie that he would have Catherine in his life.

Now I just needed to tell Catherine.

That evening when I got ready to leave for Laura's, Courtney had the affront to be miffed that I was leaving her for the evening. She was vaguely mollified by my making dinner—veal chops with mustard sauce—and showing her how to get Netflix on the television.

I fed Izzy, took her down to the courtyard to wet the pavers, and then left feeling insecure and uneasy about leaving Robbie behind—which was ridiculous since Courtney had kept him alive and healthy for the past five months.

I took a taxi to Laura's apartment. She lived in my same arrondissement so I could easily have walked but it looked like it might rain.

When I arrived at Laura's apartment I took a moment to ground myself. An extremely distraught woman was on the other side of that door and I needed to be calm and measured so I could help in any way I could.

Inside was a woman going through the very worst thing any mother can experience.

From the moment Laura opened her door to me, I felt the tension and the fear pour out of the apartment as thick and palpable as a living thing.

My stomach soured with dread and a low-grade panic as I followed Laura into her salon.

Cindy Johnson was a dark blonde with heavily kohled and startling blue eyes. She had a fragility to her that I've come to believe many men are attracted to.

I shook hands with her and saw the emotions I expected to see in her face.

Desperation, grief, and heartbreaking love so big and hopeless it hurt to look at her.

"Thank you so much for meeting with us," Cindy said.

"Of course."

I sat on the couch next to Cindy. Laura sat opposite us. On the coffee table was a laptop. A man's face was visible on the screen.

"I'm Bill Johnson," he said. "Haley's father."

"Pleased to meet you," I said. I took in a breath and turned to Cindy. I reached for her hands. They were cold and clammy.

"What did the police tell you?" I asked.

"Nothing!" Bill barked from the laptop. "They're useless. Totally incompetent. They don't even have a foreign liaison office and we can't speak their damn language!"

"I sent someone with them," Laura told me, "but the homicide detectives wouldn't allow her into the interview room."

I felt a wave of annoyance and wondered if that had been Jean-Marc's call.

"When did you last see Haley?" I asked.

"When she left for school this morning," Cindy said, her hands trembling in mine. "I told her to have a good day. She was worried about a math test. Math isn't her strong suit."

"She doesn't care about that!" Bill said. "Tell her the facts. She left the apartment at seven hundred hours. She was seen leaving school at fourteen hundred hours."

"Did she walk home with anyone?" I asked.

"Don't you think we'd have talked to them if she had?" Bill said.

I was tempted to close the laptop but reminded myself that Cindy wasn't the only one having a really bad day. Haley's father was five thousand miles away in Austin, Texas, while his worst moments as a father were playing out.

I hated to ask this next question because it truly was the monster in the room. But I couldn't take the chance that they'd been asked by Jean-Marc's people but hadn't understood.

"Did Haley know Cecily Danvers?" I asked.

Cindy pulled her hand from mine and clapped both hands to her face. I gave her as much time as she needed to pull herself together.

The last thing anyone wanted was to be reminded of the connection between the two girls, considering what had happened to Cecily.

"Of course they knew each other!" Bill said. "It's a small school. Everybody knows everyone."

"How many students are in the school?" I asked, hoping the question would serve to relax Cindy a little. I often found comfort or at least distraction in numbers and facts.

"Around two hundred," Cindy said. She looked at Laura and Laura confirmed the number with a nod.

"Do you have a picture of Haley?" I asked, wondering if Laura had told them that I wouldn't be able to take the case.

Cindy pulled out her phone and scrolled until she found one and turned it around to show me.

Haley was blonde with a broad smile of perfect white teeth. She wore her hair long and tucked behind her pierced ears.

"Can you help us, Claire?" Cindy asked, her face tear-stained and haunted. "Can you help us find our baby?"

I looked from her to Laura who deliberately looked away.

"Mrs. Johnson," I said, "*Cindy*. I'm happy to interface with you and the police. I can promise they won't throw *me* out."

"We don't need a damn translator!" Bill shouted. "We need someone to find Haley!"

This was worse than I imagined. Why did I ever agree to talk with them? How was this helping anyone?

"I'm sorry," I said. "But I'm not able to take this on as a missing person's case."

I didn't want to even *think* about the similarities between Haley's disappearance and Cecily Danvers because of what those similarities might mean for Haley's chances of coming home safely.

"But why?" Cindy asked.

"It's beyond my abilities," I said honestly.

"You think whoever took Cecily has our Haley, too, don't you?" Cindy said, her bottom lip trembling.

"I don't know," I said, reaching for her hand again. "Did the police not tell you anything of what they would do next?"

"They said they'd let us know," Bill said.

"She won't help us, Bill," Cindy said, pulling her hand again from mine, her face suddenly blank and unanimated.

"Bitch!" Bill said. "I'd love to see something like this happen to you!"

"I'm so sorry," I said.

Laura stood up, hugging herself with her arms, her eyes drilling into me. I stood up too and picked up my purse. I didn't dare apologize again. These people deserved more than an apology and I didn't blame them for hating me.

A part of me hated me too.

8

T he next morning I dressed for rain.
I'd bundled up Izzy in her little rain jacket—
which frankly she detests—for our daily walk to the
park and set out right after my morning coffee. I was pushing
the stroller that I'd bought at Monoprix on the way to the park
and felt frankly ridiculous at my age. But I couldn't leave
Robbie in the apartment with Courtney not awake yet.

After stepping through the ornately scrolled and gilded
wrought iron park gates of Parc Monceau, I went to the first
bench I came to with a nice view of the carousel.

One of the things I like best about Parc Monceau is that it
can be anything you're in the mood for. It's got all the mani-
cured grace of a perfect French garden with lawns and wrought
iron fences hemming in riotous expanses of glorious flowers.
But in the midst of all that order and studious control is the
very picture of playful fantasy evoked by arching stone bridges
over ponds filled with ducks.

I really needed a little fantasy this morning.

Unfortunately the memory of how unhappy I'd made
Cindy and Bill Johnson last night—not to mention Laura—

kept interfering with my attempts to enjoy the beautiful morning in one of Paris's loveliest parks.

I looked over at Robbie propped up in his stroller. His eyes seemed to follow the birds and his little head snapped around at every snatch of laughter from the children playing in the park. It was easy to see Bob's features in Robbie's face. I wondered more about his personality.

Not that Bob had been born a liar, of course. In my whole experience with him—up until the end—I'd never thought he was deceitful at all. But somehow, perhaps after years in the advertising business, my husband had learned to lie and lie well. I watched Robbie clap his hands in delight at a nearby butterfly.

No, Robbie Perdue was a blank canvas right now. A canvas to be written on by his hapless mother and anybody else who would become a part of his life. Catherine. Perhaps myself. And of course whoever Courtney ended up with in the boyfriend department.

I felt a tingling of dread in my chest at the thought.

In spite of the fact that Courtney and I had ultimately chosen the same man to fall in love with, I didn't have a lot of faith in who she would choose next.

I shook the thought from my mind. I had absolutely no control over what Courtney did or who she did it with or how she raised this child. The fact that Robbie looked a little like Bob was just one irrelevant fact among the thousands that clogged my mind in a typical day.

Not my problem.

A little boy ran over to where I sat, his hand outstretched to pet Izzy, but he looked at me first for permission. I smiled and he knelt in order to give her his full attention. Izzy promptly rolled over on her back. He laughed as he scratched her tummy.

"*Elle est belle,*" he said to me. Then he looked up and locked eyes with Robbie who was watching him and smiling ear to ear.

"*Garçon chanceux!*" the boy said before hopping up and running off.

Garçon chanceux. Lucky boy.

I put my hand on Robbie's head and he turned and smiled at me, a long thread of drool dripping from his mouth to the front of his little t-shirt.

I hope so, I thought. *I hope very much that you'll be a lucky boy.*

I remembered well when Catherine was this age and while she had looked more like me than Bob and so physically didn't resemble Robbie, aren't all babies basically the same? At least happy babies? Which Robbie clearly was.

Bob and I had talked about having a second child and I can't remember now why we didn't. My memory seems to suggest that Bob had always felt that the time wasn't right.

I want to be fair but I know I'd have loved a second child.

I had a girlfriend who had three daughters before she and her husband were surprised with an unexpected pregnancy and that one, finally, a boy.

My friend told me she was ill-equipped to raise a boy after three girls, offering as proof the fact that she'd given her baby a treasured family toy that all three of her girls had played with as toddlers.

She said within five seconds of putting his hands on the toy her son had gleefully cracked it into six pieces

So yeah, boys were different.

I grinned at Robbie who grinned back, blinking into the sun but not minding a bit.

I think I would've loved trying one of my own.

Izzy gave a brief yap at a squirrel who dared to venture too close and Robbie snapped his head around to see.

Yes, it was a perfect morning—in spite of my difficulty in

vanquishing all thoughts of last night—and so it was a good time to do something difficult and potentially unpleasant. Not that I always seek to ruin perfectly lovely moments but I do think that bitter-tasting medicine does go down better with a spoonful sugar.

It's the Mary Poppins in me, I guess.

I picked up my phone and punched in Catherine's number, knowing the time difference was fine.

"Hey, Mom," Catherine answered breathlessly. "Everything okay?"

I normally didn't call at this time of day and I could relate to her wanting to make sure there were no life-altering bombshells hiding in the phone call.

Little did she know.

"Everything's fine, darling. What did I catch you doing?"

"Todd just left for work and I'm getting Cameron's breakfast ready. But he doesn't get up for another hour. What are you doing?"

"I'm enjoying a lovely morning with Izzy at Parc Monceau," I said.

"Oh, I can't wait to meet Izzy some day," she said. "And that park! You always talk about it. It feels like forever since we've seen each other."

I'd flown to Florida for Christmas and she'd promised they would come to Paris for a spring visit. That hadn't happened.

"I know. I miss you too," I said.

I think parents have to be careful when telling their adult children how much they miss them in case the kids translate the comment to mean the parent is dissatisfied with how much attention they're getting. The last thing I wanted Catherine to think was that I spent my time sitting around Paris hoping she'd call or visit me.

"Todd thinks we'll be good to visit maybe around October," Catherine said.

I could hear the hedging in her voice and knew it would

never happen. October was too close to Thanksgiving which—although Catherine had no real family except me—would be reason enough for Todd to insist they stay home.

And then it would be Christmas and then it would be too cold in France compared to Jacksonville, Florida and from there it would be some other excuse from Todd.

It is what it is, I told myself. She married him. It could always be worse.

And in my business, didn't I know it.

"There is one thing, darling," I said, my eyes on Robbie as he leaned over the stroller front bar in an attempt to reach Izzy with his hand.

"Something good I hope?" Catherine said.

"Well, I think so," I said. "And I really hope you do too."

9

D o I turn here? Is this the way I came?
For a minute nothing looked familiar and it took a moment to see the recognizable signs.

Reaching out with a hand against the rough texture of the building for support—it was necessary to take a moment to breathe in and out—but also to relish what had just happened, to relive the exquisite bliss of it all...

The girl's screams still seemed to ring in the air.

I shouldn't have been so afraid with the first one that she'd be overheard. It was so much better when you could hear them beg.

There was a tingling sensation that seemed to be all-encompassing, on every part of the body at the memory of the girl's panicked whimpers.

Why didn't I think of it before?

It was textbook.

Engage all the senses. Not just taste and touch and what you can see—although those had of course been magnificent.

But listening too.

I should have recorded it. But no, as blissful as it might be to enjoy at my leisure something like that would be hard to explain if the cops ever got close.

Who am I kidding?

As if that were remotely likely.

The laugh welled up and expanded from the throat to chest until it burst out in one joyous ejaculation too powerful to contain.

10

Robbie fell asleep twice in the park but by the third time he was awakened by the strident shrieks of nearby playing children, I decided it was time to head back home.

During that time I discovered that even sitting on a park bench for an hour can overtire you if your emotions are allowed to run wild.

Catherine had not taken the news well.

Or, at least, I think the news about Robbie specifically had gotten lost in the general news that her father had sired another child. I don't know what I was expecting from my usually taciturn and rational daughter—or what poor Cam must have thought to hear his mother screaming—but I was not expecting her to throw a tantrum reminiscent of when she was five years old.

"I will hate him forever! I will never mention his name again to Cam! He's dead to me!"

I wisely refrained from pointing out that Bob was in fact dead to all of us. While I'd hoped Catherine could have been a little less emotional about it, I knew she needed to vent.

I also felt incredibly guilty.

Me, who *hadn't* had an affair and given birth to a child outside my marriage! *Me,* who'd done nothing but been done to! What did I have to feel guilty about?

But therein lies the job of all mothers everywhere.

As much as it hurt to hear Catherine so upset, I actually felt a little better after hearing her tirade.

I'm sure both Cindy and Bill Johnson would give anything to hear a similar one from Haley about now. At least my only child was alive and kicking. And screaming.

Besides, in time Catherine would get over her fury. She wouldn't be angry at her father forever. And when she met Robbie, I was sure she'd be open to having a relationship with him.

I knew my daughter.

I stopped at the Frère Café a few blocks from my apartment and ordered a *pain au chocolat* and a coffee and let Robbie and Izzy split the little butter cookie that came with my coffee. I could see that most of Robbie's drooling problem seemed to be because he was teething and was astonished that it hadn't resulted in more tears up to now.

I have to say that in the process of pushing Robbie's stroller down the sidewalk—and I found this to be true in the park too —I noted that I'd gotten a fair amount of approving nods from people I passed. I was clearly too old to be this baby's mother and so presumably I must be his *grandmère* and was thereby accorded all the benefits of that status. I have to say it felt good.

I surprised myself with how easy it was to sit in a café and enjoy my coffee, basking in the beautiful weather and smiling my thanks at people who complimented me on how handsome and well behaved my *petit-fils*—grandson—was.

I was in no hurry to get home. I'd left a detailed note for Courtney about how to catch the Métro to the Châtelet Les Halles and from there directions to the US Embassy. I reminded her to bring her passport and that I would watch Robbie for the day.

I think a part of me was putting off returning to the apartment because I feared I'd find Courtney still in bed. What would I do in that case? Was there any legal support for me in evicting a stranger from my apartment? I glanced at Robbie working hard at gnawing on his half of the butter cookie.

Could I even do that? What was the process of someone being kicked out of the country? Would they put Robbie in a holding cell with Courtney?

I couldn't let that happen.

My phone dinged, heralding an incoming text and I felt a spike of anticipation that it might be from Jean-Marc. I knew he was busy these days and I certainly didn't want to do anything to interfere with that. The sooner he gathered the appropriate clues on poor Cecily Danvers' murder the faster he would be able to identify her killer and find Haley Johnson.

Still it did occur to me that an *I'm-thinking-of-you* text would hardly derail his case.

The text was from Laura Murphy.

I felt a wince of guilt when I saw it, fully expecting a virtual tongue-lashing for the meeting last night. Even though I'd told her ahead of time I wouldn't take the case, I still felt I deserved her rancor.

I opened her text.

Five words.

And each one drove a spike of dread into my heart.

<Have u seen the news>

My stomach clenching, I opened the Google News app on my phone. I didn't have to search for it. It was the lead story.

American schoolgirl's body pulled from Seine.

11

A t seventeen hundred hours the light on the Seine was golden.

It temporarily masked the sick green swirl of the river water, which was choked as usual with swirling trash and debris.

Pont d'Alma was a utilitarian bridge, Jean-Marc noted. Unlike the other bridges along the Seine, it was basic metal with a low guard rail and nothing particularly decorative to recommend it.

Except for the view, of course.

Jean-Marc glanced up at the Eiffel Tower looming in the near distance across the river.

Quintessentially Parisian.

Was that the whole point? Dropping the body on this spot to remind everyone that this was happening in the most famous city in the world?

Or was it just because the school where the girl was snatched from was nearby?

Jean-Marc felt a heaviness in his limbs and a persistent lack of mental energy.

He glanced at the body on the pavement. Unlike Pont Alexandre III where Cecily Danvers' body had been found, there was no easy access around Pont D'Alma. Haley Johnson's body had been found floating in the water at the base of the stone embankment that rose to meet avenue de New York. The forensic team had had to haul the body up the stone roadway to the street which Jean-Marc's team had cordoned off.

Jean-Marc squared his shoulders and put away his phone. The call with his superior Commandant Bulie had been brief and to the point. He had asked Jean-Marc for a quick update of the scene and whether Jean-Marc felt he was up for the job.

Two girls missing. Two girls dead.

It's official.

There is a serial killer in Paris preying on the expat community.

Jean-Marc knew his supervisor's lack of confidence was a direct reference to "the incident" last summer and his subsequent disgrace. While it was true that Jean-Marc was the "acting" *Inspecteur Principal, it was only* because Millicent Elicé the last *Inspecteur Principal* had screwed up even worse than he had.

The medical examiner Janine Bedard surrounded by her technicians was kneeling by the girl's body. Bedard was late thirties and attractive. Trim, petite, with grey probing eyes. Not unlike her surgical instruments.

Jean-Marc knew she didn't like him. She remembered him from a few cases last year during which he hadn't behaved particularly well. In fact, he'd been criminally negligent.

The temperature had fallen with the approach of evening. There were even a few wisps of fog hovering close to the stone walkway near where the body lay. Jean-Marc felt a wave of sadness.

Haley Johnson had shown up the same way as the first girl —thirty hours after the abduction, raped, strangled, dumped in the Seine.

Both were American. Both had attended *Le World School de Paris*.

Sergeant Caron stood between Jean-Marc and the medical examiner. He turned to Jean-Marc, the expression on his face a clear depiction of his unspoken question: *Are we still on the case?*

Would he be asking that if I were anyone else? Jean-Marc couldn't help but wonder as he approached the medical examiner.

Would he ever be able to overcome what had happened last summer? Would his colleagues ever forget?

No matter how many second chances he was given?

And didn't poor Cecily Danvers and Haley Johnson deserve better than him?

12

The first thing I did was call Laura. The news story didn't identify the girl beyond the fact that she was a teenager. No name, no nationality.

Laura answered immediately.

"Is it Haley?" I asked, holding my breath.

"Cindy has been asked to come to police headquarters to identify a body," Laura said.

Bile began to burn at the back of my throat.

If the police had asked her to come down, they must be pretty sure. My skin crawled at the thought of what Cindy was going through at this moment.

The daughter they'd asked for my help in finding last night had in all likelihood already been dead.

"I'll call Jean-Marc," I told Laura, although that certainly would help nobody at this point. If it *was* Haley, Cindy would hear everything the police knew herself.

After hanging up with Laura I paid my bill at the café. But before I could gather up leashes, purses and diaper bags, my phone rang again.

"Have you seen the news?" Adele said.

"Did you work the scene?" I asked breathlessly. *Forget Jean-Marc*, I thought. Everything I got out of him would have to be dug out with a hammer and chisel. If Adele had worked the crime scene, she was all the source I needed.

"I did," Adele said. "They pulled her out around twenty-two hundred hours. I'm back home now. She's in the morgue being identified by her mother."

My stomach clenched again at the thought of what Cindy was doing—going through the worst experience any parent can endure.

"Are the cops thinking it's a serial killer?" I asked.

It was an obvious question. Two schoolgirls nabbed in the same way from the same school? Both killed and dumped in the Seine?

"Are you investigating this?" Adele asked. "Did Laura get you to—"

"No. I'm...I'm just interested."

"Okay. Well, there was evidence of this one having been bound like the first one. Her wrists were rubbed raw. Evidence of rape too, like the first one."

I swallowed hard. I hadn't realized Cecily had been raped.

"Strangled and dumped about three hours after death," Adele said. "So right at thirty hours from when she was taken. Like the first one."

"Any DNA?" I asked.

"If you're asking me if she was raped by the same guy only the ME and the detective on the case know that."

Jean-Marc.

"Did you pull any prints?"

"This guy is careful."

"So is that a no?"

"I need to know why you're asking."

But I didn't even know myself.

"Never mind," I said and turned to head back to the apartment.

That afternoon was interminable.

Yes, Courtney had been at the apartment all morning and I didn't even care. After giving Robbie his bath and putting him down for a nap, I set about making dinner.

It was something to do.

I desperately wanted to talk to Jean-Marc but the last thing he needed was to hear from clingy girlfriends—if that was what I was.

And it wasn't just that Jean-Marc was too busy to answer my questions but I knew him. I knew he'd take Haley's death personally.

Of course he would. I flashed back to the photo Haley's mother Cindy had shown me. She was adorable. To be snuffed out so brutally was hard to imagine.

There was no doubt that Jean-Marc was blaming himself for not finding her in time.

Fortunately Courtney was so self-absorbed that she had no idea if anyone else was going through something difficult. She kept the television set on and twice I had to ask her to lower the volume so as not to wake the baby.

I was actually looking forward to the moment when Robbie's nap was over so I could distract myself with taking care of him. When he woke, I changed him again and dressed him in a new playsuit I'd picked up at Monoprix. I was reminded that there was a children's boutique in Le Marais that I'd been wanting to wander through. At six, Cameron was too big for me to shop there for his clothes.

Ever since I moved to France I'd found renewed pleasure in cooking, even if just for one. Sifting and sautéing and cutting vegetables all tended to either distract me or focus my mind, depending on what I needed.

Today I was making the French version of macaroni and cheese, something I didn't even know existed until I came here. But it does. In the land of forty thousand cheeses? It exists in spades.

I pulled a jar of crème fraiche from the fridge and began to shred the first of five different kinds of cheese that would go in the casserole.

My Zen moment didn't last long.

"Oh, I found the note you left me!" Courtney said from the dining room. She was spooning the jarred baby food that I'd bought into Robbie's mouth.

You just found it? I thought, shaking my head and putting way more muscle into grating the gruyère than was strictly necessary.

"I'll for sure go to the embassy tomorrow," she said. "This jet lag is a total killer, you know? I just can't shake it off. Can you watch Robbie again tomorrow while I go?"

I knew she was taking advantage of me but I also knew that I was the one with an income and a comfortable apartment. Courtney may be a manipulator, but she was a manipulator who'd managed to put herself in a situation where she had no home, no friends, and no family to turn to.

I could afford to let her take advantage of me for at least a little while longer.

It was six o'clock by the time I washed the last dinner dish and by then I was so anxious to hear any news at all that I could hardly sit still. Finally, I snapped the lead on Izzy and went downstairs to walk her around the block.

Incredibly, my nightly dog walk includes a church built in the mid-1860s during the time Baron Haussmann was renovating many of Paris's streets. I was told his building project was mildly controversial because, while what he created was undeniably beautiful, he did have to tear down several blocks of slum housing leaving thousands homeless in his wake.

I rounded the corner and saw the magnificent presentation of the Église Saint-Augustin de Paris. Seeing it always took my breath away and I always took a moment to marvel that this magnificent structure was just a half block from where I lived.

The massive gold dome of the church, built to be visible from the Arc de Triomphe, is 200 feet high and gives the structure an enchanted, exalted appearance.

If it weren't for Izzy, I would have gone inside to sit and pray. I think churches are about the only place that dogs are not welcome in France. But there was a bench in the square in front of the church and that would serve well enough.

My phone rang and I nearly dropped it in my hurry to get it out of my jacket pocket, hoping it was Jean-Marc or Adele or Laura with news.

It was Catherine.

"Mom?"

"Hi, sweetie," I said, my voice tinted with disappointment. This might be the only time in my life when I felt let down to get a call from my daughter.

"I just wanted to apologize for my behavior this morning," she said.

"Darling, you have every right to be upset," I said. "I can only imagine how you must feel."

"Well, the greater injustice was done to you, as Todd said, so I feel bad hijacking your pain."

"No pain," I told her firmly. "I'm fine. I adjusted to it all months ago."

"So you weren't devastated when you heard Dad had made a baby with someone else?"

Putting it like that didn't help but I gritted my teeth to answer her.

"Nope," I said. "I just hate seeing what it's doing to you. He was your dad, Catherine..."

"I'm not there yet, Mom," she said firmly. "Not by a long shot. I think he sucks, okay?"

"Okay." My heart sank to hear her words but I told myself it was early days. She'd get there. She'd remember her dad during the good times. She'd forgive him.

"Where are you?" she said. "It sounds like you're outside."

"Izzy and I needed a little air. We're out for a walk."

"Well, be careful, okay? I know you think bad things only happen in the US but Paris is a major metropolitan city with major metropolitan crime."

I wanted to cry at that moment listening to her telling *me* to be careful. When all through her call, the only thing I could see when I wasn't seeing Cindy Johnson crying herself sick was the image of Haley Johnson's body floating face down in the Seine, bumping into tourist trash and being nibbled on by river fish.

And thinking...*what if that were Catherine?*

I felt an involuntary shudder sweep through my body.

"Gotta go, Mom," Catherine said. "I'll give your love to Cam and Todd. Take care of yourself, okay?"

"You too, darling," I said, waiting for her to hang up first as I always did.

I sat for a moment longer on the bench, listening to the vague rumble of traffic in the distance. Underneath the noise was the sound of music pouring through the open doors of nearby bars and cafés.

Izzy looked at me and cocked her head. By now she could pick up on my moods.

"I'm okay," I said to her. "It's all okay."

After that, I decided that a bath and a glass of wine would help finish off the night—and hopefully ensure sleep—so I headed back to the apartment. Once at my building, I opened the door to the lobby off the courtyard and ran right into Luc

Remy, who lived on the floor beneath mine and whom I'd briefly dated when I first came to Paris.

It had not ended well. "Good evening, Luc," I said, proud of myself for always being the one to take the high road and speak first.

He ignored my greeting as he always did.

I continued past him to the stairs.

The high road always was a little chilly, I reminded myself.

By the time I made it to the second floor, Izzy ran to Geneviève's apartment door. I laughed because I guess that meant Izzy spends so much time with Geneviève she considers her apartment as much home as mine.

On impulse, I knocked on Geneviève's door.

I think I just wanted to say hi and nothing more. It was nearly eight o'clock by now. But when Geneviève answered the door, she must have seen something in my face because she immediately advanced and held out her arms.

You have to know how significant that is. The French don't hug.

We stood there for a moment in the hall until she finally stepped back so that I could enter. I unclipped Izzy's leash and went to sit in the living room while Geneviève went to get two glasses of sherry. Within moments, she was back with the drinks.

"What has happened, *chérie*?" she asked.

"The girl I was supposed to find—the one they were asking me to find..."

Geneviève put a hand to her mouth. "*Mon Dieu*," she said, knowing immediately that it was the one found dead in the Seine today. "*Un tueur en série?*" she whispered.

A serial killer?

"I think so, maybe," I said.

"Those poor parents." She looked at me and narrowed her

eyes. "But *chérie*, you could have done nothing for them. It was too late."

"I know. That's what I tell myself."

"Because it is the truth."

We sat silently for a moment. I think that's all I really needed. With a problem so big it has no answer, certainly none that I can divine, it's all anyone can do. Just to sit with a friend.

In the midst of our silence, my phone vibrated.

"It's a text message from Adele," I said. "She was the one who processed the body today."

Geneviève shook her head.

"I do not know how she does what she does for a living."

"I know. I—"

I read Adele's text message and felt my heart fly into my throat as fear slowly spread to every part of my body.

"Dear God!" I whispered.

"What is it, *chérie*?" Geneviève said, leaning over to squeeze my hand. "What does she say?"

I looked at her. For a moment it felt as if time slowed.

"Another girl's gone missing," I said.

13

I like to think I'm the kind of person who chooses action over debate.

That can be good or bad depending on the context of course. In many cases, my urge to *do* something has made me overlook salient points that would have directed me to be more cautious.

The horror I felt when I saw Adele's text and realized that another girl had been taken by this maniac can't be exaggerated. And if I'm honest, the guilt I felt at refusing to help Haley's parents—even though *I know* that by the time I was talking to them their daughter in all likelihood had already been...but enough of that.

Suffice it to say my guilt couldn't be exaggerated either. I knew I wasn't responsible for what had happened. Of course—I knew that.

But I hadn't helped either.

Maybe that's the reason I scooped up Izzy and said my goodbyes to Geneviève in order to be ready. For what I don't know.

I was on the phone to Laura within minutes of getting Adele's text.

"Have you heard the news?" I said breathlessly into the phone to Laura as I entered my apartment. Courtney was asleep on the couch, the TV set was still on, and little Robbie was asleep on the edge of the couch ready to tumble to the hardwood floor any second.

"I just got a call from the girl's mother," Laura said.

I hurried to the couch and grabbed Robbie. He awoke and protested briefly. I went into the kitchen, swaying him until he fell back to sleep.

"She's with the police now," Laura continued. "But she's asked me for help. May I assume by this call that you want to be involved this time?"

Sometimes I really hate people like Laura. If she had an ounce of sensitivity she'd know how terrible I feel about what Haley's parents were going through. But I couldn't blame her.

"Is it just the mother?" I asked.

"The father lives in the States."

Is that pertinent? I couldn't help but wonder. This father also lived apart? Was this a coincidence?

"When can I meet her?" I asked.

"I'll set it up for first thing in the morning at my place. The cops want to stake out her apartment."

"Do they have any hope that it's something other than the same maniac?"

I only asked because staking out the parents' house is how a kidnapping was typically handled if a ransom request was expected to come in.

"I don't know any more than you do, Claire. I imagine the cops are just doing what the manual tells them to do."

I headed for my bedroom to change Robbie's diaper and put him to bed. The snores from the living room were getting louder but I had no intention of waking Courtney to escort her to her bedroom.

"Set it up with her," I said. "And Laura? Please don't get her hopes up. Serial killers are quite a ways out of my wheelhouse."

"Understood, darling," she said briskly. "Probably true for most of us."

14

J ean-Marc watched Ali Burton's mother as she was helped down the hall to the lobby. He felt a pressure building in his chest and reminded himself to breathe.

Jean-Marc didn't have children himself. And during times like these he was glad of it.

Jessica Burton had had even less to offer in the way of helpful information than the other two mothers had.

Mon Dieu, was this maniac going to kill a third time?

Oui. He is. Unless I do something to stop it.

As Jean-Marc walked to the murder room, Caron got in step beside him. The eyes of every single detective and uniform in the *préfecture* in the Place Louis Lépine followed them as they walked. The tension in the room seemed to suck all the air from it. Jean-Marc felt the tightness in his chest.

Of course he'd assured *Commandant* Bulie that he was up for it. He'd even found himself arguing that he was the best person on the team to find this man.

A serial killer.

The man who the press was already referring to as the *In-Seine Killer.*

Jean-Marc and Caron stood in front of the murder board as Dartre added Ali Burton's photo to the board. He had earlier placed the pictures of both her parents, and her boyfriend on the murder board next to her murdered American school-mates, Cecily Danvers and Haley Johnson.

"What could she tell you?" Caron asked as Jean-Marc joined him and Dartre in front of the board.

"Same as the others," Jean-Marc said. "Ali left school at fourteen hundred hours, was expected home by no later than fifteen hundred hours—she lives even closer to the school than Haley or Cecily. When she didn't arrive, her mother wasted another hour calling her friends until finally calling us."

Caron nodded and looked at Dartre.

"What do we know about the girl?" he asked.

"Name, Ali Burton," Dartre recited. "Age sixteen, on the soccer team, played flute, been in Paris since she was thirteen. Speaks the language fluently."

"She only has this boyfriend?" Jean-Marc asked.

"She doesn't have a lot of friends but here is a list of the three or four she does have. All American."

Jean-Marc took the sheet Dartre handed him. He glanced at the three names on the list. Mikayla Mcintire, Jackie Lannigan, Dezi White.

"Are we really looking at the boyfriend for this?" Caron said. "Don't we know what this is?"

Jean-Marc appreciated Caron's candor. They were treating this as a textbook abduction when it had all the markings of being anything but.

"We're looking at everything," Jean-Marc said. "We can't assume it's the same guy. It probably is but making those kind of assumptions means we might miss an important observa-tion. Somebody bring her boyfriend in."

Dartre turned to his desk and his phone.

"Has anyone checked the teachers' alibis at the international school?" Jean-Marc asked.

"We have," Caron said. "And we have four who are persons of interest."

"How do they match up for Cecily and Haley?" Jean-Marc asked.

"As of yet undetermined," Caron said.

"Okay. Let's look at those teachers again and find out where the four we were looking at for Cecily Danvers' murder were from three o'clock to five o'clock yesterday. Then call the head-master and have him shut down the school."

"The headmaster is one of the persons of interest."

"Then you'll be able to kill two birds with one call. Any word yet on the DNA found on Haley Johnson?"

He really didn't expect anything. This guy was careful. If it truly was a serial killing and this fit some sort of MO then the sperm they'd found in Haley would also be untraceable.

"I'll check, Chief," Caron said.

While both Caron and Dartre were on the phone, Jean-Marc continued to stare at the murder board. He looked at the smiling faces of the three girls—two dead, one missing. They looked classically American to him. Straight white teeth, happy, confident smiles that said they lacked for nothing in their lives, that they were convinced of their superior place in the world.

Also on the board were photographs of the four teachers from the international school that had weak or nonexistent alibis for Cecily or Haley's murders.

One was a handsome young man with a razor sharp grin. Jean-Marc stepped closer to look at his picture. The caption on the photo read: Eric Watson, American, Art Teacher.

He turned to the next photo, this one a woman. She looked mannish and stocky, her expression churlish and unsmiling. The caption read: Deb Knox, American, Gym teacher.

The third photo was of a large man, hair closely-cropped,

with a broad jaw and piercing piggy eyes. The caption read Hans Dieter, German, German teacher.

The fourth photo was of a portly middle-aged man with rolls of fat under his chin and a long bony nose. His mouth was pursed as if he'd just eaten something sour. The caption read, Cedric Potter, Headmaster.

Jean-Marc turned to Caron who had just hung up the phone.

"Dieter has an ironclad," Caron said. "He's moved back to Germany. His wife confirms it."

"Did he drive or take the train?" Jean-Marc asked.

There would be a record of it if he flew or took the train.

"Train."

Then that leaves three, Jean-Marc thought as he reached up and removed Dieter's photo from the board and after a brief hesitation Deb Knox's too.

"I think we just caught a break," Caron said excitedly, his phone still pressed to his ear.

Jean-Marc looked at him with growing hope and anticipation.

"They've got a DNA match on the sperm," Caron said.

15

M ark White opened his daughter's laptop, glancing down the hall toward the master bedroom. He didn't know why he bothered. Audrey and Dezi were both fast asleep.

On the other hand it doesn't hurt to be careful.

He opened up Dezi's Facebook account and scrolled through her list of friends. He didn't know any of them by their names.

Maybe I should send a fan letter to Mark Zuckerberg to thank him for including a picture next to the names, he thought. *No point in wasting time over a sexy-sounding name only to discover upon further research that the girl looked like an emaciated water buffalo.*

He found a picture that looked interesting and hovered his cursor over her picture for a moment before clicking.

Jan Bunting.

Terrible name, he thought as he scrolled through her Facebook posts.

But very cute girl.

Two generations before this one and he'd have seen naked pictures, drunk pictures and all manner of inappropriate content. But this generation had learned the hard lessons of their older brother and sisters.

There were memes and cartoons and God knows selfie after selfie.

But nothing from the chest down. And nothing to remotely inflame any normal red-blooded American male.

This must be the vainest most self-absorbed generation yet, he thought as he clicked through a series of Jan's photos.

She had taken her own picture from every possible angle wearing literally dozens of different outfits. Unfortunately those outfits were not revealing in any way except possibly to expose how much money her parents had.

Again, he thought in frustration, they'd all learned from the sins of their older siblings.

But oh those sins had been sweet, he thought.

He turned to look at Jan's friends and found a pretty blonde girl—Bryanna—stupid name—who had bleached blonde hair and overdone makeup.

His heart beat faster at the thought that this one might be a little less careful.

It was always smarter to go after friends of Dezi's friends, he thought. It was too dangerous otherwise.

He knew there may well come a time when it would be prudent to put a little distance between Dezi and these girls.

Oh, yes, he thought, suddenly breathing heavily as he came to a photo of little Bryanna in a lacy bikini that looked more like a bra and panties.

Now this was more like it.

16

The next morning I was up before the alarm clock could wake me, even before Izzy was awake enough to start bugging me to take her downstairs.

I wasn't, however, up before Robbie. I went to him, changed him and brought him into the kitchen where I put the water on for coffee.

Courtney had obviously gotten up some time in the middle of the night and made her way to the guest room. I put Robbie on the couch, piling pillows around him, and showered and dressed quickly. By then the coffee was ready.

I looked at the stroller and remembered how tricky it had been getting it in and out of the elevator yesterday. It occurred to me that what I really needed was one of those slings so I could just pop him in and scoot down to check the mail and walk the dog. And then I realized what I was thinking and told myself sternly that if I did find myself in the baby section of Monoprix in the next couple of days I should realize that that was a very bad sign of things to come. I told myself I wouldn't let it get to that.

I debated leaving Robbie on the rug in the living room

while I ran Izzy down to wet the pavers in the courtyard. I was pretty sure Robbie wasn't crawling yet and should be safe but I didn't feel good about it. What if Courtney woke up and came in and tripped over him? I would just have to manage the stairs, the leash and one arm full of fully-awake baby.

I wasn't decrepit yet, I reasoned. I should be able to do this.

In the end, I opted without shame to take the elevator down and back up.

Once back upstairs I was glad to see that Courtney was up and drinking my coffee. Well, I wasn't glad that she was drinking my coffee but I was glad not to have to ruin the mattress in the guest room by pouring a jug of water on her because that had definitely been my plan if she wasn't up.

"Do you not have any half and half?" she asked with a yawn as I came in with the baby and Izzy.

"I drink my coffee black," I said, handing her Robbie. "He's been changed. Feed him."

"Hello, Mister Snookums," Courtney said, kissing him.

It was right then that I realized that Courtney treated Robbie like a human doll or stuffed toy. On the one hand it might mean that he got plenty of love from her during his childhood, on the other hand it might also mean he would get accidentally left behind on a bus seat at some point.

"Do you still have the note I wrote you about how to get to the embassy?" I asked. "It's a straight shot from here if you take the Châtelet Les Halles Métro. If you have trouble, you can call me."

"With what?" Courtney said, opening up the fridge with the baby on one hip. "I had to give up my phone weeks ago."

That made me stop for a moment. Even though I hadn't had a cell phone—let alone a smart phone—when Catherine was a baby, the thought of managing without one now was daunting.

Courtney pulled out a bag of stale canelés she found on the counter and began to eat from it standing up. Not for the first time I tried to imagine what in the world Bob had seen in this woman. Aside from her body and her relative youth, what had he been drawn to?

"Honestly I don't see what the big-ass hurry is," she said. "Why can't I just stay with you? You have two bedrooms. It's not like I'm putting you out."

"You can't stay here," I said between gritted teeth as I got my notebook, and tote bag together.

"I have no money."

"How did you think moving to France where you don't speak the language was going to help that? Or did you think I'd just support you?"

"Robbie is your grandchild."

"He isn't. At all."

She settled down on the couch with Robbie in her arms and Izzy jumped up on the couch with them. I went to the kitchen to make Robbie's formula and handed the bottle to her.

"I'm sorry, Courtney. I know this is hard for you especially with Robbie. But you need to get settled somewhere."

"How? I mean I'd love to get married but how's that going to happen?" She gestured to Robbie. "Talk about baggage."

"Bringing a baby into any relationship is the same no matter what country you live in," I said patiently. "Some guys won't mind and some will see it as a deal-breaker."

"I thought the French were more tolerant. Wait a minute. Where are you going? You've forgotten the baby."

"I have an appointment this morning," I said. "No dogs or babies allowed."

"Well, what the hell am I supposed to do with him?" She struggled to stand up, knocking the bottle's nipple from Robbie's mouth.

"I don't know, Courtney," I said. "I imagine you'll do whatever it is you've been doing for the past five months."

I left before she could respond or before I could change my mind. I had a very delicate interview this morning.

And I knew that the last thing a mother needed in the current position of Jessica Burton was to see an adorable little baby with his whole life still ahead of him.

17

There was no point in taking the Métro to Laura's place since her apartment was in the same arrondissement as mine. Besides, the walk helped wake up my brain. I was all too aware that all the dangers I'd faced with the Johnson case—and the reasons I'd turned it down—were still there with this one.

Missing girl.

Deadly outcome.

Ticking clock.

No clues or leads.

No agency support.

The difference was how I'd felt in that moment when I'd heard that Haley's body had been found and I'd not done anything to try to prevent it.

I know, I know, not that I could have done anything.

I had no illusions about what I was walking into. Raw need and terror, a mother's worst nightmare. Worse, in order to help this woman I would have to forget that I was also a mother. I would have to forget how easy it would be to slip inside her skin and feel her pain.

Forget how easily my world could end with one bad, fortuitous meeting between a beloved daughter and a deranged killer.

I pulled out my phone as I neared Laura's apartment building. I'd waited long enough and now I would wait no longer. I hated to bother him. I didn't want to be the one interfering or providing a distraction when he needed to be totally focused.

But now I had a job to do too.

"Hey," I said, half surprised that he actually took my call. I could just imagine the pandemonium and intense pressure of the Paris homicide department now with what the media would surely be labeling a serial killing.

"I heard about the second girl," I said.

"Yes, it is not good," Jean-Marc said, ever the embodiment of understatement.

"It wasn't your fault, Jean-Marc."

"I don't know who *else* was tasked with stopping it."

I knew him well enough to know I wasn't going to talk him out of feeling responsible for what had happened. Since I knew nothing of what he'd done on the case so far, I also knew nothing about any leads or clues that hadn't been followed up. I didn't know if he could genuinely absolve himself of the guilt of what had happened.

"So it's a serial killer," I said, hoping the bluntness of my words would prompt him to open up to me.

It didn't.

"I must go, *chérie*."

I wondered if anybody overhearing him thought he was talking to his wife. I appreciated that he called me *chérie*. It was practically the only affectionate or intimate thing between us since there really couldn't be anything physical. I understood that too, of course.

After my own husband's betrayal—hello, Courtney and Robbie, Exhibit A and B—I appreciated a man who wouldn't break a promise just because he ended up regretting making it in the first place.

I found I was grateful for the fact that Jean-Marc was too distracted to ask me what I was doing today. I didn't like to lie to him—although I would if pushed and if the stakes were high enough—and I knew telling him I was about to meet the missing girl's mother would just be one more nail in his cross.

"Okay," I said. "Good luck with today. I guess I'll see you when I see you."

Jessica reminded me of a friend I'd had years ago in college. She was in her early forties at most, but she dressed much older in a prim long-sleeve blouse and a belted A-line skirt. I couldn't detect any makeup, but in a crisis making up your face is usually the first thing to go. Her hair hung to her shoulders, clean but unstyled.

If I had to guess I'd say Jessica, although without doubt depressed, was usually uninterested in fashion. Strange. Paris was all about clothes. I wondered if her daughter felt the same way?

We shook hands and I saw that haunted desperate look in her eyes that nearly made me flinch away.

I reminded myself that putting myself in Jessica's shoes was not going to help her. To do that I needed to be a machine, a callous and unemotional mind at work.

Laura had sent me the facts in advance of our meeting. American, Jessica Burton worked at the US Embassy as a secretary. Living in Paris was a life-long dream—one that she'd transferred to her daughter Ali. She and her ex-husband, Fred, who lived in Austin, had divorced when Ali was two.

I also knew that Jessica was currently getting the prerequisite comfort and coddling from Laura and that I needed to focus on giving her what I did best. In the end, if it helped get Ali back, that was all that mattered.

Unlike at a crime scene, a kidnapping typically gave investigators very little in the way of physical material to work with except who saw what when. In this case there was no real area to examine for clues or DNA. The stretch of street where Ali had gone missing—which was not exactly the same stretch where both Cecily and Haley had both gone missing but close enough—was too long and too frequently traveled to effectively comb for physical clues.

"Did anybody see anything?" I asked Jessica.

She took in a long breath.

"There's a CCTV camera but it only showed Ali walking down the street and then out of the frame."

So whoever took Ali knew how much the CCTV camera was capable of capturing. Or was that a coincidence? I wondered if Jean-Marc was on that angle.

"Her best friend Dezi spoke to her just before Ali left school," Jessica continued.

"Why didn't they walk home together?"

"Dezi lives in the opposite direction. And she was being picked up for clarinet practice."

"Anyone else?"

"Ali's boyfriend, Ben, saw her but again, only briefly."

"Why didn't he walk with her?"

"He had soccer practice."

"Is that confirmed?"

"You mean like an alibi?" Jessica looked stricken at the thought that Ali's boyfriend might have had anything to do with Ali's disappearance.

"I just like to eliminate everyone," I said. "I have no reason to think he's involved at this point."

"Claire is very good at what she does," Laura said, placing a hand on Jessica's.

I wish she hadn't said that, but I knew she was just trying to reassure Jessica.

"What about teachers?" I said. "Any favorites? Any she hated?"

Jessica was nodding before I finished speaking.

"Ali and her friends all loved the art teacher, Mr. Watson. And they all detested the gym teacher."

I wrote this down in my notebook.

"Any particular reason why they hated the gym teacher? What's her name?"

"Deb Knox. They felt she was too strict with them, never allowing them not to dress out when they had their periods. Ali used to say, 'it's like she thinks we give women a bad name.'"

I sensed there was something more there but I wasn't sure Jessica was the right person to ask about it.

I closed my notebook and reached for my phone.

"Can I have your contact information, Jessica?" I asked. "In case I think of more questions."

She gave me her number and then turned to Laura, her shoulders slumped in exhaustion.

"Is that all?" Jessica asked. "I need to be home with the police in case...in case..."

"Yes, of course," I said, standing up. "I've got enough to start."

I waited while Laura hugged Jessica and held her a long time before Jessica turned and made her way out of the apartment. When Laura returned, she looked at me worriedly.

"Well?" she asked.

"I don't know, Laura. Like I told her, I'll get started and we'll see. I really hope her hopes aren't up too high."

"Wouldn't yours be? What else does she have but hope?"

"I know. Of course. It's just, the first forty-eight hours are critical in any kidnapping and I'm already twelve hours behind the curve. If we're sure Ali didn't run off—"

"Jessica swears she would never do that. Besides, where would she run to? Her boyfriend is still here."

"Right. So if she didn't run off then this guy has had her for twelve hours." I waved my notebook. "I have to talk to people and run down leads. It will take time."

"Ali doesn't have time," Laura said softly.

She walked me to the door and handed me a piece of paper. "This is the headmaster at Ali's school," she said. "Cecil Potter. He's expecting a visit from you. He knew all three girls."

"Good. Thanks, Laura."

Just as I was about to leave, she touched my arm which made me stop and look at her.

"I know this is hard for you on a personal level," she said, "and in all honesty, probably hopeless. So thank you."

I squeezed her hand in response, not trusting my voice, turned and left.

18

Not unlike most streets in the Latin Quarter in
summertime, this one was full of foot traffic and lots
of tourists swinging shopping bags and talking too
loudly.

I reminded myself that I was probably describing myself
when I first moved to Paris, although honestly I couldn't
imagine that.

I was presently putting up with all the annoying tourists
because the *brasserie* on whose terrace I now sat produced an
amazing duck confit well worth the irritation of the crowds.

In the last year I'd adopted the French way of stopping for a
proper lunch—including wine—and amazingly I found it left
me with more energy and a clearer head for whatever my day's
task was than skipping lunch or just grabbing a sandwich.

Plus it was just a civilized thing to do.

The meeting with Jessica hadn't been as difficult as I'd
imagined. I'd stayed focused on the facts and resolutely pushed
aside any tremors of relatable emotion. But that method was
only as effective as I was willing and able to work at it.

Now that I was sitting at a café with only my thoughts and

two point one million Parisians milling around me, it was proving harder to emotionally disengage.

As I waited for my lunch a random thought hit me from some research I'd done last night.

One in a hundred people are psychopaths.

I looked at all the people scurrying by me and felt a tingle of unease. Could there really be so many? All around? At the grocery store, in schools, on the Métro? While it's true not all psychopaths are violent, it was still disquieting to realize that we are literally surrounded by people who have to work hard every day to control their antisocial impulses.

And then there were those who couldn't.

As I sipped the single glass of wine I'd allowed myself, I called Bill Riley, Ben Kent's soccer coach. I'd gotten his number from Jessica. He quickly confirmed that yes, Ben had been at practice the day Ali disappeared.

I thanked him and was about to put a call in to check on Courtney before remembering she didn't have a phone. Should I get her one? At least a temporary one? Deciding that was probably wise at least for the short time she was with me, I considered calling Jean-Marc again but decided against it.

I knew he had his hands full and besides, what was I going to tell him? That I was investigating Ali Burton's disappearance?

There was no universe in which he would consider that good news.

Instead, I called Adele. The call went to voicemail so I hung up and tried again.

"I am trying to sleep here," Adele said groggily into the phone.

I knew she'd been up most of the night before processing the Haley Johnson murder scene.

"I need whatever you can tell me about Haley Johnson's death," I said.

"So this is for real? You're going to investigate it? What does Jean-Marc think?"

"He doesn't know."

"Oh. That's probably wise."

"I need info on Cecily and Haley's autopsies too. Can you meet?"

"No, but I can talk. What do you want to know?"

I glanced at my notebook of jotted questions.

"Cause of death," I said.

"Ligature strangulation."

"Killed elsewhere and transported to the river?"

"Affirmative."

"Time of death?"

"Between fourteen and sixteen hundred hours."

That meant between two and four in the afternoon.

"How was Haley dressed?"

"In the same outfit she was snatched in. A school uniform, long socks, shoes. She even still had a barrette in her hair."

"At what point was she put in the river?"

"That we don't know. But she ended up at Pont d'Alma. I heard your boyfriend LaRue had it roughly narrowed down to between Bir Hakeim and Austerlitz—which is basically the whole river but I don't know how he's figuring that. I know my firm hasn't been called in to throw a crime scene tape over any place other than Pont d'Alma."

"If you know when she died, and we know she was found two hours later," I said, "can't someone figure out how long she was in the water?"

"Are you asking can we figure out how long it took her to float to the point where she was found?"

"Yes."

"No. Anything could have held her up. There's so much trash and debris in the Seine, she could've gotten hung up somewhere for an hour before the wake from one of the tourist boats pushed her free."

"How did she get found?"

"A couple was making out on the upper embankment and saw her bob up near them. Pretty horrific end to their picnic, I'll say that."

I looked at my notebook and felt a fleeting sensation of despondency.

What made me think I was any better at this than Jean-Marc? Surely he and his team had gone over this information a hundred times.

"Was there any reconstructive evidence at the scene?" I asked, grasping at straws.

"Claire, no. Just the body. The work of a very smart, very brutal maniac."

"And you didn't find any DNA or prints on anything?" I asked in frustration.

"I never said that, Claire. We found plenty of stuff on the girl. She fought back so there was skin under her nails."

My stomach turned at the image of this seventeen-year-old girl fighting for her life.

"Was there a match for any of the DNA you found in CODIS?"

CODIS was the acronym for the DNA index system that the FBI used for its criminal justice databases which had been expanded to include most European countries too.

"Oh, wouldn't that make things easy?" Adele said. "Not for the first one, no. I haven't heard about Haley. But there was something very bizarre about both the rapes."

I swallowed hard at the reminder that Haley had been raped too. What a nightmare. Cindy and Bill Johnson would have been informed of that development this morning.

"Or should I say *so-called* rapes?" Adele said.

"What do you mean? Were they not really rapes?"

"I don't know. That's above my pay grade although the ME indicated that there were no tears or abrasions to indicate a forced entry on either girl."

"So the sex was consensual?"

"Possibly but doubtful."

Scientific people can be so infuriating. They tend to see the world as a grouping of facts. They don't often see connections between facts and God forbid make any obvious deductions as a result of them.

"Are you saying the rapes happened post-mortem?" I asked.

"That *is* what I'm saying. But that is not the most interesting thing."

"I'm all ears," I said eagerly.

"The two semen samples found in the girls were from two different men."

19

"How can that be?" I said, my heartbeat racing. "This is a *serial* killer."

"I only know what the science tells me. Listen, Claire, I'm getting another call. That's pretty much all I know until the lab results come back."

"Sure, okay, Adele," I said. "Thanks for this."

My head was swimming by the time I disconnected and while part of that had to do with the four espressos I'd had this morning, most of it was the massive wrench that had just been flung into the works by Adele's bombshell.

Two different men?

And neither of them was in the crime database or they wouldn't have deliberately and blithely left their DNA behind.

Are the cops looking for a criminal with no record?

While I'd read that the prisons were full of psychopaths who were unable to control their violent impulses, most psychopaths lived lives of quiet, benign evil until they showed up on the police's radar. Even their relatives would be surprised to realize a serial killer's true identity.

How were the police supposed to find a man who'd left no trace of his crimes over the years? Worse than that, if this was truly a serial killer, it meant he had no motive either.

Not having a trail of evidentiary clues to follow made it nearly impossible to find him. Which was one of the probable reasons why he'd been able to remain undetected for as long as he had.

But two different DNA samples found in the girls?

I glanced at my watch to see it was nearly time to leave for my interview with Cedric Potter, the headmaster of Le World School de Paris. Looking at my watch made me think that I was also looking at the hours and minutes that Ali Burton had left to live.

I felt an ache in the back of my throat and realized my appetite was gone. I signaled for the bill at the same time my phone dinged to signal an incoming text message.

It was from Laura.

<International school summer classes closed for the remainder of the summer by order of police. Potter to meet you in his office>

I paid the bill and headed in the direction of rue St-Charles.

Closing the school would've been Jean-Marc's edict. And it made sense.

Two girls dead.

Probably past time to close the doors.

The streets surrounding *Le World School de Paris* in the fifteen arrondissement were as landscaped and stylized as you'd expect from a school that charged eighty thousand euros a year in tuition.

In addition to the Eiffel Tower looming in the distance I noticed there were several upscale boutiques and shops nearby and a large outdoor café on the corner—Café Bleu—which was less than a block from the school. I imagined it was probably a popular hangout of the students.

The front doors of the building, a nondescript two-story brick structure, opened onto a wide atrium lined with awards and plaques, children's pictures and various sporting outfits and dance costumes. As I entered I detected a scent of wood polish and flowers and perhaps garlic and onions.

This was France after all.

I walked down the hall past several empty offices, peeking into them as I passed. Some of the rooms were obviously meant for very young children with colorful pictures of fruit and animals spelling out their names in French.

Laura had said Cedric Potter was expecting me so I wasn't worried that I found no one in the building to announce me. At the end of the hall there was a beautiful mahogany door with a golden plaque on it that read *Directeur*.

The door was open a crack and as I didn't want to force Potter to hop up and let me in, I pushed the door open and entered.

It was a handsome room, lined with built-in shelves and carpeted with an Aubusson rug. A massive oaken desk anchored the center of the room and backed up to a series of floor to ceiling windows that faced the street.

The headmaster was seated at his desk, his head down unaware of the fact that I'd entered.

He was squinting into his computer screen. Balding, with thin lips and a long nose, Potter wore round John Lennon glasses. I studied his face to see if there was anything about him that might help me remember him were I to see him again. Because of a brain anomaly I find it impossible to remember people's faces. Ever. Even faces I've seen mere minutes earlier.

Maybe the glasses would be a tipoff. But only if he was the only one in the crowd wearing them.

I cleared my throat and Potter jumped violently, fumbling quickly for a button on his computer screen. He stood up at once, wiping his hands on his pants as if they were wet.

I hate to say this about myself, because I pride myself on prioritizing clues and facts over gut instinct, but I found myself almost immediately registering that I didn't like this guy.

Once something like that happens, I'm then tasked with working even harder *not* to listen to my gut when dealing with the person—unless of course I need to rely on my gut at some point to fill in missing puzzle pieces. I didn't totally discount the merit of judging someone by instinct but just because I didn't like someone for whatever reason didn't mean he qualified as a serial killer.

That's what I needed to remember. I needed to remember to *lean on the facts*.

But first I needed to find them.

Potter stuck out his hand and grimaced at me, withdrawing it almost as soon as our flesh connected.

"Mrs. Baskerville," he said. "Please take a seat. I doubt I can be of any help but if I can of course I want to be."

Which was the most bass-ackward way of saying he didn't really want to help I'd ever heard.

For a school headmaster with the name Potter, I was surprised he didn't work the Hogwart's angle a little more. But right off the bat I could see Cedric Potter was your basic inherently unhappy camper.

"It's a terrible thing that's happened," I prompted. "Three girls missing in a little over a week? I assume you are working with the police?"

That flustered him nearly as much as if I'd accused him of doing the nabbing himself.

"Of course," he said defensively.

"I have some questions," I said. "But first I need to ask you where you were during the three timelines when the girls went missing."

"Are you serious? In what capacity do you believe you have the right to ask me that?"

"Oh, none at all," I said. "I should have made that clear. I am not in any way connected to the Paris police or the US embassy."

He snorted as if vindicated in his initial assessment.

"My right extends only to those granted me from the missing and dead girls' parents who have hired me to follow behind the police to ensure nothing has been missed."

"So in other words you have no right to ask for my alibi."

"None," I said with a smile, feeling my stomach clench with dislike of this man. "Except I suppose whatever rights a public social media platform might allow me."

"What?"

"Answer my questions, Mr. Potter, or I will go on social media to announce to the world that you refused to."

He sputtered in fury.

"A few of my colleagues might go much further," I continued. "They might actually post a suggestion that the police were looking at you as their prime suspect."

"That's not true!"

"Oh, Mr. Potter, bless your heart! What does that have to do with anything?"

He glared at me.

"You would go public with a lie like that?" he asked.

"Well of course not *me*. I said some of *my colleagues* would stoop to that. Myself, I always endeavor to stay on the straight and narrow until of course I'm convinced there's no other way. Character assassinations can be very messy, if effective. Just ask any innocent teenager who's been bullied online with stories that weren't true."

"What do you want to know?"

"Where were you when Cecily was taken?"

"I was here in my office. As I was with Haley and Ali too. My secretary and the assistant headmaster can vouch for that."

I poised my pen over my notepad. "Their names?"

He flushed angrily.

"Marie Zimmer and Nicole Danton."

"Their phone numbers?"

He gave them to me very ungraciously.

"I also need the home addresses of Eric Watson and Deb Knox," I said.

He arched an eyebrow at me. "What for? Are they suspects?"

I ignored his question.

"And finally, can you confirm that the school is closed for the summer?"

He grunted an affirmative. I wondered if he was able to hide his general animus from the parents of prospective students or were the expat parents just so desperate to get their kids into an English-speaking school that they overlooked his rudeness?

It was possible he was just a difficult person. Not everyone who didn't behave the way I'd like was a sociopath. Or at least I kept reminding myself of that. But in any event, I couldn't help but notice that Mr. Potter seemed to share some rather unsettling characteristics with the textbook sociopath.

He appeared to exhibit shallow emotions with a grandiose sense of self and pathological lying. In fact, the only thing he lacked was the sociopath's glibness and superficial charm.

"That's really all I have for now, Mr. Potter. I suppose you take a good deal of teasing because of your name?"

"The little brats never let it go," he muttered, standing as if to encourage me on my way out the door. When he stood I couldn't help but notice his eyes darted to the screen on the computer on his desk which twigged my memory of something he'd done when I entered his office.

Now that I remember it, when I'd taken him by surprise, he'd reacted by immediately pushing a button on his computer to make the screen go dark.

20

C edric watched her from his office window as she made her way down the sidewalk in front of the school and disappeared around the block.

What a perfectly ghastly woman.

He sat down hard in his chair and his glance fell on his dark computer screen. He raised a hand to wipe the sweat from his face.

Anger swept through him as he registered a roiling heat in his belly.

How dare she come here and ask those kinds of questions? The *police* weren't even asking him those sorts of questions.

Americans, he thought in disgust.

Still. You never knew who she might talk to, or who she might infect with her suspicions and conjecture.

He found the folder on his desktop and clicked it open. Inside were the twenty video files. He licked his lips. Did he dare erase them?

Could he live without them?

Don't be absurd, he thought as he right-clicked the nearest video file and selected *Delete* from the pull-down menu. The resulting sound, one of an ugly jaw crunching through bone, was the most gut-wrenching sound he'd ever heard.

I can't do the rest.

After everything I did to get them? To just throw them away because one nosey American came in here and acted like she knew something?

Something there's no way she could know!

Still, his hand wavered over the next video file.

Protect yourself, Cedric, he thought. *You can always find more girls. You can always make more videos.*

He right-clicked on the second video and heard the same awful crunching sound as it removed the file to his trash can.

What if she comes back with the police? What if they confiscate my computer?

And found these?

A light sheen of sweat developed on his top lip.

He couldn't bear to do this one at a time.

He right-clicked on the entire folder. It disappeared and amazingly, he felt instantly lighter when it did.

He leaned back in his chair and stared at his blank computer desktop.

It's the right thing to do.

He should have done it sooner.

He listened to the birds in the trees outside his office window and took a moment to truly enjoy their song, feeling freer than he had in weeks.

That Baskerville woman has actually done me a favor, he thought with renewed spirit as he opened his computer's application files and began to search for the cache files that would lead an IT technician to recover the damning videos.

He erased all trace of them and their source files and felt a shimmer of pleasure vibrate through him when he was done.

I should have gotten rid of the videos right after Cecily, he thought.

He got up and reached for his jacket. It would be beautiful on boulevard de Grenelle this afternoon. And a nice cold beer with a view of the Eiffel Tower would be just the ticket.

He turned at the door to his office, his hand on the light switch, and glanced back at his office to see if he'd left anything behind. His eyes fell on his desktop computer.

Besides. I can always make more.

21

I f it weren't for the fact that every minute that passed was ticking off the last minutes of Ali's life—or I had to assume they were—I would've felt pretty good about my interview with Cedric Potter.

As it was, I didn't feel very good about anything.

Ali had been snatched yesterday afternoon. If Cecily and Haley's killer stuck to his MO, it meant Ali had only a few hours left to live.

Isn't everything I'm doing hopeless?

My next stop was Dezi White's apartment. Jessica had told me that Dezi's parents, Audrey and Mark, were classic helicopter parents but well-grounded and what she called "good people." Mark was a sales rep with Mammotome, a French medical devices company, and Audrey spent her time taking French classes and shopping.

They lived in the sixteenth arrondissement, an upscale section of town not close to the school. I headed for the École Militaire Métro station since it would take me forever to walk to their neighborhood from where I was across the river.

Once on the Métro, I put a call into Ali's boyfriend Ben Kent but the call went to voicemail. I left a message asking him to call me and then called the number I had for Dezi White.

"Yes?" a woman's voice said, answering.

"My name is Claire Baskerville," I said. "May I speak to Dezi?"

"With regards to what?"

"I've been asked by Ali Burton's mother to look into Ali's disappearance—"

"I'm sorry," the woman said. "This is Dezi's mother. We've already spoken to the police and Dezi doesn't need to be upset any more over this than she already has been."

She hung up.

I was at the Métro stop for Dezi's neighborhood by this time but I wasn't so callous as to not understand a mother's desire that her child not be upset by all this. On the other hand, Dezi was Ali's best friend and could very well be a source of important information on Ali's mindset as well as her actions leading up to her last moments before her disappearance.

But of course I understood.

Nonetheless, I got off at the stop, deciding to at least get a sense of the neighborhood before getting back on the train to head home.

I hadn't gone two blocks when I felt my phone vibrate in my pocket. I glanced at it to see I'd received a text message.

<Can u meet me at Dune's? In 30 min?>

It was from Dezi White.

Dune's was a corner café at the corner of rue Michel Ange and rue d'Auteuil. It was not crowded at this time of day—halfway between lunch time and *apéro* time—and I quickly found a table near the street and ordered two coffees.

I didn't have to wait long before a pretty dark-haired

teenage girl walked up and began looking around at everyone on the terrace. I assumed it must be Dezi.

I waved to her and she hurried over to my table.

"Thank you so much for meeting me," I said as we shook hands.

I could see that Dezi, though not really overweight, probably struggled with her weight. I knew that could be problematic as far as fitting in when it came to high school. Her eyes were red-rimmed as if she'd been crying recently.

"I want to do anything that might help find Ali," she said, her bottom lip trembling with her effort to hold it together.

"Well, anything you can tell me about what Ali was doing just before she disappeared," I said, "would be very helpful."

Dezi shrugged helplessly.

"She didn't do anything different than how she usually went home," she said.

"Was there anything upsetting her yesterday?"

"More than usual?"

"Was she usually upset about things?"

Dezi shrugged again. "Aren't we all?"

Right. Teenage girls. Full of angst and despair.

"How about your teachers? Anybody giving her a hard time?"

That question lit up Dezi's eyes.

"We all hate Miss Knox," she said. "She's the worst."

"Any reason in particular?"

"She thinks we give women a bad name. Can you believe that? It's because she hates men and she wants everyone else to hate them too."

I wasn't sure how helpful this information was.

"Anybody else?"

"We like all our other teachers."

"How about Eric Watson?"

"Mr. W? He's a beast."

I knew enough about kid-speak to know that this was meant as a positive.

"The cops have been questioning him and it's so unfair. He would never have done anything to hurt Cecily or Haley or Ali."

"And there's nothing you can think of that Ali did differently yesterday?"

"No, nothing. Oh, wait! There is one thing," Dezi said, her eyes alert and suddenly worried. "I can't believe I didn't think of this before now."

"What is it?"

"Desdemona! There you are!"

Both Dezi and I turned our heads to see a large man storming over toward us.

"Dad, no," Dezi said as her father reached our table.

Mark White was a very large man with a bull neck and red veins protruding across his forehead. If I'd had the time or inclination to imagine him other than the picture of enraged fury in front of me, I might have said he was handsome.

But that was very difficult to see at the moment.

His eyes were cold and hard. He jutted out his chin as he regarded me.

"How dare you meet with my daughter without an adult present!" he said loudly. "I can have you arrested for this."

"Dad, stop it," Dezi said, softer now.

Beads of sweat had formed on her lip and forehead. He reached over and grabbed her wrist. I was on my feet. A few other diners—all French—craned their necks to watch us.

"Daddy, no!" Dezi said. "I wasn't doing anything wrong."

"Oh no? Thank God your mother put that tracker on your phone, now get up!" He pulled her out of her chair and she squealed in pain.

"Let her go," I shouted as my hand went to my purse.

He turned on me, his face flushed with fury and pent up

violence but before he could say anything, I pulled my Taser out of my bag and pointed it at him.

Instantly he released Dezi's wrist.

"How dare you!" he screamed at me.

"I dare because child endangerment is against the law in France," I said, aware that my heart was thundering in my ears.

Dezi stared in horror at my Taser as she rubbed her wrist.

"Go home!" Mark snarled at her. "Now!"

Dezi bolted away, knocking over a chair in the process. Mark began to back away from me. He pointed a finger at me.

"I don't care how old you are," he said. "If I see you near my daughter again, you'll regret it."

22

I could really have lived without that *I don't care how old you are* crack but regardless I had sufficiently recovered from Mark White's verbal attack by the time my train pulled into my home Métro station of Saint-Augustin.

What normally would have been just an unpleasant incident morphed in my mind into a possible lead. Either I was just that desperate or I really had seen something more in Mark White's unpleasant behavior.

The typical serial killer has above average intelligence and a strong will to dominate and victimize.

As far as I'm concerned that was exactly what I'd witnessed in the altercation at the café today.

I sent a quick text to Dezi from the train to ask if she was okay but there was no response. I even called her number and when I did I heard the flat and truncated ringtone which told me the recipient had blocked the number.

That would be her parents, I thought. Specifically her psycho father.

I don't know what made me pull the Taser out of my bag. They're as difficult to own in France as a Glock nine millimeter.

Fortunately no police saw me with it and none of the diners appeared inclined to jump in and make a citizen's arrest.

All I can say in my defense is that I was prompted by pure adrenalin and a mother's protective instinct.

No, I corrected myself. He was hurting Dezi. I reacted as anybody would.

I decided I wasn't in the mood to cook tonight so I stopped at an Indian restaurant near the apartment and ordered take-out. While I was waiting for them to put the order together, I called Cedric Potter's assistant headmaster, Marie Zimmer. The call went to voicemail.

Next I called his secretary, Nicole Danton. The call was answered by a woman in a very guarded voice.

"Madame Danton?" I said.

"Who is this?"

"My name is Claire Baskerville. I am a private investigator working with the police on the Haley Johnson murder case. I was referred to you by Cedric Potter who said you would be able to confirm his whereabouts the day Haley went missing?"

"He said that?" she said incredulously. "How would I remember where he was?"

And then she hung up.

One of the things I love about living in a Paris apartment building—and there are many—is that at a certain time in the evening you can smell the beginning aromas of all the wonderful dinners in the process of being prepared. Mostly it's onions and garlic—since that is the start of just about every French dish in existence—but sometimes there are spices too in testimony to the growing Middle Eastern population in Paris.

I walked into my apartment and set down the Indian takeout on the counter.

As usual, Izzy ran to greet me for all she was worth and I took a moment to make sure she knew I was glad to see her too.

"Wow, you're finally home," Courtney said, coming into the dining room with Robbie in her arms. I saw he was wearing the same outfit he'd slept in. "We're starving here."

"Why don't you set the table?" I said as I clipped Izzy's leash to her collar. "I'll be back in a minute."

Feeling guilty about having been gone all day, I let Izzy have a good quarter of an hour to sniff and squat on every bush, plant, weed and stone in our courtyard before going back upstairs.

When I did, I found Courtney on the couch with a plate of Indian food that she'd dished up for herself from the kitchen. Robbie was on his tummy on the floor. Izzy instantly ran to him and licked his face.

Stifling my irritation, I went to the kitchen to make Izzy's dinner before plating up my own meal. I set it down on the dining room table and opened a bottle of wine.

"Oh! I'll have some of that!" Courtney said. "I couldn't find the wine opener anywhere."

I poured two glasses of wine and sat down to my dinner. Courtney hurried into the dining room and claimed her glass.

"How did it go at the embassy?" I asked.

"Yeah, about that," she said, bringing her wine with her back to the couch. "I didn't go."

I took in a covert breath and reminded myself that there were other ways to get rid of her. Possibly even some noncriminal ways.

"Why not?" I asked.

"What are they going to say?" she scoffed. "Are they going to give me a place to stay in Paris? Or money for food?"

"Probably not."

"No. They're going to put me on the first flight back to the States and that is not a part of my plan."

"So you have a plan?"

"Yes and it doesn't involve living in the States! I told you, every guy I meet there thinks I'm either too old or too much trouble because of the baby. I'll never find a husband there. American men are just too conventional."

"Your plan is to marry a Frenchman?"

"That would be cool. Or maybe a German or a Switzerland person."

"And meanwhile you intend to live with me?"

"You have plenty of room and this way you get to be with the baby."

I was ten seconds from deciding to believe that the best thing for Robbie was to be taken away from Courtney and put into care. I know from what I've read that foster care isn't wonderful but at least it's stable.

Because if I were to take a more aggressive route to getting rid of Courtney, the first thing that would happen is that she would lose Robbie.

As I watched her drink her wine and click through the TV channels, I thought that she might not think that was such a tragedy.

I finished my dinner and brought my plate to the sink.

It had been a long day and ultimately a hopeless one. Maybe that's what made it so disheartening for me, knowing that all this shoe leather and knocking on doors—and being publicly screamed at by irate fathers—wasn't going to help Ali. Not if she really was in the clutches of a serial killer. I was too far away from knowing anything that might help.

Have you ever undertaken an important task knowing it was hopeless?

It's really hard to stay motivated.

Izzy began barking seconds before a light tap on the door

could be heard. I frowned because Izzy wouldn't bark if it was Jean-Marc or Geneviève on the other side of that door. And with my security system, it was virtually impossible for anyone else, i.e. a stranger, to get inside the building.

"Company?" Courtney said hopefully.

I went to the door and opened it. There on the doorstep was a teenage boy. His hair was cropped short which accentuated his youth and his large brown eyes. He had bad skin but even now you could tell he would grow into a handsome man.

He wore jeans and an Atlanta Braves T-shirt and carried a bright red skateboard with the outline of a white skull on it.

"Mrs. Baskerville?" he asked. "You wanted to talk to me?"

I nodded and beckoned him inside.

"Ben Kent, I presume?" I said.

23

On second thought I decided to talk with Ben downstairs in the courtyard. Courtney was already too interested in my visitor and I didn't need the constant interruptions that would inevitably accompany her fascination with him.

I put Izzy back on her leash and directed Ben to the stairs.

The evening was warm but not humid. As we came out onto the courtyard, Izzy ran to her usual favorite spots and I let Ben take his time.

There was still the scent of roasted garlic in the air as many of my neighbors were clearly eating late. There was also the barest hint of honeysuckle from the large stand of it in a pot beside the wrought-iron outer door to the building.

I watched Ben as he put his skateboard down and then picked it up as if he didn't know what to do with it or himself. He rubbed his hands on his jeans and looked toward the gate as if thinking of leaving.

Then he looked at me and his face struck me as so sad and helpless, I decided to make it easy on him.

"What can you tell me about Dezi's dad?" I asked.

"Oh, wow. I can't believe you just asked me about that."

"Why?"

"He came on to Ali, that's why! Made her real uncomfortable."

I'd seen Mark White's violent temper firsthand. But Ben was saying he had predatory tendencies too?

"Ali wasn't the only one either," Ben said. "The whole girl squad told him to eff-off at least once."

"Girl squad?"

"Yeah, the sisterhood of the traveling pants, you know."

You are speaking a totally foreign language, I thought, frowning in frustration.

He clearly saw my confusion because he immediately clarified.

"The girl gang," he said. "The BFFs. Ali, Dezi, Mikayla, Jackie."

"Was Cecily or Haley a part of this girl group?"

Ben screwed up his face in thought.

"I don't know. It's not an official group."

"But they all hung out together."

"Kind of."

This was frustrating.

"So they *didn't* hang out together?"

"Well, Dezi and Ali are best friends, you know? And there are others, every now and then, you know, that get together."

I pulled out my phone.

"Can you give me Mikayla and Jackie's phone numbers?"

"Sure." He pulled out his own phone and read off the numbers to me and then knelt on the stones to pet Izzy.

"Can you help Ali?" he said, looking up at me, his face haunted by a fear he didn't want to give in to.

I didn't want to lie to him. I didn't want to say I was just going through the motions because the fact was any hope Ali had rested with the Paris police. With Jean-Marc LaRue specifically. And I could only pray they were several steps closer to the answer to this than I was.

Several *big* steps.

"I'm going to try," I said.

"You think Dezi's dad might have had something to do with it?"

"Not really," I said. "He appears unpleasant. That doesn't usually qualify a person for being a murderer. Well, not just that."

"Yeah. He's a dick. But he's Dezi's dad."

"I appreciate you coming to see me."

He didn't speak for a moment, his head turned downward as his fingers massaged Izzy's ears and neck.

"Ben?" I said gently.

"Is it going to happen like with Cecily and Haley?" he said, his voice breaking as he turned to look at me, his face streaked with tears. "Is it too late? Do you think Ali's alive?"

I knelt and put my arms around him.

Young love is full of extreme emotion. That's just the nature of the beast. The first cut and all that.

But to lose your first love to a murdering psychopath?

That is a pain I'm not sure anybody ever comes back from.

24

I spent the rest of the evening holding my breath and waiting for the phone call that would say that Ali's body had been found. In the meantime, I did more online research about serial killers.

There weren't many surprises. Most serial killers tended to have a clear victim type—as evidenced by the three blonde American schoolgirls. Plus they usually devised very specific methodologies that they religiously stuck to—their MOs. In this case, both girls had been killed in the same way. Strangled and dumped in the Seine. Plus, most serial killers were arrogant, narcissistic and displayed a marked lack of remorse.

Again, nothing I didn't already know.

I took my laptop into my bedroom with Izzy and Robbie while Courtney watched TV in the living room. My mind drifted back to my visit with the headmaster Cedric Potter and also Mark White. I'm no criminal psychologist, but as far as arrogant, narcissistic and unremorseful tendencies went, both seemed like textbook definitions to me.

I reminded myself not to get ahead of myself by suspecting people I only had a gut aversion to.

I needed *evidence*. Not Wikipedia definitions.

I put another call into Cedric Potter's assistant headmaster Marie Zimmer. This time she picked up.

"*Allo?*" she answered pleasantly.

"Hello, Madame Zimmer, my name is Claire Baskerville. I'm a private detective working with the police on the disappearance of Ali Burton."

"What can I do for you?"

"Cedric Potter has given you as part of his alibi for the time that the three girls went missing, Cecily Danvers, Haley Johnson and Ali Burton. Can you confirm that?"

"I can confirm that I haven't worked at the school since before Christmas," Madame Zimmer said.

"Thank you," I said. "That's all I needed to know."

After we disconnected I thought back to my interview with Potter and remembered again how strangely he'd acted when I first entered the room. Like he'd been caught in the act of erasing something on his computer. What was on his computer that he was ashamed of?

I texted Jean-Marc. <*Did u examine cedric potter's computer?*>

I didn't expect an answer any time soon from Jean-Marc. He had two murders to solve and one missing person—before it became *three* murders.

After I bathed Robbie and put him to bed and ran Izzy back downstairs for her last call of the night, I decided to take a sleeping aid and go to bed myself.

There was no question I would never be able to sleep tonight without help. My mind was simply not going to allow it.

The next morning, I went through the motions of my new daily round—change the baby, feed the baby, take Izzy out, make coffee.

Notice how *my* needs went to the bottom of the list?

When Courtney finally emerged from the guest room, she went straight to Robbie to kiss and cuddle with him before putting him back on the floor and turning to the kitchen to find her breakfast.

"Cute guy last night," she said as she poured the last of the coffee into her mug.

"He's seventeen," I said.

She shrugged. "Bet he's got all his functioning parts."

"I thought you were looking for a husband."

"That doesn't mean I can't have a little fun in the meanwhile. Are we out of Nutella?"

I definitely didn't miss the "we" in that question and reminded myself that this was not a permanent situation. Just as soon as I had a plan—and not a missing sixteen-year-old girl to think about—I would enact that plan.

I have to say I took great comfort in the fact that I hadn't awakened to grim headlines or texts from Adele or Laura. It was long past the thirty-hour mark that the killer had established with both Haley and Cecily.

I'd fallen asleep last night praying that whoever had taken Ali was somebody else entirely than who had hurt Haley and Cecily. I prayed that it was somebody not driven to racking up a string of copycat killings. Somebody sloppy and new at the game.

Somebody who would leave a trail.

Courtney was dressed in sweatpants and a cropped top. She sat on the couch eating the remnants of yesterday's macaroni and cheese.

"I'm bored," she said. "Can we go shopping today?"

"You're going to the US embassy today," I said.

She groaned. "I thought we settled that."

I'd decided that navigating a foreign city with a baby was

probably too much for Courtney to handle. So I intended to remove all obstacles today.

"I'll take Robbie off your hands again today," I said.

She turned and smiled. "Really? That would be great. Okay, sure. You're right. I'll go to the embassy."

I know when I'm being snowed and Courtney wasn't even trying to hide it.

"Do you still have the directions I gave you?" I asked.

"Yep."

I went to my purse and pulled out the pre-paid cell phone.

"Here," I said. "You need to be able to give a phone number to your case worker so they can reach you."

She grabbed the phone and began ripping off its packaging.

"My case worker?"

"At the embassy," I said.

"Oh, right. Sure. Thanks! I better get dressed." She bounced up from the couch and ran to the guest room.

I had no hope that she was really going to the embassy.

The weather today was still warm but I'd worn slacks and a long sleeve shirt because I didn't trust it to stay nice and I had a long day ahead of me. I left my building with Izzy and Robbie in his stroller and headed down rue de Laborde, toward Boulevard Haussmann.

Le World School de Paris—which is a stupid name for an international school although probably a smart public relations maneuver since it's half English and half French—was located in the fifteenth arrondissement which is a fair hike from where I live. I'd need to take the Métro there and back because of the baby stroller and the dog.

Again, because Parisiennes tolerate if not love their doggos, riding the Métro in itself wasn't the problem. But it still presents certain logistical obstacles for a sixty-year-old woman needing to manage said dog and stroller up and down a set of lengthy train station stairs, not to mention squeezing through the waist-high turnstiles.

The fact that the day hadn't started with the discovery of Ali's death gave me hope and energy for the rest of my morning. Every hour that went by with no body was a gift and increased the hope that Ali's disappearance was not a part of this serial killer's *modus operandi*.

Would it hold? If it *was* the same killer who'd taken her, why was he altering his MO? Had something happened? Something out of his control?

The case studies of the serial killers I'd read about were all about their obsession with control. The fact that this guy wasn't able to adhere to his own self-imposed rules might be nearly as pernicious to his victim than if everything had gone smoothly. Of course, that only counted if the cops were able to use the change in MO to identify and locate him before he killed his latest victim.

Before he killed Ali.

Thinking of the cops and what they were or weren't doing with this case made my thoughts drift to Jean-Marc. It was unusual for him not to call me last night, especially after our less than great phone call the day before. But I'd be damned if I called him.

Not that I play games but if I did play games the ball would definitely be in his court.

After wrestling the stroller down the stairs of the Saint-Augustin Métro station and onto the first train car whose doors opened, I sat down heavily.

Robbie was looking everywhere at once, his little smile plastered across his face. How could Courtney *not* love this little guy? I thought with a smile. I put my hand on his arm and he turned to give me his widest wet smile.

This person would be a life-long friend of my daughter's.

As the train lurched forward I allowed my thoughts to go where they needed to go, specifically, to Adele's news yesterday that the semen found in the two dead girls was from two different men.

I wasn't sure if that meant this was still a serial killing or not. I'd give anything if I could hear Jean-Marc's take on it. I wondered how he was going to address it. What could it mean?

The first stop on my train route was *Madeleine*. I could either switch trains to take a different train that went quite close to the school or I could stay on this train for nine more stops and give myself a walk of at least ten blocks on the other end. As nice a day as it was, I decided to switch trains.

As I waited for the train to pull into *the station,* I thought about what Ben had said last night about how predatory Dezi's father had been with Ali and the other girls, Mikayla and Jackie. I couldn't help but wonder if Mark White's DNA was on file with the cops? But why would they take White's DNA? He was just a parent at the school, unconnected to the murders.

But even if they *had* taken his DNA, if they had nothing to match it to—which they wouldn't unless White was some kind of criminal back in the US—taking his sample would only work to eliminate him for the next murder.

Didn't that mean that White couldn't be the serial killer?

Not that I was seriously considering him anyway. Again, I was giving in to my bias against him which I really needed to do a better job of managing. In any case, thinking of White made me think of Haley and Ali's fathers, both of whom were overseas with iron-clad alibis to prove it. I wondered what the story was on Cecily's father?

At the very least I needed to assume—for the sake of my sanity and my baseline confidence in the human race—that both Haley and Ali's fathers were incapable of killing their own daughters. In any case I was sure, knowing Jean-Marc, that he would have taken everybody's DNA.

I glanced at my phone before the train car doors opened and was tempted to fire off a text to Jean-Marc asking him exactly that but I resisted.

Once the train doors opened, I maneuvered Robbie's stroller out onto the platform and was quickly engulfed by a swarm of tourists. I scooped up Izzy and settled her into the stroller with Robbie to his sheer delight and went to find the elevator to the next level.

As I walked I texted Laura.

<What is family situation of first murder?>

She answered quickly.

<father deceased>

Well, that solves that, I thought. Cecily's father was dead, and Ali and Haley's fathers have probably both been ruled out by their DNA and the obvious impossibility of their being anywhere in France at the time. I made a mental note to go online tonight to see if I could track Haley's and Ali's fathers' travel through credit card receipts in the last few weeks.

Even so, I thought as I stepped into the elevator that would take me to the platform heading toward *Balard*, a credit card receipt can be faked.

25

So angry I can hardly breathe.

Mustn't let anyone see me like this.

I'd been wrong about not gagging them. This one's screaming was ghastly. I can't believe nobody heard her and I still can't get the ungodly screeching out of my head. I'll have a headache for the rest of the day.

On top of that, she'd gotten away from me.

Dear Lord, what a mess that would've been. Just the thought of how close I came makes my hands shake.

And in the process of reclaiming her the little bitch actually marked me!

Picking up a mirror and squinting into it showed a subtly swollen bottom lip.

Oh, she'd paid dearly for it but what did that matter? I still have to show my face in public and explain a fat lip.

Or do I? The idiot police don't seem to look at anything very closely.

I could probably have a police interview with half my jaw hanging off and they wouldn't even notice.

Them being so stupid almost takes all the fun out of this.

Almost.

Easing back against the brick wall of the *building* helped make it easier to breathe normally. *I needed to wait until I could catch my breath and recover.*

How many times I've wondered how it is people don't just take one look at me and know the truth? I mean, my face has to give it all away—the jubilation, the bliss, the pure joy of it. Right?

And yet nobody ever has.

And I'm pretty sure they never will.

26

J ean-Marc looked at Claire's text message from the
night before.

<did you examine cedric potter's computer?>

He didn't know how these things worked in the US
but unless he was ready to formally charge Cedric Potter he
had no hope of examining his computer. Still it made him
wonder why she'd asked the question. He was tempted to call
and ask her when he saw Caron enter the interview room
ahead of him.

As it happened, because Potter's alibi hadn't checked out,
Jean-Marc had brought the man in for further questioning. He
was waiting inside one of the interview rooms at this very
moment.

Jean-Marc and his team were well aware that the killer's
usual thirty hours had come and gone on Ali Burton and no
body had appeared yet in the Seine. There could be many
reasons for that and Jean-Marc did not allow himself to feel too
optimistic.

*The bastard might've had trouble moving the body out without
being seen.*

The bastard might've been held up and unable to finish the killing.

The girl might have escaped.

Jean-Marc didn't hold out much hope for that last one.

The fact that the first two bodies both had semen in them but from two different men, Jean-Marc took as simple bragging on the part of the killer. It didn't mean necessarily that the man wasn't raping the victims as well. The only absolute known was that the bastard was goading the police.

Unfortunately, the one break they'd gotten in the case—traceable DNA found in Haley's body—had turned into a dead-end when the man matching the recovered sperm DNA turned out to be a homeless man living under the Pont Marie bridge who was found in his cardboard box with his throat slit.

Jean-Marc still didn't know how to process that. The man was in ill health, and been known to live by the river for years. The thought that he might be able to somehow walk unobserved down a street in the wealthy neighborhood of Le World School de Paris and manage to push a healthy big girl into his car—when he had no car—was ludicrous.

But how had his semen found its way into Haley Johnson's body? It was becoming clearer that the homeless man's death had likely been at the hands of the serial killer himself. That theory was confirmed by the fact that the DNA found under Haley's fingertips was found not to match the DNA found in semen.

Jean-Marc stepped into the interview room which held a long metal table and three chairs, all riveted to the floor. A pair of handcuffs hung on a chain from the table. Jean-Marc had given instructions to Dartre to crank the thermostat to a sultry twenty-four degrees Celsius.

Potter sat at the table, his hands folded in front of him, the sweat dribbling off the back of his neck. He looked up when Jean-Marc and Caron entered the room and licked his lips.

"You have been made aware of your rights, Monsieur Potter?" Jean-Marc asked as he took the seat next to Caron.

"Why am I here?" Potter said, his eyes darting from Caron to Jean-Marc.

"We are having some difficulty with your alibi, Monsieur," Caron said.

"Pardon?" Potter said, the sweat now pouring off him.

"My men have spoken to both your assistant headmaster and your secretary, neither of whom can confirm your whereabouts during the times in question," Jean-Marc said. "Want to try again?"

Potter rubbed his neck and pulled at his collar.

"I don't know what to say except they're lying," he said, wiping the sweat from his face.

"Marie Zimmer was not even working at the school on the dates in question," Jean-Marc said. "She left the job three months ago."

"I...that...I..."

Potter crossed his arms over his stomach and stared down at the desk in front of him.

"Margo Danvers, the mother of Cecily Danvers," Caron intoned, "also told us that her daughter had a private meeting with you the week before she went missing."

"I...that is not unusual," Potter said.

"What was the meeting about?"

"She...I...she was wearing inappropriate clothing," Potter said, his chin quivering.

Caron wrote down Potter's words and Potter watched him in apparently growing concern.

"Our investigation has also revealed that both Haley Johnson and Ali Burton had private meetings with you in the weeks before their disappearance as well," Jean-Marc said.

"I...there were discipline issues!"

"Where is Ali Burton, Monsieur Potter?"

"I...I have no idea! I swear to you!"

Potter covered his face with both hands and began to weep, his broad shoulders heaving with the effort of his wracking sobs.

Jean-Marc and Caron both stood up and stepped out of the room. Caron immediately turned to Jean-Marc.

"He's guilty," he said.

"Agreed," Jean-Marc said. "Of something anyway."

The man was definitely hiding something. But serial killers don't cry easily. They brag. They strut. They smirk.

Something didn't feel right about Potter's performance.

"What should we do with him?" Caron asked.

Jean-Marc pulled out his phone to see he'd missed a call from Chloe. Something was off with her lately. Normally she called at least five times a day and if he didn't answer she left long rambling messages. He tried to remember the last time she'd left a message.

In fact, now that he thought of it, this phone call was only the second time in a week that she'd called him. That might not be so significant if it weren't for the fact that he hadn't been home in four days.

"Chief?" Caron prompted.

"Let him go," Jean-Marc said. "But put a tail on him."

"Do we have the budget for that?"

"No. But we can't afford not to."

27

Cedric practically ran down the sidewalk in front of the police headquarters where he'd just spent two of the most intensely unpleasant hours of his life.

He forced himself to slow down. In case someone was watching. In case the CCTV cameras had zeroed in on him or any one of the many people he knew who had been planted to surveil him were taking note. He mustn't be seen as being in a hurry.

They mustn't know they've upset me in any way.

It will all be over very soon.

He'd already made that decision when he was in the midst of speaking with that horrible, arrogant frog detective.

This will be on your head, he'd wanted to tell him, in fact nearly said. *The ensuing bloodbath will be laid at your feet. And oh! There will be blood!*

That gave him some comfort. Some little bread crumb of comfort.

Do you deserve that, do you think? The Voice asked him as Cedric waited at the corner of Pont au Change and Quai du Marché Neuf for the light to change.

Cedric looked around him, stealing a look at the tight-faced woman beside him, oblivious of him and The Voice. He turned to his left where two young men stood. Filthy creatures with their dreadlocks, mottled skin and horrible clothes.

But they hadn't heard The Voice either.

I do, he whispered silently. *I do deserve some comfort after what I've been through.*

The light changed and he charged across the street forcing a compact car who'd been in the process of running the light to slam on its brakes. Cedric shot him an angry look and hand gesture to match. Instantly it rocked him out of his head, breaking the spell.

He reached the other side of the street and felt his breathing begin to slow and steady. The day was a nice one. A good day to sit outside on the terrace and drink a beer, to watch the girls go by, to imagine and dream that life was as good as he'd planned.

You know what you have to do, The Voice intoned.

Cedric flinched and felt his breathing accelerate again.

He felt the blood rush to his face, his groin, his extremities. His mouth went dry just thinking of the inevitable next step.

Because he didn't need to be told what to do.

He already wanted to do it more than he had ever wanted anything in his life.

28

I pushed the stroller to the front of the school. Looking around, I was grateful that there was nobody in sight. Fortunately there were only three shallow steps to the front door and I was able to manage to get the stroller up them fairly easily. I went to the front double doors and pulled on the handles. They didn't open but I hadn't expected them to. The school was closed after all for the summer.

I just needed to make sure it was as unoccupied as I thought.

Robbie gave an ear-piercing squeal that made me grab my heart in fright. He had noticed a squirrel racing up one of the massive beech trees in front of the school. When Izzy bolted after it, I tightened my grip on her leash just in time—nearly garroting the poor dog in the process.

I had every reason to assume that security at the school was twenty-first century when students were on campus but possibly less so when they weren't. I took out my phone and called up the schematic I'd found on the Internet last night. The map showed me the location of all exterior entrances. Descending the front steps, I followed the sidewalk around the side of the building, glancing behind me as I pushed the stroller.

I have to say that one of the few benefits to being sixty and pushing a baby stroller with a dog on a leash is that nobody and I mean *nobody* would ever assume I was up to no good. Clueless, possibly, lost, absolutely. But sneaking around to find the best port of entry to break into a school?

Not in a million years.

Unlike a typical school campus in the States, there was no designated parking lot to help determine if anybody was inside the school building. I would just have to watch my step once I got in. I glanced down at Robbie who had now upped his noise quota considerably with laughing and chortling.

I imagined that, once inside, Robbie's voice would echo exponentially in the empty hallways. But there was nothing for it. I had a few other plans for today but the first to-do was to see Ali's classrooms and locker. I'd thought about looking at Haley's and Cecily's lockers too but in the end I didn't have time. I wasn't here to catch a serial killer. That was Jean-Marc's job.

I was here to find Ali.

Behind the school building there was a paved play yard enclosed by a tall chain link fence. I went to the fence gate, fully expecting an electronic keypad, and was surprised to see there was only a padlock.

"That's good news for us," I said to Robbie. "Forget everything you are about to see."

He giggled and turned his face to the sun.

I knelt by his stroller and pulled out a leather pouch. From it I took a teething biscuit which I snapped in half, giving one half to Robbie and the other to Izzy. And then I withdrew the lock-picking kit I always carry but rarely have an opportunity to use.

I've discovered that there are actually lock-picking clubs out there with many active members, which I suppose is more reassuring than the fact that there are whole groups of people who make it their business to learn how to open locks that are locked for a reason.

I've played with lock-picking for years, even got my first kit on Amazon over a decade ago. Of course as locks went electronic, those skills were no longer needed.

But in France, while apartments had definitely modernized their security, many of the older shops were still old school.

This lock was pretty sweet. It was new but quickly opened with one twist of my trusty number seven pick.

I was inside the play yard in under a minute. I'd already scanned the perimeter to confirm that there were no cameras back here and quickly made my way across the black tarmac to the back door of the school. There was a window in the door and I peered through it to see if there was any sign that an alarm might go off when I opened the door.

Again. Old woman with a baby and a dog.

If the alarm did go off, I could always punt to being confused and one hundred percent of the time the police would believe it. Sigh. It really is one of the few benefits to being elderly.

Holding my breath, I pushed open the door.

There was no alarm.

I wheeled Robbie's stroller into what appeared to be a sort of mudroom or anteroom. Benches lined the walls on both sides of the hallway and I imagined that this was where squads of students sat before and after school.

I moved quickly into the next room which was a locker room. If I was planning on rifling through Ali's locker, I was out of luck. None of the lockers were personal, they were just used for the hour of class needed to safekeep a student's purse, books and personal items.

There was a drain in the cement floor of the locker room which made me think that the showers must be somewhere nearby. I continued walking and saw them to the right off the hallway facing an office with a window.

A plaque on the door to the office read *Miss Knox Physical Education Director.*

I heard what I thought was a sound of approaching footsteps and stopped for a moment and held my breath but the sound didn't repeat itself.

I pushed the office door open and stepped inside, maneuvering the stroller to park it by the door.

A wooden desk was positioned near the far wall with just enough room for the chair behind it. Shelves in the room were filled with soccer balls, basketballs, hockey sticks, stacks of towels as well as binders and paperback books. A metal armoire was adjacent to the desk and two wooden chairs with no padding were squeezed in front of the desk.

On the desk was a dying African violet in a pot, a stack of papers and a framed photo of an older man with his arms crossed and a look of anger on his face. Next to him stood a young girl with worried eyes.

I went behind the desk and pulled open the first drawer. Inside were paper pads, pens, pencils and other office supplies, along with several golf balls. The next drawer contained a large supply of tampons. I tried the bottom drawer, but it was stuck hard.

I pulled harder and finally succeeded in jerking it open. Looking inside, I couldn't believe what I saw.

A headband, a scrunchie, and a wrist band with the initials H. J.

I gasped as I picked up the wristband in my hands.

H. J.

Haley Johnson.

I felt the adrenaline rush all the way down to my toes.

I was pretty sure I was looking at a serial killer's trophy collection.

29

"What the hell are you doing in my office?"

I never even heard her come in.

At the sound of her voice, I dropped the wristband back in the drawer and straightened up. My eye went first to Robbie since he was between me and the woman I assumed was Deb Knox. When I did, Knox pivoted to stare in astonishment at the baby in the stroller in her office.

"What the hell is going on here?" she said, now looking over at Izzy who had taken up her post next to the stroller and was eyeing the gym teacher with growing menace.

I hurried out from behind the desk and put my hand on the stroller handle.

"I'm sorry," I said. "I was lost."

"In my *desk*?" she said incredulously, pushing past me to look at her desk and what I'd been looking at.

Deb Knox was a large woman, easily two hundred pounds. Her hair was cut short and framed a blotchy and very angry face.

"Who let you in here?" she asked, slamming shut the desk drawer and turning to face me.

"A very nice older gentleman," I said, praying that the likelihood of the school having some old custodian should be fairly high. "He was very helpful."

"Well, he's just lost his job on account of you!"

I decided to take a different approach.

"Mr. Potter said I was to have free run of the place for my investigation."

How's that for a pivot? From lost old lady to investigator in under ten seconds.

If I were called on this lie by Potter, I would say I had misunderstood him, believing that I'd left him with the understanding that I could search the building and that he'd said he'd do whatever he could to help in the investigation of Ali Burton's disappearance.

It should at least help the poor custodian keep his job.

"Well, Potter never said anything to me," Knox said, still glaring at the baby, the dog and me.

"Be that as it may," I said primly. "Can you tell me what these items are in your desk drawer and how they came to be there?"

I was less interested in whatever lie she would spin for me about the items than actually possessing the items themselves. I cursed the bad timing of Knox's arrival since I knew I badly needed to take them with me to be tested for DNA.

"That drawer is the Lost and Found," she said.

"So you have no idea who they belong to?"

"Would they be in Lost and Found if I did?"

Good point.

"Why would Potter give you free run of the place?" she asked, narrowing her eyes at me. "What do you mean *investigation*?"

"I am employed by the parents of Ali Burton," I said.

If I thought that might change her belligerent attitude, I was sadly mistaken. If anything, she snorted in derision upon hearing it.

"The cops already talked to me when Danvers disappeared. And then again with Johnson."

It took me a second before I realized she was referring to the dead girls by their last names.

"I'm the last person to be surprised they got themselves kidnapped and killed," she said. "They were both classic victims."

"And Ali Burton?"

"The same. Weak. Pathetic. Are we done here? I have work to do."

"What work are you doing when the school is closed and there are no students?"

"That is none of your business."

"One thing that is my business," I said, "is ascertaining where all the teachers were during the time that Ali Burton went missing."

"Oh, give me a break. How would a teacher have enough time to get out of here at two o'clock and nab a student? And why would they? We have enough of the little buggers all day long."

"Nonetheless. Where were you?"

"Yesterday? Home sick and my partner can confirm that. During the time that Johnson and Danvers were taken? I was in London. Again with my partner. Happy now? Will you kindly piss off?"

The fact that Knox possibly had a confirmable alibi—and of course I would confirm it—was one thing but the other thing that didn't make sense was the fact that she had a partner. Serial killers tended to be loners.

Not to mention the fact that she was a woman.

In the history of the world there have only been a handful of female serial killers.

I maneuvered Robbie's stroller out of the small room, tugging Izzy along on her leash.

Regardless of how excited I'd been over my discovery of Knox's office drawer, the fact was unless she was a hell of an actor—which, let's face it, most sociopaths are—*and* she can teleport, Deb Knox was probably not the one I was looking for.

30

W*ell, this sucks.*
Now there's now no way I can make it happen in
thirty hours.

A jab of anger punched hard to the chest at the thought.

Am I the only one who cares about style? Or process?

Do the police even know that the girls die within thirty hours of being taken? Have I given them too much credit?

It was infuriating that there were no details in the press. At least then there would be some accounting, some indication of how the police were assessing the crimes.

Do they think I'm stupid? Or sloppy? Do they not see the symmetry of this?

It was infuriating beyond measure that there seemed to be no one who understood the structure of it all.

Do I need to paint them a frigging picture?

And now what? Now that there was no way to dispatch the next girl in a timely fashion?

The rage boiled up into a cauldron of vitriol until even breathing felt difficult.

Here's a thought. Let's mix things up a bit, shall we?

I'm not changing my MO.

I'm deepening it.

A shiver of pleasure shimmied through the killer, dissipating the earlier anger and leaving in its place a low-grade hum of euphoria.

Yeah, that's right. Deepening it. Are you ready?

Let's see if you can figure out this next move.

31

Beads of water gathered on the café's tabletops and morphed into a hypnotizing stream.

It started out as a light sprinkle but was soon dripping off the overhanging awning of the terrace where Jean-Marc sat at the café near Claire's apartment. He recognized that he was playing a game with himself, one he'd unconsciously created in an effort to make himself feel better about what he was doing.

Instead of going up to her apartment to see her, or calling her, he would sit at the café and wait for just a few precious minutes of peace and quiet before going back to the office. If she happened to stroll by—not at all unlikely—then he would be rewarded by a visit with her.

If she didn't, then it wasn't meant to be and he would finish his coffee and go back to work.

His mind was roiling with the status of the three cases. Each of them seemed similar yet not. It had now been forty-eight hours since Ali Burton was taken and Jean-Marc took comfort with every passing minute that her body had not shown up.

He sat at the café, feeling the pressure build up in the darkening clouds that had gathered overhead, and once more obsessively ran through the details of all three cases from the beginning.

The first case: Cecily Danvers, American. Nabbed on the way home from school. Raped, strangled, dumped in the Seine.

The second case: Haley Johnson, American. Nabbed on the way home from school. Raped, strangled, dumped in the Seine.

The current kidnap victim: Ali Burton, American. Nabbed on the way home from school.

In every case except the latest, the girl had been dispatched quickly, the ME putting time of death right at thirty hours after abduction.

For some reason Ali was different.

Unless the bastard had already killed her and was just having trouble dumping the body. Nausea rippled through Jean-Marc at the thought.

Could he see Cedric Potter hauling these big healthy girls—athletes most of them—upstairs and across bridges? The man looked too hesitant to have a plan for his next breakfast let alone a *modus operandi* to baffle the finest detectives in France.

He flinched at the thought.

If only someone else was on the case. These girls might at least have a shot.

His eye caught the sight of Claire coming toward him. She was walking briskly down the sidewalk, her little dog on its leash.

Pushing a baby stroller.

He watched her come, feeling his heart lift in his chest like a balloon trying to escape. A part of him couldn't help but imagine that this is how she would have looked if they could have had a life together years ago, a life with children.

He brusquely pushed the thought away and stood up, raising a hand to get her attention.

"Claire," he called.

Her face, which only seconds before had been clenched in thought, cleared at the sight of him and when it did he felt his love for her beam out of him as if it would pool around them both.

She came to his table and he kissed her on both cheeks and then on the lips before holding the chair out for her.

"So this is the little love child, *non*?" he said, nodding at the infant who was eyeing him seriously.

"I don't tend to refer to him as that," Claire said with a grimace.

Jean-Marc laughed.

"Of course not. Sorry. So how is all that going?"

"You mean with Courtney? I'm a little worried that I'm not going to be able to get rid of her."

"But you are always taking in strays, yes? That is your way?"

"How dare you?" Claire said with mock indignation. "I'll have you know that Izzy is a purebred French bulldog."

The waiter came to take her coffee order.

"How long have you been here?" she asked. "Why didn't you come up to the apartment?"

"I can't stay," he said. "I am sorry, *chérie*."

"No word yet about Ali Burton?"

"You know I cannot talk about an active case."

"You can tell me if she's been found or not."

He realized he wasn't meeting her eye.

"She has not been found," he said.

"Do you have any idea at all where she might be?"

"Don't you imagine I would be there if I did?" He pressed his lips together in a severe line.

"No, you're right, of course. I'm sorry. It's just so frustrating. What about her teachers? Have you talked to them?"

"Claire, enough. I must go." Jean-Marc stood and signaled for the bill.

"Is it true that Deb Knox was in London during the time of both murders?"

Jean-Marc's eyes widened in surprise.

Is she questioning my suspects?

"It's just that I happened to bump into her this morning," Claire said hurriedly. "And she said she was in London with her girlfriend. Did you confirm that?"

"We are in the process of confirming it."

"Plus she has a desk drawer full of headbands and things that belonged to the girls, including a wristband belonging Haley Johnson."

"So?" he said, drumming his fingers on the café table in irritation.

"So you should test them for DNA. They could be trophies."

"I thought you said you would leave this case alone," he said.

"I told Jessica Burton I would do what I could."

"*Non.* This is not good for you emotionally and also you will get in my way."

"I gave my word."

"Listen to me, Claire. This case isn't like the others."

"What about Cedric Potter's alibi?" she asked, ignoring his comment. "I called his secretary and she said she couldn't remember seeing him that day. So he might not have an alibi. I called the assistant headmaster too and—"

"I mean it, Claire. Let it *go.*"

And because he knew he was already late getting back and because all she wanted to talk about were things he couldn't discuss and things he was failing badly at, he left abruptly, not even kissing her goodbye.

He strode down the sidewalk to his car feeling her hurt rippling in the air behind him.

～

As I watched Jean-Marc go stomping off down the sidewalk it occurred to me that he'd probably think twice before he decided to spontaneously surprise *me* with a midday visit.

I was sorry about that. Not only did I get no information from him beyond the fact that Deb Knox's alibi hadn't been confirmed, but I'd pissed him off in the bargain.

The only brief glimmer of good news was the one I'd started out with: no word yet on Ali Burton showing up dead somewhere.

Of course Jean-Marc's admission that he had no idea of where to find her rather canceled out the meagre joy of that little feel-good bump.

After I finished my coffee I turned my swirling mind to the dregs in my coffee cup—I really needed to stop drinking coffee so late in the day. It was worrisome that Jean-Marc seemed to have no leads or sense of direction with either the serial killings or Ali's disappearance—and I was working very hard to consider them both as separate cases.

My phone gave an innocuous chime, indicating I'd received a text message. With mounting dread, I dug my phone out of the diaper bag and saw it was a text from Ben Kent.

<forgot to mention last night! do you know about Maurice?>

32

After his disastrous rendezvous with Claire it took Jean-Marc a good hour to shake off his bad mood. Even the long walk to where he'd parked his car and the drive back to police headquarters hadn't aided in dissipating it.

She must think I'm an idiot, he thought as he strode to his desk, nodding curtly at Caron and Dartre.

She honestly thought I had a lead!

That was when he realized his real anger was at himself for having to reveal to her that he was still flailing away for answers.

With a young girl's life on the line.

He entered the department bull pen, nodding at a few detectives he knew and who hadn't totally frozen him out for past gross conduct. Both his sergeants were at their desks and looked up when he entered the room.

In the old days he might have expected some news when he came back from a long lunch. But these days any news worth hearing he would've gotten on his cell phone.

No new leads. No breaks in the case.

He dropped his car keys on his desk and turned and walked over to the murder board. Every time he looked at it, he harbored the hope that something might jump out at him that he hadn't seen before.

His eyes went to Ali Burton's photo. She was taken forty-eight hours ago.

What did that mean? Why had the killer changed up his MO? Could it be Potter after all? It would explain why no body had shown up during the time he was in police custody.

"Dartre," he said turning to the younger sergeant. The young man looked up, ready and eager. "Check the CCTV cameras again on the walk from the school."

Dartre frowned. "For which date, Chief?"

"For all of them! Check all the abduction dates."

"Right, Chief."

He appreciated the practiced look of consideration on Dartre's face but he could read his thoughts as clearly as if the boy had shouted it out, *This was hopeless.*

They were going over old leads for the tenth time.

What was it Claire had said? That Deb Knox didn't have an alibi?

Jean-Marc groaned. That was even more useless information than he already possessed.

A woman did not do these crimes.

He picked up his phone, noting that he hadn't heard from Chloe today. He put a call in to her to let her know he wouldn't be coming home again tonight.

Not with Ali Burton's body about to show up at any moment in the Seine.

"*Allo?*"

"*Allo, chérie,*" he said. "How is your day?"

"Who cares how my day is?"

He was used to this.

"I'm sorry, *chérie*. I have to stay here again tonight. This case I'm working on is time-sensitive and the—"

"You don't need to bother lying to me, Jean-Marc," she said and hung up.

Jean-Marc held the phone for a moment, surprised. And then felt a surge of relief. He didn't have time to deal with Chloe's hurt feelings at the moment. But it did remind him that she had been acting much less clingy lately.

And more secretive.

"Chief," Dartre said, standing up, his phone to his ear. Jean-Marc turned and saw the stricken look on the boy's face and he stopped as if turned to stone.

"It's Dispatch," Dartre said. "They just got a call from another of the school's parents."

Mon Dieu, non, Jean-Marc thought. *It can't be.*

"Another girl is missing."

33

I immediately called Ben.

"Who's Maurice?" I asked.

"He's the pervert who waits tables at Café Bleu on the corner crossroads of the school."

I remembered that café from when I'd spotted it from a distance yesterday.

"Why is he a pervert?" I asked.

"I don't know. Maybe something in his childhood?"

"No, I mean why do you call him that?"

"Oh, because he was always leering at the girls, you know? He'd touch 'em too. Most of the girls thought because he was French it was a cultural thing, you know? So they'd let him get away with it without flying all over his shit."

I made a note to go to the café. The sun was hot where I sat and seemed to sap me of my energy by the minute. And then I thought of how Ali was out there somewhere and the minutes probably felt even longer to her.

"Okay," I said. "Now where can I meet these two girls Mikayla and Jackie you were telling me about?"

"I'm meeting them at the Bois de Boulogne in fifteen minutes."

The Bois de Boulogne was a famous and quite large Paris park, perhaps a hundred times the size of Parc Monceau and two and a half times the area of Central Park.

"Where exactly in the park?" I asked.

He gave me directions and I disconnected. Robbie had fallen asleep in his stroller about five minutes before Jean-Marc left. I really needed to change him but I didn't want to wake him if I could help it. I debated running him upstairs on the hopes that Courtney might be back but if she wasn't I'd be stuck with him anyway and then I'd be late for my meeting with Ben and the girls.

"I guess I don't need to ask *you* if a little longer walk is okay?" I said to Izzy who sat in Jean-Marc's seat watching all the sidewalk pedestrian traffic go by.

I gathered up her leash, paid the bill and headed toward the park. The Bois de Boulogne was a long walk from here and I was already tired—welcome to being sixty—but for some reason after seeing Jean-Marc I was even more aware of every passing moment.

And what that meant for Ali Burton.

I think I knew that to a certain extent Jean-Marc was just trying to protect me. He knew what an emotional time bomb all these cases were for me—and for any mother experiencing anxiety over her children's safety. But he also was keenly aware that the anxiety was ultimately useless. It wouldn't help him find Ali Burton any faster, it wouldn't help him identify and bring Haley Johnson's or Cecily Danvers' killer to justice.

The park was on the far side of the eighth arrondissement on the right bank, so technically it was still in my neck of the woods—but only technically. It was also not that far from Le World School de Paris.

By the time I arrived at the park I was exhausted and coated in sweat. Robbie was wet and hungry.

And telling the world about it.

Just the sheer size of Bois de Boulogne reminded me that it used to be a royal hunting preserve. It wasn't just a park but a series of greenhouses and botanical gardens with several lakes thrown in for good measure. I'm pretty sure you could come to this park every day for a year and not have the same experience twice.

Currently my experience was bordering on the very unpleasant.

Robbie's howls were effectively chasing the very birds from the trees above us. I found a semi-shaded bench in the first clearing in the park I came to and put the brake on the stroller. I tied Izzy to the stroller handle and quickly changed Robbie's diaper. That was one problem solved but not the one that appeared to matter most to Robbie.

As I worried that I was ruining everyone else's peaceful park experience, I saw three teenagers approach me from the winding gravel path that meandered through the park.

"Hey, little man!" Ben said as he walked over to my bench with his red skateboard in one hand and two blonde teenage girls behind him.

"Oh, he's so cute!" one of the girls said. "Can I pet him?"

I looked to see she'd untied Izzy's leash and was kneeling next to her.

"Sorry about this," I said to Ben. "I didn't mean to make quite such an entrance."

"Wow," the other blonde girl said, frowning at Robbie, who Ben had now picked up and was doing an expert job of swaying and jostling to calm his crying. "Is he yours?"

"Don't be stupid," Ben said to her good-naturedly, patting Robbie's back. "He's gotta be her grandkid."

"Why's he unhappy?" the girl asked.

"He's hungry," I said, rummaging in the diaper bag for a bottle of formula. I held it out to Ben questioningly.

"Sure," he said, taking the bottle and sitting down on the bench with Robbie who eagerly clapped both hands over Ben's hands to hold the bottle to his mouth.

"Wow!" Ben laughed. "Look at him go!"

I wiped my hands on some wet wipes and turned to the two girls.

"I'm Claire Baskerville."

"Yeah, Ben told us," the girl with Izzy said. "The private detective."

"I was hoping I could ask you a few questions."

The girl with Izzy held onto the leash but sat on the bench with Ben and peered into Robbie's face. Between her and the other girl I knew there was no way I'd ever recall these two girls' faces again. They were both blonde, about the same height and weight, with normal noses, blue eyes and absolutely nothing I could use to distinguish them.

Story of my life.

"So which one's Jackie?" I asked,

The girl on the bench with Ben raised her hand but didn't tear her eyes away from the sight of Robbie enjoying his lunch. I turned to the other girl who was standing and watching her two friends on the bench.

"So you must be Mikayla," I said.

"Wow. You really are a detective," she said with a curl of her lip.

I sized her up quickly, deciding the brash mouth was an act. I know some kids take strength and self-protection from sarcasm. I totally get that. I know some adults do too. But getting to the truth usually requires getting past that particular defense mechanism.

"Ben said that Dezi White's father sometimes behaves inappropriately with you," I said.

Mikayla laughed and shook her head. "Really, Ben?"

"Well, he does," Ben said, blushing. "I'm not making it up."

"*Does* he get inappropriate?" I pressed Mikayla.

"I hate that word," Jackie said. "It doesn't say what it really means."

Before I could rephrase the question, Mikayla spoke.

"Yeah, he's a letch," she said with a shrug. "Annoying but harmless. And some of the uglier girls even appreciate the attention. You know what I mean?"

Jackie giggled.

So it's true. Mark White flirts with the girls his daughter's age. Not good but probably not illegal.

"What about your teachers?" I asked. "Are there any who might have wanted to hurt Cecily or Haley?"

Both Mikayla and Jackie looked at each other. "Miss Knox," they said in unison.

"Why is that?" I asked.

"Because she hates men and she hates girls who don't. She basically hates everyone who isn't like her," Jackie said.

"Yeah, except for Haley," Mikayla said thoughtfully.

"Miss Knox didn't hate Haley?" I asked.

Or was she saying Haley was gay too?

"Yeah, you're right," Ben said. "Knox didn't hate Haley because Haley was her best soccer player. She'd never do anything to hurt her."

"We'd never win another game if she did," Jackie said. "Oh. I guess this means we're not going to win any more games."

I let the silence seep in for a moment.

"What about Ali Burton?" I asked softly. "Did Miss Knox hate her?"

"Definitely," Mikayla said, her eyes going over to Ben. It was then I realized she had a crush on him.

But Ben was in love with Ali.

"Of course she hated her," Ben said, sitting up with the baby, his eyes fierce. "Because Ali was beautiful and sexy. She was everything someone like Miss Knox wanted to be but wasn't."

"I gotta go," Mikayla said. "Jackie, you coming?"

"Yeah, okay," Jackie said as she gave Izzy one last pat on the head. "We loved her too, Ben."

"I know," Ben said, focusing for all he was worth on feeding Robbie and not lifting his head.

After the two girls left, I sat down on the bench with Ben and took Robbie from him to burp him before putting him back in the stroller. I gave him a flower to play with, checking first to make sure it wasn't toxic since it would almost certainly end up in his mouth.

"Have you heard anything about Ali?" Ben asked. "Any news at all?"

"No news is good news," I heard myself say.

"Do you think it's possible Miss Knox could have her somewhere?"

Honestly, it seemed unlikely.

"I don't know. I'm still following up leads. Thanks for the tip on Maurice, by the way. I've given the cops a heads-up."

"What about Dezi's dad? He could've killed Cecily and Haley both. And Ali thought he was a perv. Could it be him?"

I hesitated. One thing I knew about investigative work was that it was tempting to create scenarios or conclusions too early in the case. That was almost always a disaster. Once you got attached to one theory or suspect over another there was a tendency to build your case to fit your prejudice.

And then what if you're wrong?

Mark White appeared to be a seriously unstable blowhard

with a big temper. While it was true that most serial killers were psychopaths who felt they were smarter than everyone else, they tended to have iron-clad grips on their emotions and actions.

If Mark White really was the serial killer he was rewriting the definition of what it took to be a murdering psychopath.

34

It was a classically elegant apartment which, after seeing the outside, didn't surprise Jean-Marc. After all, the Whites lived in a fashionable neighborhood in what many believe to be the most expensive city in the world.

It was after seven in the evening but the scent of coffee coming from the large American-sized kitchen and the crush of people in the halls and living room of the apartment belied the time.

When an abduction occurs there are specific protocols and everyone has a job to do.

He and his two sergeants had been among the first to arrive at the White's residence. From the kitchen, Jean-Marc now watched the parents of the missing girl. What he saw was not unexpected. He hadn't witnessed it exactly when the other three girls had gone missing because in each case the fathers had not been present.

Is that significant?

Audrey White was a tall, attractive woman in her early forties with dark auburn hair and a pale complexion. She was dressed simply but tastefully in a pair of cream colored slacks and a cashmere sweater with small gold studs at her ears.

The living room where the parents sat was tastefully furnished. No one piece jumped out as screaming money. Every piece of furniture looked expensive but not ostentatious so that the overall effect was subtle elegance. The sitting area walls and seat cushions were a combination of repeating damask patterns and floral prints. They should have clashed but they didn't. The entire living room was gently illuminated with small wall sconces.

Yet the tension in the room was as harsh as if Jean-Marc were standing in a boxing ring surrounded by howling adversaries.

From where he stood by the entrance to the kitchen he could see Mark and Audrey White with their arms around each other as they sat in their magazine-cover living room. Audrey sobbed quietly into Mark's shoulder while he gazed around the room with a stunned expression on his face as though not able to believe what was happening.

It had been four hours since Dezi White disappeared.

Both of Dezi's parents had given preliminary statements. The appropriate agencies and the wheels of their care and service had been set in motion—social services to see if there had been problems at home (there hadn't been, or at least none reported), psych services to aid the parents in the current process, and of course all auxiliary police agencies throughout the country to be on the lookout for a seventeen-year-old girl, five-foot tall, one hundred and twenty pounds, no scars or outstanding identifiable features.

And all of it a big waste of time.

There wasn't a person standing in this room—her parents included—who didn't know exactly what had happened to Dezi White.

Jean-Marc took in a deep breath and exhaled slowly before

entering the living room. Immediately the husband spied him and broke away from his wife.

"You're in charge?" Mark White said, standing up to confront Jean-Marc.

"I am, Monsieur White," Jean-Marc said. "Will you sit?"

"I've had enough sitting! What are you doing about finding my daughter?"

"We have a procedure for—"

"Screw your procedure!" White yelled, prompting his wife's sobs to become more pronounced.

"Did your *procedure* help Dezi's friend Ali? Or Haley? I want to know what you're going to do *different!*"

"Monsieur, if you would just calm yourself," Jean-Marc said.

"Don't try to *handle* me, you French bastard! This is my little girl we're talking about!"

"I understand that, Monsieur. But our procedures enable us to get the information we need to go forward. Please."

White ran a frustrated hand through his hair, his eyes rheumy and bloodshot. His puffed-out chest seemed to collapse under the weight of Jean-Marc's reasonableness. He turned back to his wife and they reached for each other again.

Caron and Dartre stood in the living room and were watching the couple closely. Dartre had already gone through Dezi's bedroom and bagged her phone and laptop. None of the other missing girls had had anything on their computers that suggested a lead to someone who could have done this and Jean-Marc did not have high hopes for finding anything on Dezi's.

Still. Procedure.

Jean-Marc signaled to Dartre to wait outside the apartment door. With uniformed police securing the premises, as well as forensic techs dusting for prints and a department social services agent to aid the Whites get through the next few hours of this crisis, there were already too many people in the small apartment and the crush of the crowd might derange even the sanest, most mild-mannered person.

And Mark White did not strike Jean-Marc as anything remotely like that even on a good day.

"Monsieur and Madame White," Jean-Marc said as he stepped over to them. "Please take a seat. I know you have already given a statement but I would like to hear it from you myself."

Sitting down, Mark and Audrey perched on the edge of the couch as if expecting the need to jump up at any moment. They gripped each other's hands tightly. Audrey's tears still fell down her cheeks onto their clasped hands.

"What do you want to know?" Mark said hoarsely, the fight nearly completely gone out of him now.

"Where were you and Madame White this afternoon?"

"We went out for lunch," Mark said, giving his wife a sad look. She squeezed her eyes shut as if she couldn't bear to remember that she'd opted to enjoy an afternoon out instead of standing guard over her only child.

"We often do that on a Friday," he said.

"But Dezi is not usually home on a Friday, yes?" Jean-Marc prompted.

"No. The school was closed so she was doing some reading and I think practicing her flute."

"Why would she be outside alone?" Jean-Marc asked.

He had already walked the small outdoor space earlier when he arrived. It featured a narrow wedge of lawn but was largely a pavered courtyard. Rows of oleanders framed the area. A linen-covered teak lounge chair sat in the middle of the lawn patch, the basket beside it was filled with paperback books.

"She likes to sit out there and get some sun," Audrey said. "And read."

Jean-Marc didn't bother asking if there was any access from the courtyard other than from the house. He already knew there was a gate off the courtyard that led to a narrow brick alley that emptied onto rue Erlanger.

"What time did you leave the house?" Jean-Marc asked.

"Noon," Mark said, angrily wiping away a tear.

"And when you returned?"

"Perhaps three o'clock," he said. "We stopped at L'Etiquette first."

Just the mention of that extra stop sent Audrey back into uncontrollable sobs again. Jean-Marc wanted to be able to reassure her that the extra stop very likely altered not at all what had happened to Dezi.

But of course, he didn't know that at all.

"What happens now?" Mark asked, his eyes hopeful and pleading. It struck Jean-Marc that this man rarely felt the emotions he was feeling now—a complete lack of control and an utter dependence on someone he might normally have every inclination to disdain.

According to Jean-Marc's background report on Mark White, he was a supervising sales representative with Mammotome, a French medical devices company. He led a team of over sixty people of all nationalities. From past annual job evaluations to which Jean-Marc had access, White was not typically diplomatic with his team members.

"One of my people will stay with you at all times," Jean-Marc said. "The phones will be monitored in case there is a ransom—"

"You know that's not what this is!" Audrey nearly shrieked. "There will be no ransom!"

Jean-Marc watched Mark White cringe as his wife voiced the thought that nobody else wanted to say out loud.

Jean-Marc's phone dinged and he glanced down to see he'd received a text message from Claire.

<Call me>

He turned his attention back to the couple on the couch in front of him.

"It is just a part of the drill," Jean-Marc assured her. "We have every team and resource of the Paris police department sweeping the streets of Paris, canvassing your neighborhood for anyone who might have seen anything, scouring Dezi's social media contacts, and following up on the leads we already have from the other cases."

Mark and Audrey White looked at him with matching looks of hope and desperation. It was all Jean-Marc could do to meet their eyes.

For while it was true he would do everything within his power, the fact was he had absolutely no idea who could have taken Dezi White from her backyard in broad daylight.

35

The weather had gone from decent to crap in less than two minutes. One minute it was all sunny skies and the next you were walking in wet shoes looking like a drowned poodle.

Deb Knox shifted her position from where she stood on the street corner. A skateboarder was headed in her direction and she took a step off the sidewalk and into his path to force him to veer off.

She took in a breath to focus on her phone conversation with Becky. Becky, who for some reason was acting not at all like herself. Becky, who for some reason, was being a total bitch.

"All I'm asking you to do," Deb said patiently into the phone, "is to confirm we were in London when I said we were!"

"But that's a lie," Becky said, her voice a plaintive whine.

God! Has she always sounded like this? Like a frightened wimp?

"It's not a lie!" Deb said between gritted teeth. "We *were* in London!"

"But not for the second murder we weren't. And technically we were back in time for the first one, too."

Deb scrubbed a hand over her face in frustration.

What is the matter with her? she thought. *What is her deal?* She turned to look up at Le World School de Paris in front of her. She instantly flashed to an image of the open drawer of her desk and its contents.

The wristband. The hair bow. A lipstick tube. A cheap beaded bracelet.

"That doesn't matter!" Deb said tightly into the phone. "You just need to *say* we were in London. The guy the cops are looking for is a serial killer so the fact that *we* couldn't have killed Danvers—"

"What do you mean *we*? I've never been anywhere near your school."

Deb's jaw clenched painfully.

"Yes, alright," she said. "*I* couldn't have killed Danvers—that fact will get lost when they see I don't have an alibi for Johnson. Don't you see?"

"I don't, really. If this is a serial killer, and you have a sort of alibi for the first one—"

"*Sort of* doesn't cut it! The only thing the cops will see is that all the little bitches hated me—"

"Gee, I wonder why."

"—and that I don't have an alibi for the second and third murders."

"What do you mean third? There's only been two murders in total, hasn't there?"

"Yes, yes. Slip of the tongue."

"Are you already counting the third girl? She hasn't showed up dead yet, has she?"

"Becks, no. I told you. I misspoke. So how about it? Will you back me up for the first two abductions? That's May fifth and seventh."

"You don't have an alibi for yesterday either," Becky

reminded her. "Since I wasn't home when you were supposedly home sick."

Deb strained to hear the background noise from wherever Becky was calling. It didn't sound like office noises. It sounded like she was out at a park or an outdoor café. Deb tried to think where Becky said she was going to be today.

"Look, whose side are you on?" Deb said bitterly, now suddenly sure that Becky had lied to her about going in to work today.

The lying bitch is playing hooky. Probably with that Scandinavian skank in her office.

"I'll tell you whose side I'm on," Becky said, raising her voice. "I'm on the side of whoever isn't asking me to lie to confirm an alibi! My last girlfriend never even used the word *alibi*! Or *prime suspect*! Or *possible murderer!*"

"Well, maybe you should go back to her. What was her name? Taffy?"

Deb felt her pulse elevate and her vision begin to narrow.

Could Becky be with Taffy right now? That would explain so much!

"Maybe I will go back to her," Becky said, lowering her voice menacingly." And don't change the subject. I'm not lying for you anymore, Deb. We were in London for one night. *One.* That puts you in the clear for the first abduction if they don't hold your feet to the fire about what time we got back. But you're on your own to explain where you were for the other two —assuming the third girl shows up dead."

"Well, you know she will."

"I don't know anything. It worries me a little that you do."

"What is that supposed to mean?"

"Nothing, Deb. Except maybe we need to take a break."

"Oh, no you don't! I've got a freakin' private detective on my ass who thinks I'm involved in these abductions! I need you to help me throw her off my scent."

"Sorry, Deb. I wish you the best. I really do. I just think—"

"I'll make you sorry for this. Do you hear me? Good and sorry!"

Deb's hands were shaking. As much as she wanted to hang up on Becky, a part of her held out hope that they might yet patch this up.

Somehow.

"Bye, Deb. I can give you until the weekend to clear out your stuff."

And Becky disconnected the phone.

36

I'd only just stepped over the threshold of my apartment, my mind a whirling cacophony of thoughts about Mark White and how much he might be involved in the disappearance of his daughter's friends, when my phone began to blow up with voicemails, first from Adele and then Laura and then Jessica.

My first thought was that this was the bad news we'd all been waiting for, the news that they'd found Ali's body.

I called Jessica back first.

"Claire, have you heard?" Jessica said in rush. "Another girl is missing. Dear God. I'm going to lose my mind. What does this mean? Where's Ali?"

I was stunned. Of all the things I'd been expecting to hear, this wasn't one of them.

"Where?" I asked. "How?"

"I don't know the details. What do you think it means?"

I heard the cold dread and terror in Jessica's voice.

It meant that Ali was in all likelihood dead, her body not yet discovered.

"The police say it doesn't mean anything," Jessica sobbed as I unclipped Izzy's leash and handed Robbie to Courtney.

"He needs changing," I said to Courtney before turning my attention back to the phone. "And they're right," I said to Jessica. "It doesn't mean anything."

"Except he always kills before he takes the next one!" Jessica wailed. "You know he does! The police know it too! Oh dear God, I can't bear this!"

"Jessica, call Laura. She'll tell you the truth which is that nobody knows. Do not give up hope. I need to call the police and—"

"Yes! Call them! They'll tell *you* the truth."

"I'm sure they're telling you the truth too," I said, knowing that was not at all the case. "I'll call you when I know something."

I disconnected and stood for a moment in the middle of the living room before turning to Courtney who had not changed the baby.

Her annoyance at being told to take care of her own baby told me in no uncertain terms that a come-to-Jesus moment was upon us.

But I didn't have time for it.

"There's *chouquettes* in the bag," I said, referring to the sugared puff pastry knots and turning to go to the kitchen to make Izzy's dinner.

"Did you get the second key made like I asked you?" Courtney said.

Robbie's tolerance for riding around in a wet diaper was about at its end and he began to fuss and squirm in her arms.

"Please change him," I said firmly. "I don't have time to—"

"Don't tell me you're going out. Because I have a date tonight."

I nearly dropped the can opener and it took all my effort not to stare at her, my mouth open in astonishment.

"You don't have to look like it's so unbelievable," she said.

I set Izzy's food bowl on the floor and reached for Robbie, who automatically stretched his arms out to me. I took him to my bedroom and began stripping his onesie off him.

Forcing myself to block out Courtney's yammering from the other room, I began to run through all the things that I had to do next. First go on the Internet and see if there'd been any news on the media that I'd missed. Then check out Ali Burton's parents' credit history or any recent big money shifts they'd made.

When you're desperate, you go back to basics.

How long had her father been at his job in Texas? Why did Jessica stay in Paris after he left? How long had she worked at the embassy?

I felt a little better thinking of all the things I could still do.

All the useless, irrelevant things.

Because in the midst of outlining these various avenues that I could still explore, my stomach was buckling as I steadfastly worked to block what my brain was trying to tell me.

He always kills before he takes a new one.

Ali is dead.

In my mind I saw Jessica screaming in agony as Jean-Marc told her that they'd found Ali's body. I blocked the image.

No! Don't give up! Don't go there before time!

"Do you hear me, Claire? I'm serious," Courtney was saying.

I finished changing Robbie's diaper and turned to face her just as there was a knock at the door.

"That's him!" Courtney squealed.

I stared in stupefaction as she ran to the door and flung it open. There in all his glory stood Luc Remy, my downstairs neighbor.

In truth, Luc had started out a lot more than just my neighbor about a year ago but things had gone unfortunately south since then and now we avoided each other like the latest mutation of the coronavirus—I guess unless one of us was dating a roommate of the other.

"*Bonjour*, Luc!" Courtney sang out as she joined him in the hallway.

He looked at me with a smug expression as he slipped an arm around her waist and turned her away from the open door and into the waiting elevator.

37

J ean-Marc got up from his desk. He hadn't slept in twenty-four hours and had only meant to put his head down for a moment but his wristwatch told him he'd slept for nearly forty minutes. He stood and tried to massage the kinks out of his back for a moment. The weariness of his failure seemed relentless, never ending.

Two dead girls.

Two missing girls.

Zero suspects.

And going into the briefing room to stand in front of the murder board wasn't going to change any of that. He rubbed a hand across his face.

His phone vibrated on his desk and he saw it was a call from Chloe. Instantly a familiar ache in the back of his throat began. He hadn't been home in six days now. He knew physically she was fine. The hired in-home nurse made regular text reports.

He picked up the phone.

"Hello," he said. "I'm sorry, I know I've been difficult to reach."

"I want a divorce," Chloe said. "I'm tired of living like this."

Jean-Marc felt a wave of weariness crest over him. It wasn't the first time she'd asked. He'd probably ask too were he in her shoes. She needed *something* to change.

She was never getting out of that wheelchair. She was never going to have a life as she once knew it.

But as much as he knew he couldn't make her happy, he knew that divorce wasn't going to make things better for her either.

"I'm sorry, *chérie*," he said. "It's this case."

Such an easy lie and one she'd never accepted before. Why did he still bother?

"That's bullshit. It's just the excuse you need not to come home."

"Not true," Jean-Marc mumbled, sitting back down under the crushing weight of his guilt.

But of course it was true.

"No more excuses, Jean-Marc. Just stay away. Stop calling. Quit pretending."

"Chloe, I—"

"*Non!* I have fired the nurse. If I see her on the property again I will call the police."

She had done this before too. Many times.

"Okay, Chloe."

"And don't patronize me. My pain is real."

"I know it is."

Your pain is second only to that of the one who knows he can do nothing to relieve it.

"Come get your things or I'll throw them in the street."

So it was a test after all.

"I can't come," he said.

"Fine. I warned you." She disconnected.

Jean-Marc sat for a moment staring at his phone before

shaking off the echo of her voice in his head—sibilant and needling.

There was no hope or new answer for this so he wouldn't spend any more time trying to find any. He stood up, glancing without meaning to at the framed photo on the shelf across from his desk.

It was the one where they'd just been to Mürren in the Swiss Alps. The one where they'd sunbathed and hiked and discovered small mountain *brasseries* and stayed in a charming auberge. The one where they awoke one magical morning to a fresh dusting of snow. In June.

The one where they'd come back to Paris knowing they needed to separate.

And then the accident.

"Chief?" Caron came to his door and knocked. Jean-Marc looked up with a desperate, hopeless expectation that there was news.

"Jean's making a coffee run," Caron said.

"Sure, yes," Jean-Marc said. "Thanks. No news?"

Translation: no ransom requests? No bodies turn up in the river?

"No, nothing." Caron turned and left.

Jean-Marc still had his phone in his hand and for a moment he was tempted to call Claire. To say what he didn't know. Mostly just to hear her voice. He tucked his phone in his pocket and followed Caron out into the hall and into the briefing room. Jean Dartre gave him a curt nod before leaving on the coffee run.

Jean-Marc went—like a lemming to the sea, he thought bitterly—to stand in front of the murder board

The photos on the board showed the two dead girls and the two missing girls.

Cecily, Haley, Ali and Dezi White. Next to them was a photograph of Cedric Potter—their only lead and their only suspect. And then only because he was in occasional contact with the girls, was roughly near the spot three of them had been abducted, and had no alibi.

Jean-Marc pulled out his cellphone and called the medical examiner. Janine Bedard answered instantly.

"Tell me again the similarities between Cecily Danvers and Haley Johnson," he asked.

"It is in my report," she said.

"I'm afraid I'm not seeing something," he said.

"If you can read then you're seeing everything."

He paused. He knew she didn't like him and he didn't blame her. He also knew that much like a suspect in his interrogation room, with enough uncomfortable silence she would start talking to fill it.

Or hang up on him.

"Both victims were interfered with but not raped," she said briskly. "Semen found in Cecily was not matched in any data base. There was a DNA match for the semen found in Haley Johnson. Neither girl was a virgin. There was no other DNA or prints, no footprints, no eyewitnesses, no valid associative evidence."

How was that possible? Jean-Marc thought. *It is like this man is a ghost.*

"Thank you," Jean-Marc said.

"Don't call me when you're capable of reading my reports," she said. "It's why I write them." She hung up.

Jean-Marc turned back to the murder board.

Semen but no sex. Two different semen samples. One unknown. One from a homeless man who was in the database for a prior vagrancy charge.

"Chief!" Caron said, coming over to his desk, his phone to his ears and his eyes round with excitement.

Hope warred in his chest as Jean-Marc turned to face his sergeant. His mouth was dry.

Please let it be something other than Ali Burton's body floating in the Seine.

"What is it?" he asked. "What has happened?"

"It's Potter," Caron said, grabbing his jacket. "He's at Hôpital Hôtel-Dieu."

"The hospital? Why?" Jean-Marc asked.

"He tried to kill himself."

38

I spent the rest of the evening on the Internet systematically going through the Facebook pages of Jackie, Ben, and Mikayla. I found nothing but typical high school angst and silliness. Facebook pages of Dezi and Ali were nowhere to be found.

With the news of the recent missing girl, I desperately wanted to call Jean-Marc and ask him to notify me if he found Ali's body. But a part of me didn't want to start that ball rolling, like I was tempting fate to even ask it.

Instead I sent him a text message. *<What is identity of girl taken this afternoon?>*

I got up to check on Robbie, who was sleeping quietly in the corner of my bedroom in his laundry basket. I poured myself a glass of wine. As I came back to my laptop in the dining room, I noticed the mess of magazines and dirty wine glasses that Courtney had left in the living room, which made me think of her grand exit with Luc.

Is she even attracted to men who haven't been with me first?

I sat back down at the dining room table. I hadn't done much with this room since I spent most of my time either eating on a plate on the couch or eating out. It was a pretty room, though, with good lighting.

Joelle had put up a mural wallpaper with the subtle suggestion of a summer park. I found it very peaceful and regardless of the fact that I never failed to think of her when I noticed it, I quite liked it. Which instantly made me realize I needed to remove it.

My dining table—a solid round piece of indeterminate age and pedigree that I'd found at one of the city's flea markets—was almost always covered with papers, magazines, electronic equipment and now disposable diapers and formula containers.

I sat down at the table and pushed the papers away. I felt as if a terrible weight was tied to my neck and realized that a big part of me had given up all hope of Ali being found safe. I was just waiting for word of what everyone knew was the truth— she had been murdered along with her friends, Cecily and Haley.

I found myself grinding my teeth in anger.

Don't give up on her yet!

She might have escaped. That could be the reason why we haven't heard anything yet. And just as quickly as that admonishment came to me, another part of my brain surged to the front.

What kind of fairy tale do you live in? How does it help to fool yourself like this?

It helps, I thought as I picked up a pencil and straightened the paper pad in front of me, because it keeps me motivated so I don't collapse into a helpless puddle of despair.

I wrote down *X* to represent the latest missing girl whoever she was. I had no idea of where she'd been snatched or when. But even ballparking her abduction to fit in with the other girls, it meant the MO of the killer gave her roughly only twenty-four hours left.

Except Ali was still alive, I reminded myself. And *she'd* been taken over thirty hours ago.

Unless the killer was changing up his MO.

I opened up my laptop and went to the skip-tracing site that I use in France. Within seconds I had the information that Jessica and Fred Burton owned a condo in Austin, Texas—presumably the one he was living in—and no other property. They were separated, not divorced. I also knew that Jessica had worked at the embassy for three years and was well-liked and had only positive evaluations from her supervisor. She rented her apartment in Paris which had been located for her by the embassy.

I was following the money but it was leading me precisely nowhere.

I tapped a pencil against my bottom lip. I needed to take a different approach. I needed to forget what I thought I knew and look at this from a totally different angle.

For example...

What if Ali *wasn't* taken by the serial killer?

Because if she had then why had he changed his MO? Had something stopped him? Was she still alive? Or had he killed her but been prevented from dumping her body on schedule?

Tonight's the night.

Shivers ran through me at the thought and I felt a throb of desperation.

Why would he have taken a new girl if he hadn't finished with the one before her?

Tonight's the night.

It didn't make sense that someone else had taken Ali. The police had been very careful to let out only the minimum information on Cecily and Haley's murders. There was no way for a copycat killer to copy what he didn't know about!

I reviewed my notes from my interviews with Cedric Potter, Deb Knox, Ben Kent and the girls. There was nothing there that even remotely suggested a clue or a lead, except possibly—

very loosely possibly—Deb Knox and her drawer full of trophies.

The only problem with that was that at some point in the day I started to remember my own gym teacher keeping a box of lost items.

Had I jumped the gun? Wasn't a drawer full of scrunchies and lip gloss exactly what you *would* find in a gym teacher's office?

I felt numb and all the urgency I'd felt before just drained out of me.

I had no leads. Not a single one. I needed more time!

But Ali didn't have more time.

My phone rang which made me jump. I picked it up with my heart in my throat, dreading any phone call tonight.

Tonight's the night.

"Mom?" Catherine said. "Am I calling too late?"

I felt a wave of relief.

"No," I said. "Not at all. Everything okay on your end?"

"I'm still processing everything," she said. "But I got to talking with Todd and I wondered if you could send me a picture of him. You know. The baby."

"Sure," I said, careful not to say anything that would make her change her mind. I sent her a video I'd taken this afternoon of Robbie grabbing both his feet and trying to put them in his mouth.

"You used to do this too," I said, feeling a knife jab into my heart when I said it.

There was silence on the line as she watched the video.

"He's cute," Catherine said finally. "Do you think he looks like Dad?"

I took in a long breath. We were over the hard part. She would forgive her dad in time.

"It's hard to tell," I lied.

"When do I get to meet him?"

"I don't know. His...mother is still trying to sort out her options."

"And she's staying with you? That is just so bizarre."

Tell me about it.

"Oh! I gotta go, Mom. Cameron's calling me."

Ten o'clock France time meant it was four p.m. Atlanta time.

"Okay, sweetie. Give him a kiss for me."

"Will do. Love you!"

I sat holding the phone for a moment, grateful for the respite from the terrible burden of my evening, grateful that it looked like Catherine had already turned a corner with regards to Robbie.

I forced myself to go back to my laptop, back to social media to see if any clues had been posted in the last thirty minutes.

It all felt so hopeless and I fought not to give in to the feeling.

With the taking of the fourth girl—whoever she was—Facebook posts had spiked with rumor and paranoia. The neighborhood around the school—and to a very large degree the whole expat community—was now in virtual if not physical lockdown—not unlike the 2020 Paris coronavirus shutdown except of course all the shops were still open.

I went to the *American Expats in Paris* Facebook page and saw thread after thread talking about how the police were completely baffled and couldn't keep any of them safe—and because of suspected xenophobia they didn't want to bother trying. Social Media had named the killer of the three girls— and the presumed kidnapper of the one after that—the *In-Seine Killer.*

The whole community was a tense ball of fear and anxiety.

Worse, there had been so much conversation about the murders throughout the school—including with the two dead girls' parents—that any hope the police might have had of keeping certain details of the murders from becoming known was officially blown.

Any copycat killer who had access to the expat social media venues would know that both Cecily and Haley were blonde, slim, went to Le World School de Paris and were taken on their way home from school.

Just like Ali.

I drained my glass of wine, got up and washed it out, then checked on Robbie again. He was sleeping peacefully.

I came back to the dining room table, and steeling myself, reached for my phone and called Laura.

"I was just about to call you," she said when she answered.

Instantly my gut tightened.

"I've been talking to Jessica," Laura said, her voice flat and devoid of emotion.

I held my breath.

"The police came to her apartment five minutes ago to bring her down to the police station..."

Oh God no...

"...to identify the remains of a girl's body found floating in the Seine."

39

T he sound of the water rushing past Jean-Marc seemed to filter into his very soul. At this time of evening, even in June, the light was long gone and with it any semblance of warmth or clarity. The relentless slap of the river's water as it pounded against the bulkhead was almost soothing in its regularity.

The scent of algae, diesel fuel and fish hung like a noxious cloud over the stone embankment where he stood.

Jean-Marc turned into the wind to look again at the canvas-covered body. Only her shoeless foot protruded from beneath the tarp. Janine Bedard was squatting next to the body with a team of four techs. Jean-Marc had recognized Adele as soon as he got to the scene.

Which means Claire will know as much as I do about how Ali Burton died, he thought.

He felt a brief wave of nausea as he watched the forensic technicians work.

But the really sickening thought was that he had never even been close to saving this poor girl. From the moment she'd been taken through all those long hours until the moment this monster had finally put her out of her misery, help had never been anywhere near.

They'd been on their way to the hospital to interview Cedric Potter when the news had come in through official channels that another body had been found.

His notebook in his hand, Caron walked over to Jean-Marc. He'd questioned a few people on the upper embankment, mostly dog walkers and residents of the nearby neighborhood. This section of the river was near the Pont Des Arts, an entirely pedestrian metal bridge which bordered an upscale neighborhood. In good weather, which today was not, it would have been crowded with people eating picnic lunches.

Was it a message? Another rich American kid killed and dumped in her expensive playground while thousands of hardworking Parisians labored to feed their families?

It was a stretch. And in the end just another wild guess. There seemed no motive for this madman to do any of this.

"Anybody see anything?" Jean-Marc asked Caron.

"No. Nothing."

Jean-Marc hadn't expected anything else. This guy was too careful.

And Jean-Marc and his team were just too damnably unlucky.

"What did the ME say?" Caron asked.

"Too soon for definitives," Jean-Marc said. "But at first glance, it's our guy."

"Raped?"

"She can't tell yet but definitely strangled."

Caron swore and Jean-Marc looked at him, remembering then that Caron had a teenage daughter at home.

"Where's Dartre?" Jean-Marc asked.

"Canvassing along the upper embankment. It's hopeless, but..." He shrugged and then turned to Jean-Marc. "Could it have been Potter?"

Jean-Marc had been asking himself that same question relentlessly since they'd gotten the call about the body in the river. Did Potter have time to snatch both girls and dispatch Ali before attempting to kill himself?

The only way to construe his suicide attempt was the inevitable consequence of a guilty conscience.

"We'll need to question him as soon as he regains consciousness," Jean-Marc said.

If he regained consciousness. Jean-Marc's contact at the hospital said Potter had taken a drug overdose and was comatose. No word yet on brain damage.

Jean-Marc took a deep breath and let it out.

Brain dead or not, he most definitely had his man. He'd finally bagged the bastard.

"Get over to Potter's apartment," he told Caron. "Then go to his office at the school, especially his computer."

Now that he had probable cause, he could get a warrant for the search.

Caron frowned. "Do you know something I don't?"

"Just let me know what you find," Jean-Marc said. "I think we should be able to wrap this whole mess up pretty quickly now."

"Thank God. The expat community was getting pretty jittery."

"I know."

Jean-Marc had already had a steady stream of impatient emails from Commandant Bulie asking him how it was coming along and when he could let the media know it was finished. Tomorrow's headlines practically wrote themselves:

Paris In-Seine Killer apprehended with discovery of latest victim.

Now, if he could only add the fact that he'd recovered the latest kidnapped girl as well—he'd have the whole thing tied up in a neat bow.

But before Potter woke up, how was that going to happen?

The medical examiner walked over to Jean-Marc. As usual, she was all business. She pulled off her latex gloves and didn't look Jean-Marc in the eye when she addressed him.

"We're going to move her now," Dr. Bedard said coldly. "The mother is waiting downtown to identify her. I'll have the toxicology and autopsy results in thirty-six hours and no, I can't get them any faster."

"That's fine," Jean-Marc said. "Obviously the *Commandant* will want to tell the media as soon as possible if there are any similarities between this murder and the two that went before."

"Between you and me," Bedard said, "they are nearly carbon copies. But I won't commit to that until after I get her on the table."

"Understood. Oh, one more question," he said, turning to her as the doctor prepared to leave. "Time of death?"

Janine Bedard looked at the body as her team lifted it onto a stretcher.

"I'd say she was killed in the last hour to two hours," she said.

Jean-Marc shot a hand out to grab her arm.

"*Pardon?*" he said tensely, feeling his heart begin to beat faster. "Did you say *in the last hour?*"

"Or possibly two. No more than that."

Then Bedard turned and walked away and Jean-Marc felt an urgent need to sit down.

Ali Burton was killed during the time when Potter was in the emergency room.

He couldn't have killed her.

He blinked rapidly in disbelief and struggled to bring his thoughts together.

Potter couldn't have done this.

Which meant the *In-Seine Killer* was still out there.

And so was one more missing girl.

40

I disconnected my phone call with Laura and went into my bedroom where I woke up Robbie, changed him, and packed a diaper bag. I wrote a brief note for Courtney, called for a taxi and then, leaving the apartment door unlocked so she could get in, I took Robbie and Izzy downstairs to Geneviève's apartment.

Geneviève answered the door in her dressing gown, but I could tell she hadn't been asleep. As soon as she saw Robbie she held out her arms.

"No," I said. "Just tell me where I can put him."

She directed me to the couch in the living room and began creating a barrier of pillows at the edge to contain him.

"I'll make something more secure after you're gone," she said.

"I'm sorry to do this," I said.

"Don't be," she said. "Just do what you need to do."

I handed over Izzy's leash and gave Geneviève a brief hug.

"I'll call later," I said. And then I turned and left.

The taxi took me straight to the police department on the

Île de la Cité. It was a large, warehouse-like building that housed the forensics laboratory, medical examiner's office and police morgue.

It was bad enough to be here on a bright sunny Paris day, I thought as I paid the taxi and hurried toward the front steps of the *préfecture*.

But at close to midnight on a muggy rainy night, the only word for it was *bleak*.

As soon as I entered through the automatic double doors to the inner atrium, I saw Laura in the waiting room. Her face was white and grim. Beyond her was the police receptionist sitting behind a bulletproof glass partition. Beyond her I saw the black and white directional signs indicating the way to the morgue.

Where presumably Jessica was.

I hurried over to Laura who looked up as I came in.

"What do you know?" I asked in a low voice.

"It's Ali," Laura said.

I felt like I'd been punched. I felt like I wanted to jump on a transatlantic flight and race over to my daughter's house and hold her in my arms and never let go.

I sat down heavily next to Laura. We were the only people in the waiting room.

"Oh, dear God," I said.

"I know."

I can't say I've ever been extraordinarily impressed with Laura in the past. I thought she was too frivolous, too rich, and too vain by half. But seeing her now in her cream cashmere knit jogging pants and matching linen t-shirt, sitting in the Paris police department morgue waiting room, waiting for the emergence of a woman in the throes of the worst hour of her life, I have to say I've never been more impressed with anyone.

She was a rock. And not a heartless one either. The streaks of dried tears down her cheeks were testimony to the fact that she was feeling the horror of this every bit as much as I was.

And she was still here anyway.

"He broke his MO," I said.

"I'll add it to his list of crimes," she said dully, her eyes looking down the hall to where she knew Jessica would soon be arriving.

"No, I mean, it's weird because serial killers are very consistent."

She turned to look at me, her eyes searching mine.

"Were you close to finding her at all? Did anything make sense to you?"

"No, not really," I said, feeling sick to have to admit my failure. "I needed more time."

She nodded. She hadn't expected anything more.

"Did you hear about Cedric Potter?" she asked.

I shook my head.

"He tried to kill himself today."

I felt a lightness in my chest at her words. "Why?"

"I don't know. Guilt maybe?"

"So he's the cops' prime suspect?"

"I don't know that either." We were quiet for a moment before she spoke again.

"I guess you've heard about Dezi White?" she said.

I felt sick. "I knew he'd taken another one. I didn't know it was Dezi."

Laura straightened the creases out of her linen t-shirt but they eased right back. Nothing was going to fix this night. Not for anything or anyone.

"There's nothing you can do here, Claire," Laura said, straightening her shoulders and turning to face me, her expression one of determination. "I'll take care of Jessica. But the clock is ticking for Dezi."

I hesitated for a moment and then she said more forcibly, her eyes glittering with determination, "You need to go. *Now*."

I stood up. Aware that the only thing I knew for sure was that I had no idea of where to go.

But I needed to go anyway.

41

The first thing I did upon leaving the *préfecture* was to find an open café, order a coffee, and call Adele. I prayed she knew something about the body in the river tonight.

The body.

That poor girl. Her poor mother...

I shook the enervating thoughts from my head. They wouldn't help.

"I thought I might hear from you," Adele said as she answered.

"What can you tell me about the body in the river?"

"You know it was the last girl kidnapped? Ali Burton?"

"I do. Tell me if it fit the same MO as the others? Was she raped?"

"That I don't know yet. She was strangled someplace else and dumped in the water around twenty hundred hours this evening."

Eight o'clock.

"Why didn't he wait until the middle of the night like with the others?"

"You'll have to ask him that."

"Strangled how?"

"With a ligature."

Like the others.

"Rope?"

"I'd say a necktie or bathrobe tie. Something like that. But it's the ME's call. I'm still writing up my report."

I could tell she wanted to get off the phone. I was sure she was exhausted.

"Can you keep me informed?"

"You know I will," she said, dropping her voice. It reminded me that she could lose her job for sharing any of this information with me.

My stomach was churning with what I knew Jessica was going through right now but I had to banish those thoughts. Yes, I'd failed her. Spectacularly. But I had to bury those feelings too and focus on whatever I could do for Dezi now.

I disconnected and paid my bill. The *café* that Ben told me where Maurice was a waiter would surely be closed at this hour so that just left one other place I could reasonably go at this time of night.

It was late, not the ideal time for knocking on people's doors who weren't expecting you. Mind you, I always find that the time that people are *not* expecting you is the best time to question them.

Besides, I didn't have the luxury of time. It was only a little after midnight. Eric Watson was thirty years old. Chances are he wouldn't be in bed yet.

Not alone anyway.

Eric lived in the thirteenth arrondissement, not really close to anything, and a good two kilometers from the police head-quarters where I started out.

The Métro closed at 12:30 so my only option was a taxi or walking. I called a taxi and within twenty minutes I was standing in front of Eric Watson's apartment on rue Tagore.

Like most apartment buildings in Paris, the security system made impromptu visits extremely difficult. On the other hand, one of the benefits of being sixty years old—and trust me there are damn few—is the fact that nobody and I mean *nobody* looks at you as any possible threat. So my hanging around a street corner in the middle of the night would make nobody nervous or suspicious as to my intentions.

I stood by the wrought-iron gate by the outer door. To the first person who opened the door to exit, I smiled apologetically and said I'd forgotten the security code to get in. Because most younger people have such a low opinion of their elders and their abilities, I got a disgusted head shake but was able to step inside to the protected courtyard.

Cedric Potter had been kind enough to also give me Watson's apartment number, so I took the elevator up to the second floor and knocked firmly on his door.

I knew there was every possibility that he might be out for the evening but I was prepared to wait if he was.

Within seconds of my knock, the door was opened and I was confronted by a man I assumed was Eric Watson.

He glowered at me as if in a low-grade fury, which made me take an involuntary step back.

Well, fury and the fact that he was completely naked.

42

Thankfully, Mr. Watson turned from the door and grabbed a robe from the couch in the living room. I stepped into his apartment, my hand on my purse with the Taser inside.

"You're not Yvette," Eric Watson said, turning to eye me skeptically. "What do you want?"

"Just a word, Mr. Watson," I said.

I noted that he was good-looking and probably late thirties. He was also arrogant and condescending. There was a whiff of the predator about him, if I was honest with myself. I'd learned a long time ago not to rely too much on these first impressions. But not to totally discount them either.

"American?" He frowned at me and stood with his hands on his hips and then waved away his own question. "Who are you?"

He was trying to understand how I could possibly fit into his world. I was clearly too old to be a parent of one of his students.

"My name is Claire Baskerville," I said. "I'm looking into the disappearance of Ali Burton."

I nearly said *Dezi White* but stopped myself in time. If Watson wasn't the killer, I didn't want him to know the name of the missing girl. And if he was the killer, I didn't want to show all my cards just yet.

I glanced past him into his living room. It was tidy, possibly obsessively so. No pillows on the couch, no television that I could see. Blinds on the windows. As sterile and antiseptic as a living space could be.

"I don't know anything about that," he said.

But he wasn't looking at me when he said it.

"Ali is your student?" I asked.

"Yes, of course. I never said I didn't *know* her. I said I didn't know anything about her disappearance."

Good liars are hard to read. Sometimes that's because they don't believe they're lying. Those of course are the hardest to discern. The other kind of good liars are just natural actors. I didn't know whether Eric really believed what he was saying or if he was just a great liar.

All I knew for sure was that he was lying.

The nauseating thrill of that knowledge made me realize I was on to something. I just didn't know what.

"Did her ridiculous mother send you?" Eric asked, sitting in a chair, and crossing one foot over his knee, unmindful of the fact that his robe was not adequately covering his nether regions. "Give me a break."

"Why would her mother send me?"

"They all complain because their little darlings scamper all over me and that's hardly my fault, now is it?"

He grinned when he said that as if totally delighted by the fact. It was true he was good-looking and I could see how naive schoolgirls could develop crushes on him.

I guess the real question was: did Eric Watson take any of them up on it?

"That must make teaching difficult for you," I said.

"Not really." He continued to agitate his knees back and forth until I realized he was doing it on purpose. He was trying to make me uncomfortable.

Honey, I lived through the sixties. If you think being flashed by a middle school art teacher with a net worth of twenty-three thousand euros is going to unsettle me, you're deluded on top of being full of yourself.

And yes, I'd done my homework. One of the first things I did for all the suspects was to look up their income on one of my skip-tracing sites.

Whether Watson's attempt to unsettle me was because he was attempting to distract me from my line of questioning—as in, he was guilty of something—or whether he was just a jerk, I didn't know. But it didn't matter. I didn't take my direction from my subjects.

"Where were you when Cecily Danvers was taken?" I said.

"You must be joking."

"I assure you I'm not," I said.

"Who can remember that sort of thing?"

"Since I'm sure the press made a big deal of her abduction, and she attended the school where you teach I would assume you would remember."

"I didn't teach Cecily in my class."

"So you didn't know her?"

"I just said so, didn't I? Why is it you're here asking me questions in the middle of the night? Shouldn't you be home in bed?"

"What about Haley Johnson?" I asked. "Did you teach her?"

"Yes, and no, I don't remember where I was when she went missing. And if you're going to ask me about the other girl, you can save your breath. I don't remember."

"Have the police questioned you?"

"Why the hell would they?"

"Uh, because you don't have an alibi for the time that the girls went missing and you're someone they all knew."

"Who says I don't have an alibi?" he asked.

"You just said you don't remember where you were."

"Of course I have an alibi should the police be interested, which they're not, and I'm not telling you."

"So you can prove you were someplace other than driving the van that snatched these girls?"

"The cops think they were taken by a van?"

I hesitated. Of course I don't know that at all. The police don't know that. I was just spit-balling.

"How else would they be snatched off the street without causing a scene?" I said.

"I have no idea and I'm not telling you a single thing more except to tell you to get the hell out of my apartment before I break my rule about manhandling little old ladies and throw your ass out."

Eric stood with his back to the apartment door and steadied his breathing. Even with the threat of bodily removal, it had still taken another five minutes before she decided to leave.

Mind you, she was good-looking for her age, but he'd have to be a lot more desperate than one French prostitute failing to show up for her normally scheduled appointment before he'd throw a leg over anything past the age of forty.

Whatever the old girl had been looking for, he was pretty sure she left without getting it.

He grinned again at his double entendre.

But his smile dissolved as his glance tracked the living room from the perspective of her location near the entryway to see what her view had been.

If she hadn't been distracted by his constantly opening and

closing the front of his robe for her benefit—and unfortunately he hadn't picked up that she had been—then she would have seen a relatively normal looking living room. Maybe a little messy but par for the course surely for a bachelor?

Had she seen anything else? Heard anything else?

He actually felt momentarily faint at the thought and then chills raced down his arms. He pulled on his jeans, a t-shirt and his Adidas sneakers and slipped out the apartment door. He could hear the elevator descending so he turned toward the stairs and, without turning on the lights, took the stairs down to the lobby.

His wasn't a heavily populated building and at midnight he didn't expect to run into any of his neighbors. He paused on the ground floor when he heard the elevator arrive at the lobby level.

He heard her open the wrought-iron grill door and then step out onto the hard tile floor of the lobby.

She didn't see anything. She couldn't have.

He waited until he heard the lobby door open and then shut before descending the rest of the stairs to the lobby. From there he stood at the door and watched her move across the darkened courtyard to the outside security gate. He'd give her two minutes— she was elderly after all—to get the door open before he followed.

He just needed to see some evidence in her comportment or her pace that she'd found something while in his apartment.

The waiting was interminable and, unlike his other more recent bouts of waiting, this one wouldn't end with the physical reward that he craved.

He finally stepped out into the courtyard and felt the bite of the night air. He hurried to the security gate, walking as quietly as he could. If she had stopped, perhaps gathering her wits about her on the other side of the door, she would be able to see him.

He needed to risk it.

He slowly opened the security door and stepped out onto the sidewalk. There were no other people out at this time of night. That wasn't a surprise.

But he *had* expected to see her.

Where had she gone?

He looked in both directions down the sidewalk, even taking a half dozen steps in each direction before realizing the impossible.

He'd lost her.

He strained his eyes down the shortest segment of the road which intersected with rue des Malmaisons.

He'd only been hoping to determine if she was walking away with purpose—which would have told him she'd seen something in his apartment she shouldn't have. Or if she was walking away in resignation or failure. Which would have told him she'd seen nothing and was just an old woman hoping to find a taxi stand on Avenue de Choisy before being mugged on a damp June night.

But now he had nothing.

He ran a hand across his mouth, his mind racing.

If she *had* seen or heard something...if she'd suspected something before she even came upstairs...but that was impossible!

To be safe he should dismantle the room.

He groaned at the thought. It would take forever to get everything set up again. All the hooks in the walls, the cameras and the soundproofing.

No, he thought to himself. She didn't see anything. There was no way she did.

As careful as he'd been? Even the cops didn't have a clue. He'd answered their stupid questions when they interviewed him at the school and they never asked to visit his apartment!

He turned and opened the security door to go back inside his building.

No, it would take a genius to figure out what he'd done and how he'd done it.

A frigging genius.

He felt a pleasant fluttering sensation in his stomach.

And one thing he knew if he knew anything was that there was nobody who was anywhere near that smart.

43

I put my phone down on the café table. He would either call me or he wouldn't.

I knew Jean-Marc had had a busy day and was having an even busier night. It was already half past one in the morning. I was at an all-night café a block from Eric Watson's apartment. I didn't spend much time in this section of Paris. The only thing I could think that was remotely close by were the famous Paris Catacombs.

The Catacombs of Paris are an enormous underground ossuary that holds the remains of over six million people killed in the riots in the Place de Grève, as well as the hapless monarchists trapped and murdered here, not to mention all thousands of dead in Les Innocents cemetery when it was moved in the seventeen hundreds as part of Hausmann's urban renewal.

Nowadays the Catacombs was a favored event setting for concerts and parties—especially Halloween parties—not to mention a popular touring destination. Creepy but fascinating.

The café was fairly far from my apartment. But I couldn't go home yet. Not yet. Not with absolutely nothing to show for my night.

Not when I knew how Jessica was spending her night tonight.

Dezi had been discovered missing at three o'clock today. That meant I had roughly twelve hours to find her—*if* the killer was still trying to play by the rules. His own rules.

I made a list of suspects in my head which was pretty easy since there were so few.

Eric Watson, Cedric Potter, Deb Knox.

I wouldn't be able to see the guy Maurice whom Ben had told me about until tomorrow at the earliest.

I focused on Cedric Potter's name. I wasn't sure if I could cross him off the list since I didn't know the specific times when Ali was killed or when Potter tried to kill himself.

For good measure, I added Mark White's name to the list even though I mostly did it because I personally didn't like him. *Hey, I'm human.*

My phone vibrated in my hand and the words UNKNOWN CALLER appeared on my screen.

An uncomfortable chill ran through me. The last time I'd answered a message from an unknown caller it had been an ambiguous text from someone who seemed to be referencing an involvement with Bob's murder. Since I was never able to trace the number to identify the sender I had nothing to base that on but gut instinct.

In the months since Bob's death—and again based on little more than intuition—I'd started to believe the mysterious sender might be my biological father.

I shook the thought away.

Focus.

I answered the phone. "Yes?"

"What have you done with my baby?!" Courtney shrieked into the phone.

I was actually heartened to hear some motherly concern from her. Honestly, before tonight I wasn't sure she even cared about Robbie.

"He's with Geneviève. I left you a note."

"I didn't see any note."

"Did you think I kidnapped him?" I asked wryly and then was sorry for the word choice.

"Well, when I saw the dog was gone," she said, "I wasn't sure you hadn't moved out on me."

I wanted to say: *Did you really think I'd want to get rid of you so much I'd leave you my two-million-euro apartment?*

But the last thing I wanted her to know was how much money I was sitting on.

"In case you're curious, Luc was a total gentleman tonight," Courtney gushed.

"I'd be careful if I were you," I said. "I'm pretty sure he's the possessive type."

"I like being possessed."

Why doesn't that surprise me?

"I'll be home shortly," I said.

"Aren't you interested in hearing about my date?"

I hung up.

Instantly I was overwhelmed by the feeling that I was wasting time. It was all very good to stay out half the night but if I wasn't finding any helpful information I might as well go home. I checked my watch and decided that it wasn't too late to see if Mikayla was still up.

When she picked up the phone—not at all sleepy-sounding —I dispensed with the pleasantries.

"This is Claire Baskerville. Tell me again why you weren't worried about Dezi's dad flirting with you."

"Ben told you that," Mikayla said. "And Ben's a nut job."

"So you *didn't* have a problem with Dezi's dad?"

"I mean, yeah, okay, he complimented us and stuff and we had a good laugh behind his back, he's so pathetic but no, he never made us feel worried or anything."

"What about Mr. Watson? Did he ever come on to you?"

"Not me personally."

"I don't have time for this, Mikayla. You do know that your friend Dezi's life is in danger, right?"

"There's no way Mr. W would take her. He can have any girl in the school he wants."

"People who catch and strangle young girls don't do it because they can't get dates," I said testily.

"I'm just that saying no girl at school would fight him off if he asked for it."

"I think you're a very silly girl if that's what you really think."

I let her chew on that for a second and was gratified that she decided not to hang up on me.

"You said Haley was your best friend," I said, trying again.

"We've known each other since middle school."

"You must be terrified after what happened to her."

"Well, I've got three brothers and all my dad does is gas on about how he'd love to get his hands on this guy, so not really."

When she said that, something flitted along the outer bands of my brain but it was elusive and I couldn't capture it.

"But still," I said. "I can't believe you haven't thought of what she went through. Your *best friend*?"

I'm not proud of that but when the clock was ticking down to the last minutes, you start doing things you never would have thought you'd do before. I didn't want to upset Mikayla but if upsetting her helped me get information that allowed me to find Dezi in time, then I was going to give her both barrels and not look back.

Mikayla's voice caught and I heard the emotion in her voice.

"Well, yeah, of course," she said. "Haley was...Haley was..."

She broke down then and sobbed.

I refrained from consoling her. I didn't want to stop her, I wanted her to feel every inch of this pain so that she might tell me something that could help Dezi.

"I mean, okay, Haley was flirty. I mean, she was really cute, you know?"

"Did she flirt with Dezi's father?"

"No. I mean, not that I ever saw."

I sighed and decided to let her bake in her own silence for a bit. People always tend to fill up the silences sooner or later. After her sniffling stopped, she spoke in a soft little-girl voice that a part of me realized was the real Mikayla.

"Is it true about Ali?" she asked. "Did she really get killed like Haley and Cecily?"

"Yes, it's true," I said bluntly.

"Was she raped?"

"I don't know."

Even us tough broads have our limits. I'd give Mikayla something to hold onto. And the idea that this monster hadn't raped Ali—when I knew he very likely had—seemed like a small bone to throw her way.

And then, just when I was sure this was one more conversation tonight that was going precisely nowhere, Mikayla surprised me with a pure gold nugget tossed right into my lap.

"Whoever hurt Ali," she said, her voice stronger now, "it can't be Mr. Watson. That's for sure."

"Why do you say that?"

"Because he didn't need to! Ali was already sleeping with him."

44

It took me less than a quarter of an hour to speed walk back to Eric Watson's apartment. At this time of night there were even fewer people available who might allow me to slip in behind them, so I buzzed the first apartment number I found and when they answered, I deliberately slurred my words and the door promptly buzzed open.

I was sure it wasn't the first time one of their neighbors had come home too drunk to remember the security code.

I rode the elevator up to Eric's floor and pounded on his door. I saw the light change from this side of the peep hole on his door and realized he was on the other side looking at me.

It took a full ten minutes, during which time I continued to pound with both fists before he finally opened the door.

"What the hell?" he said, slamming his hand across the doorjamb to prevent me from entering.

"You slept with your students," I said.

The look on his face told me everything I needed to know. *It was true.*

"Who says so? I deny it!"

I pulled out my phone and called Jean-Marc. I had no

reason to think he would take my call when he hadn't taken any of my others except I almost never call him at two in the morning. When he answered, I began speaking before he could say anything.

"Did you know that Eric Watson who teaches at Le World School de Paris slept with two of the three victims?" I said on the phone.

"That's a lie!" Eric said, his eyes darting manically around his apartment. "It was only Ali!"

"You are with Watson now?" Jean-Marc said.

"That's right," I said, drilling Eric with my gaze. "And I have a girl who will testify that this piece of work slept with both Haley Johnson and Ali Burton."

"Who told you that?" Eric yelled. "Lying little bitch!" He rubbed his ears in agitation, his face flushed.

Jean-Marc swore on his end of the line. Then I heard him turn to someone on his end and order them to go to Watson's apartment and bring him in.

"Bring a warrant, Jean-Marc," I said. "He keeps looking around his apartment like he's got a body buried in the couch."

"Go home, Claire," Jean-Marc said. "It is late. You should not be out."

"I have to be out," I said fiercely before disconnecting with him. "For the same reason you do."

I stood on the corner of Avenue d'Italie and rue Tagore and watched an unmarked police car stop in front of Eric's apartment. Because of my disability I wasn't able to recognize the two detectives who got out of the car as the two who usually work with Jean-Marc, but who else could they be? The detectives went inside the apartment building.

I felt satisfied with my night's work but also a little let down.

Was I really going to just go home when Dezi was still out there somewhere in a closet or basement or trunk of a car?

But what else could I do?

I started walking in the direction of the nearest taxi stand. The thirteenth arrondissement is not a big tourist area and so taxis at this time of night were not plentiful and I was exhausted to the bone.

As I walked, I sent a text to Jean-Marc.

"BTW. Ali's boyfriend—Ben Kent—told me a waiter at Café Bleu near the school preyed on the girls. First name Maurice. Have you spoken to him?>

He texted me back.

<Go home!>

With images of a terrified Dezi begging for her life swirling in my head, I trudged in the direction of the nearest taxi stand down what had to be the darkest, most wretched street in all of Paris.

45

T he sounds and scents of the *préfecture*—coffee and loud boasting conversations—seemed particularly enhanced today. Perhaps that was testimony to Jean-Marc's own level of excitement and hope that he might actually have someone who could lead him to something besides a brick wall in this case.

After leaving the crime scene at Pont des Arts, Jean-Marc had come back to the *préfecture* to spend a painful thirty minutes with Jessica Burton as she sobbed her heart out over the body of her daughter in the police morgue.

She'd had very few questions for him since, with her beloved daughter lying on the slab before her, there were no answers that really mattered.

This is the part of the job I will never get used to.

They'd picked up Eric Watson at two o'clock this morning and Maurice Dubonnet at eight o'clock.

On the face of it, neither of them looked particularly viable, but they were more than he'd had before.

Cedric Potter's condition in the hospital was unchanged, and so was any premature tendency on Jean-Marc's part to let the man off the hook just because he was in the clear for Ali's murder.

That still left Cecily's and Haley's murders who Potter doesn't have an alibi for.

The preliminary report on Ali Burton's autopsy from the medical examiner has been a mixed bag. First and most noticeably between her murder and the first two were not the similarities but the differences.

Specifically—no semen had been found in Ali's body.

What did that mean? Had the killer been rushed? Or was he changing his MO?

That was a question he hoped to have an answer before the end of the day.

It had been Jean-Marc's decision to put Watson in a holding cell and talk to Dubonnet first. Although he didn't appear to be on drugs, Dubonnet's behavior was jumpy, irritable and unfocused.

Jean-Marc studied Dubonnet across from him at the table in the interview room.

"You've got the wrong man," Dubonnet said. "I don't know anything about anyone."

"So you've said."

Caron came in then with a coffee for Jean-Marc and a printout. There'd been an overload of the department Internet servers this morning and only now was Jean-Marc finding out exactly what they had on Dubonnet.

He looked at the printout, his eyes widening as he read. He glanced at Caron who was grinning at him.

Dubonnet was on the sexual register for the attempted rape of a fifteen-year-old girl six years ago. He'd done five years in prison for it. He'd been released only three weeks before.

"I know what you're looking at," Dubonnet said. "It doesn't change the fact that I could never hurt those girls."

With barely suppressed excitement Jean-Marc laid out the

pictures of the three girls before Dubonnet: Cecily Danvers, Haley Johnson and Ali Burton.

"Do you know these girls?" he asked.

Dubonnet looked at them and shrugged.

"They came to the *café* where you work every day after school," Jean-Marc said.

"Okay," Dubonnet said, scratching his face. "So I have seen them. Look, I hate what happened to these girls. I'm not a monster. I could have wept for what their parents went through. I mean it."

Jean-Marc slid a fourth picture of Dezi White in front of him.

"And her?" Jean-Marc said.

"Probably. I can't say for sure."

"She's missing."

"I don't know anything about it."

Jean-Marc tapped the other photos. "These three were found in the Seine. Raped and strangled."

Dubonnet's eyes met his and Jean-Marc detected fear in them.

"You know I didn't do that," Dubonnet said.

"I don't know that at all."

"You have my record!" He gestured to the paper that Jean-Marc had laid on the table. "I don't kill! You can see that in my file, right?"

He stood up in agitation, his eyes going from Jean-Marc to Caron.

"Sit down, Maurice," Jean-Marc said.

When Dubonnet sat down, he began gnawing on his nails, his eyes darting around the room.

"It wasn't me," he said. "I could never have done something like this!"

"Well, it's true you hadn't up to *now*. That we know of."

Dubonnet pushed away from the table. "This wasn't me! I'd kill *myself* first."

Jean-Marc waited for him to calm down again.

"You're not supposed to reside or work within six-hundred meters of a school."

"A kiddie school."

"No. Not any kind of school."

"I didn't know that."

"Does your boss know about your prison record, Maurice?"

Dubonnet swallowed hard and looked away.

"Maurice?"

"Even if he does, he's not going to be happy now, is he?" Dubonnet said, still chewing his nails, his eyes on the pictures of the girls.

"Where were you on May fifth of this year?" Jean-Marc asked.

"How would I remember that?"

"It was only two weeks ago. How about May seventh?"

Dubonnet threw up his hands in frustration.

Jean-Marc stood up.

"Take him back to his cell," he said to the policeman standing in the room by the wall.

"Wait!" Dubonnet said. "So can I go now?"

Jean-Marc left the room and headed back to the bull pen. Detective Caron met him in the hallway.

"What do you think?" Caron said.

Jean-Marc grunted.

Claire had been right. Maurice Dubonnet was definitely a person of interest in this case. His background and proximity to the school made him an automatic suspect.

Why hadn't he shown up on their radar before?

It would take a while to pin the pieces of Dubonnet's connection to the girls—either the ones who were killed or any girls from the school who could testify against him. But Jean-

Marc's gut told him that Dubonnet didn't commit these murders.

If he had, the first thing he'd have done was create a plausible alibi.

Any serial killer worth his salt would know that.

But at least he was off the street for the short while. If Dubonnet *did* take Dezi and hadn't already killed her, they at least stood a chance of getting him to tell them where she was.

He'd give him an hour to pace his cell and try again.

Jean-Marc stood in front of the murder board and stared. Eric Watson. Cedric Potter. Maurice Dubonnet.

First, Dubonnet. Jean-Marc's gut said no but he was in no position to listen to his gut. Beyond that there was no direct evidence linking Dubonnet to any of the girls. Not only that, but in the back of Jean-Marc's mind was the nagging doubt that Dubonnet was smart enough to plan any of this.

Then there was Potter, somebody who looked good on paper but who didn't fit the basic profile for a serial killer. And who physically couldn't have done the last murder.

Was he just that good during the interview that he made me believe he didn't have the basic characteristics of a serial killer?

What about his suicide attempt?

Had that been a ruse that had gone wrong for Potter? Had he meant to take himself off the police radar and gone too far?

Jean-Marc turned to Dartre who appeared to be on hold on his phone.

"What did you find in Potter's apartment?" Jean-Marc asked.

"I thought he wasn't a suspect any longer," Dartre said with surprise, glancing at Caron as if for support.

Jean-Marc felt a sliver of agitation.

"Did I tell you to stop investigating him?" he said tightly.

"No, sir," Dartre said, turning to his computer screen. "I'll get that information for you."

Jean-Marc turned away.

It was true that Potter was a long shot. He didn't fit the time-line for the Ali Burton murder nor did he fit the profile for a serial killer.

But Jean-Marc couldn't take him off the board yet. He couldn't admit defeat even in the face of the facts.

He looked at the third photograph on the board. Eric Watson, currently sitting in a holding pen among last night's drunks and male prostitutes. He'd been peripherally inter-viewed for both Cecily and Haley's disappearances but no red flags had come up. Except for *possibly* sleeping with one of the victims, Watson had no obvious motive or means to commit any of the crimes.

"What are Eric Watson's alibis for the first two murders?" Jean-Marc asked Caron.

Caron turned to his computer. "I'll look it up," he said.

Jean-Marc felt his anger pulse out of him.

We have three photos on the board and only three suspects for one of the highest-profile serial killings in the city in the last two decades. Why isn't information on all three of them at our fingertips?

Why isn't it seared into our brains?

"Chief?" Dartre said from his computer. "They found some-thing at Potter's office at Le World School de Paris."

Jean-Marc's anger morphed into an alert hopefulness. "Yes?" he said.

Dartre hesitated as he stared at his screen.

"Out with it!" Jean-Marc barked.

"They found home videos on his work computer," Dartre said, his face flushed with excitement. "Seems he'd been secretly filming the girls' locker room."

46

Jean-Marc took a long bitter sip of his coffee, feeling it burn all the way down his throat. He stared at the murder board, knowing he would see this board in his dreams all the rest of his days—regardless of whether they ever caught the bastard or not. The image of this board with its map of the river and the black and white photos of the three dead girls were branded in his memory forever.

The discovery at Cedric Potter's office had been a morale boost but nothing more. The headmaster still couldn't have killed Ali Burton but there was some comfort in the knowledge that if he ever woke up, he'd do a minimum of fifteen years in prison on charges of child pornography, voyeurism and possessing sexual recordings of a minor. Claire had been right about that.

Jean-Marc looked at the girls' faces in their photos.

Cecily, Haley, Ali and Dezi.

Each one of them had a story to tell and together they held the key—in their faces and in their backgrounds—as to who had stolen them away. Something was right there to be seen. If Jean-Marc could only see it.

They were all pretty and except for Dezi, all blonde. They all went to Le World School de Paris. They were all American. They all knew each other well.

Was the killer someone who hated Americans? But except for Dubonnet and Potter all Jean-Marc's suspects were themselves American.

He tried to make Dubonnet fit the mold. A serial killer working from inside the school like Watson and Potter would have a much harder time maintaining his innocence. But a predator watching from a corner *café*? It was a perfect setup.

Except Dubonnet didn't feel right to Jean-Marc. Not for these crimes.

He put a call in to Claire. She answered immediately.

"Tell me you are home," he said.

"I will if you tell me you got some sleep last night."

"It was not a good night for sleeping."

"Do you have any new leads?"

"We brought Maurice Dubonnet this morning. He has a record."

"Do you think he's your guy?"

"My gut says no. He appeared truly horrified about the murders."

"Psychopaths can express empathy, even regret."

"It sounds like you have done your research," Jean-Marc said dryly.

"What about Eric Watson?"

"We have him but we're letting him stew for a bit."

Caron had been unable to ascertain what alibis Watson had given for Cecily and Haley's disappearances. Jean-Marc wasn't sure how he had fallen though the cracks. Probably Watson hadn't seemed viable at the time and there had been no follow up. Even now, Watson felt wrong as a serial killer candidate. Too fresh-faced, too All-American. Still, Jean-Marc knew the masks any psychopath worth his salt would wear.

"And the gym teacher that all the girls hated?" Claire asked. "Deb Knox?"

"These murders were committed by men."

"You don't know that! I heard two of the bodies had semen in them from two different men."

"How did you—?" Jean-Marc started and then sighed. *Adele, of course.*

"And Deb Knox is strong enough to grab and strangle any of these girls," Claire said.

"We talked to her. Hating pretty girls is not a motive."

"Jean-Marc, I hope you're not looking for motives because you know as well as I do that serial killers don't need them to kill."

He was tired. Of course he knew that.

"Do you know how many female serial killers there have been in the history of the world?" he said tiredly.

"You can't discount anyone, Jean-Marc."

"I'm doing my best not to."

"You've got to find her," Claire said. "She must be so frightened."

"I know."

"At least grab thirty minutes of shut-eye. You're no good to anyone dead on your feet."

"I will."

"Liar."

"I'll call you if anything breaks," he said wearily. "Thanks for the lead on Dubonnet. It was a good one."

"Go get that nap. I mean it, Jean-Marc."

"*Bien sûr.*"

47

After hanging up with Jean-Marc, a wave of sadness hit me. It was as if somewhere inside me I knew that the story was over and there was nothing more to be done. I think it was testimony to just how helpless I felt and how utterly powerless I was to change the trajectory of this terrible narrative.

This monster was calling the shots and nothing Jean-Marc or I did was going to slow or revise what was going to happen.

How many hours did Dezi have left? I wondered. If the killer went by his previous MO, she was long past the deadline. Wherever she was, Dezi was either breathing her last moments or already dead. And no amount of guilt or helpless feelings on my part was going to change that.

I sat for a moment on the couch with my phone in my hands before I realized that the apartment seemed oddly quiet. When I'd come home late last night I'd just gone straight to bed.

I jumped up and made a quick check of the guest room which confirmed that Courtney was not there. I suppose that meant she'd spent the night at Luc's. Well, good for both of them.

After showering and dressing for the day, I went downstairs to Geneviève's apartment. She met me at the door with Robbie on her hip and the scent of fresh coffee behind her.

"*Bonjour, chérie,*" Geneviève said, handing the baby to me. "A productive night, I hope?"

Izzy ran to me and began to jump against my knees, so I knelt to love on her.

"Not really," I said.

Sometimes when you're working a case you can't see what you're building because it's done in incremental pieces and it takes a while to see the whole picture. But in this case—with the pressing timeline always uppermost in my mind—incremental building was little better than no building at all. It was just too slow to help.

On top of which, the picture never changed.

"The girl has not been found?" Geneviève asked gently.

I shook my head.

"So she has not been killed yet either," Geneviève said as she set down a steaming mug of coffee in front of me.

"That's not a given," I said.

"You are doing your best, *chérie.*"

My best. What was my best? My best was tracking people through their credit card purchases or their job histories and sometimes their social media posts. Was I fooling myself to think I was really doing any *detection*?

My "best" was going to mean precisely nothing to Dezi White and her distraught parents.

"Will you go back out today?" Geneviève asked.

"I don't know." I sat on the couch with Robbie in my lap. He curled up happily, laughing and grabbing for Izzy when she got too near him.

"Have you spoken with the baby's mother about her plans?" Geneviève asked.

"Courtney has no plans," I said. "None beyond those that have me supporting her."

"And are you okay with that?"

"No," I said, feeling a weariness descend upon me I didn't usually experience this early in the day. I set Robbie on the floor and took a sip of my coffee. It immediately seemed to infuse me with energy.

Geneviève was smiling at Robbie who was flailing uselessly on his stomach, unable to crawl. It was hardly a surprise that Geneviève would become fond of him in the time she'd been forced to care for him.

I pulled out my phone and Geneviève stood up as if to give me some privacy. I don't know how she knew I needed it.

I called Laura and she picked up after a few rings, her voice subdued and tired.

"How's Jessica?" I said when she answered.

"Don't ask."

"I wish there was something I could say to her," I said.

"There isn't. Trust me. Just find Dezi so *her* parents don't have to go through this."

"Have you heard from Dezi's parents?" I asked.

"No. They weren't active in the expat community. Plus..."

Her voice trailed off but she didn't need to finish the sentence. *Plus* whatever help Laura had offered Jessica and Cindy in the way of my involvement had not changed the terrible outcome one bit.

"Please give Jessica my deepest sympathies," I said, knowing how lame that sounded.

"I will. How goes the hunt for Dezi?"

"The police have a couple of new leads," I said, knowing that was an exaggeration if not an outright lie.

"Well, that's something anyway. It's more than they've had up to now."

I saw a call coming in from Adele.

"I've got to take this call, Laura. I'll let you know if I hear anything."

We disconnected and I picked up the incoming call.

"Hey," I said.

"Are you busy?" Adele said, the excitement evident in her voice.

"Not really. Why?"

"Meet me at Ladurée, yes? I have found something."

48

D ubonnet could not believe his good luck.

Freed when that bastard LaRue had clearly intended to keep him.

Incredible.

LaRue thought he knew so much but he was as stupid as the rest of them. He couldn't believe how he had bought all his crying about how awful he felt for the girls! And LaRue had believed him! In the end they were all so easy to fool.

And then a disquieting thought came to Dubonnet and he felt a rush of heat.

How had the cops gotten on to him? Someone must have told them. But who?

Dubonnet scrolled through in his mind everyone he thought he knew who might have given him away. Could it have been his boss? But no, he was all right. He was always bragging about giving ex-cons a second chance.

How about one of the kids? It could be any one of the little shits. Although why they might do it wasn't clear. But now that he was on the cops'radar it was only a matter of time before they tried to pick him up again. He couldn't go back to Café Bleu. He'd probably have to leave Paris.

A perfect situation had turned to *merde* and all because someone knew something they shouldn't and talked about it.

Someone just ruined my life and all my brand new chances.

Before he did anything else he'd need to find that someone. He'd track him down—or her!—and he'd make sure they never had the chance to ruin another person's life ever again.

49

I n case there's someone in the world unaware of the fact, Ladurée is an amazing luxury bakery and sweets store that's been around since 1862. It was just a straight shot down the Champs-Élysées half way between the famous George V Hotel and the Disney Store.

Sometimes I think of all the ladies who wore full-skirted crinoline petticoats complete with multiple flounces and tiers to the floor sitting where I'm sitting and sipping *noisettes* and enjoying a lavender macaron or two as I sometimes do. It always makes me think that perhaps life hasn't changed all that much in a hundred and fifty years.

Well, at least not the important things.

I tell friends that Ladurée is just a few blocks from my apartment, but as I walked it today I realized it was much farther.

It didn't matter. Adele said she'd found something. I would've traveled a lot farther to hear what she had to say. And then there wouldn't have been macarons.

I'd settled in at a corner table in the window by the time Adele showed up—in a rush for a change, her face flushed with excitement. Just seeing her so charged up made my pulse quicken in anticipation and hope.

She was wearing a stunning Stella McCartney jogging outfit and heels. It was one of her favorite outfits and very chic although how she could run in those heels was beyond me. And to get here from her flat in the time she'd done it, she must have run.

We both ordered Americanos and because it was Ladurée, macarons of course. I could feel my hopes ratcheting up as I soon as I registered Adele's excitement.

"Is your news about Ali?" I asked.

"It is," she said. "Turns out this one *was* different. He didn't rape her."

I frowned since, while it was true that any difference between the murders was a lead that could be followed up on, Adele and I had already ascertained that none of the girls had really been raped—at least not in the traditional sense.

"Okay," I said, waiting for what I was sure must be more to come.

"There was no semen found in her at all."

This was good news. It was definitely a change from the others. I'm not sure what it told me but it was better than the nothing I'd had five minutes ago.

"Plus it looks as if she was killed forty-eight hours after she was grabbed."

That was a significant alteration from the killer's MO. Serial killers typically took pains to plan their methodology. They saw it as leaving a signature for the clueless authorities. It made them feel even more superior.

And from John Gacy to Ted Bundy, they didn't like to alter their patterns.

Something had made this guy change his MO.

"The medical examiner thinks Ali was dumped early in the

evening, while it was barely dark, but with people still walking around.

"Do the cops think someone could have seen him?"

"Maybe," Adele said as our coffees arrived. "They're still canvassing the neighborhood."

"That is incredibly time-consuming," I said.

And the one thing we don't have is time.

"There's more." Adele leaned in closer so as not to risk being overheard by the handful of tourists and diners sharing the dining room with us.

"We found DNA under Ali's fingernails just like with Haley."

"That's great!" I said. "So they match each other?"

"Yes, but not anything in the…"

"Yes, I know, nothing in the criminal database," I finished for her. "But still. It might mean he's getting sloppy."

"Also," Adele said. "Do you remember the semen I told you that was found in the other girls?"

"Of course."

"The lab said it was dead when it entered the body."

I frowned. "Meaning?"

"Sperm needs moisture and warmth to survive," she said, delicately selecting a pistachio macaron. "The second the ejaculate is in the air the seminal plasma begins to break down."

I shrugged in confusion. "So?"

"So," she said patiently, "it means whoever did this didn't have the capability of keeping it alive. The semen found in the girls likely came from a container of some kind."

Hadn't we already established this? The girls' wounds were not consistent with rape.

"So I guess you're saying this confirms that the killer didn't really rape them," I said.

"Exactly."

"But he wanted to give the appearance of it," I said, my

mind racing to put together the implications of what this might mean. "How weird."

"Isn't it?" Adele said. "Plus, did I tell you there was a match for the semen found in Haley?"

"Seriously?"

"Yes, but remember, our evidence suggests that the *killer* didn't rape the girls," Adele said.

"But then who was the DNA match for?"

"Some homeless guy they found under a bridge with his throat cut."

I felt my fingers begin to tingle.

"So you're saying the guy whose DNA they found inside Haley was later found murdered?" I said.

"About the size of it," Adele confirmed.

I thought about this for a moment. From my research I knew that most serial killers were driven by a strong sexual impulse to commit their murders.

"I wonder why the killer didn't rape them himself?" I murmured more to myself than Adele.

"That's the twenty-million-euro question, isn't it?" Adele said, relaxing back in her chair and picking up her coffee cup. "He may be impotent or in some other way unable."

I raised an eyebrow at her.

"What do you mean in *some other way?*'" I asked.

"You know, like if he's really a woman."

50

A fter Adele left the restaurant I sat and reflected on what she'd told me. As far as I was concerned, this new information opened up the possibility that Deb Knox was the killer.

It was a quiet day at Ladurée—unimaginable but true. Normally I feel guilty if I linger there since there's almost always a line out the door. But for whatever reason, today the restaurant was quiet. I ordered another *noisette* and, God help me, two more macarons.

I pulled out my notepad and looked at my list of possible suspects.

Eric Watson, the art teacher, who I thought seemed to resent teaching rich kids, had slept with at least one of the dead girls. Plus, he'd essentially bragged to me that he had no alibi and didn't need one.

I wrote in the margin next to his name: *Would a proper serial killer not have an alibi for the time in question?*

My answer to myself came back: if he was arrogant enough, then very possibly.

Cedric Potter, Le World School de Paris headmaster, gave

out definite vibes of hating the rich expat parents he had to suck up to in his job. Plus, he had no alibi. Worse, he lied about having one. Plus, while Potter and his rampant narcissism might fit the textbook definition of a serial killer, the singular outstanding feature that marks the difference between your average psychopath and a serial killer was impulse control. Potter struck me as one sneeze away from a total meltdown.

As evidenced by his suicide attempt.

I called Adele on my phone.

"What is it?" she asked. "I just left you."

"Is there any way Cedric Potter could have killed Ali?"

"You mean DNA-wise?"

"That or time-wise."

"Hold on a sec," she said.

I waited while she put me on hold, assuming she was calling up one of the Medical Examiner's reports on the murder.

Was I looking at this the wrong way? Was I being distracted by who did or didn't have a motive? It's like I told Jean-Marc, *a serial killer has no motive.* He kills to relieve pressure or for reasons known only in the dark recesses of his own diseased mind.

Or *her* mind.

"They ruled him out," Adele said when she came back on the line. "Ali Burton was killed between fifteen and nineteen hundred hours. Potter was on his way to the emergency room by that time."

I felt my shoulders sag but whether from relief or disappointment, I wasn't sure.

I crossed Cedric Potter off my list.

"Thanks," I said. "Go get some sleep."

"I will if you'll stop calling me!"

I wrote down the name *Deb Knox*. If I took away the fact that she was a woman, would she qualify as a suspect? The only thing that argued against it—besides two hundred years of history of predominantly male serial killers—was Knox's alibi.

I didn't bother texting Jean-Marc to see if he had confirmed it. He wouldn't tell me. Instead, I texted Laura. I hated to do this to Jessica—remind her that she was the mother of a student at Le World School de Paris—but I needed Knox's partner's contact information.

<pls ask Jessica for Deb Knox's contact info; specif her partner name and number>

I glanced back at my list of names and wrote down one more.

Mark White. Dezi's father looked suspicious to me because of the way he behaved around all the schoolgirls. If I discounted him because it was unbelievable to me that he could do this to his own daughter, that might be exactly what a psychopath would want me to think.

Then there was Maurice Dubonnet. Because I had no hope of immediately interviewing him, I didn't know how he might fit the serial killer's profile. I'd have to trust that Jean-Marc had that covered.

Laura texted me back.

<No clue as to phone # but J remembers Knox's girlfriend named Beckie Kirkland>

I sent a quick thank-you text back to her and opened up a search engine on my smartphone. It took me five seconds to locate the phone number that Rebecca Kirkland had opened her Paris utility bill with.

When I called the number, she answered guardedly. I knew my number would have shown up on her phone screen as UNKNOWN.

"Yes?"

"Beckie Kirkland?" I said. "My name is Claire Baskerville. Do you have a moment?"

Normally I hate to give any subject an opportunity to turn

me down but I was going to try to get her to tell me the truth even if she ended up incriminating her partner—so I figured a more delicate touch was warranted.

"What's this about?" she asked.

"I'm working with the Paris police," I said briskly. "And they've asked me to confirm some statements that they gathered in reference to a homicide that occurred last week."

There was a pause on the line and I forced myself not to fill it.

"This is about Deb's alibi, isn't it?"

I felt a rush of excitement. That statement right there told me that she and Deb had discussed the topic. And that Beckie wasn't happy about it.

"I need to confirm that Deb Knox was with you in London on May fifth through the seventh," I said.

There was that pause again.

"Miss Kirkland?" I prompted.

"We were in London on May fifth."

"But not on the seventh?"

May seventh was the Haley Johnson abduction.

"No."

My mind began to compute in double time. I wasn't sure what it meant that Deb Knox was alibied for one of the murders but not both. The only thing I knew for sure was that she lied.

"All right," I said. "That's all I need."

"Look, I know Deb didn't do this," Beckie said. "She couldn't. Well, maybe she could but she didn't. I've known her a long time."

She could but she didn't? Was Beckie Kirkland telling me her partner was capable of the murders? I made a mental note to have Jean-Marc bring Knox in for more questioning. Maybe, just maybe, he'll find out she wasn't in London on May fifth either.

After I disconnected with Beckie I looked at my notepad and underlined Deb Knox's name.

I felt a sheen of perspiration on my skin and recognized its source was the underlying panic I was trying to ignore as the minutes and hours ticked by and I was still so far from finding a single lead.

If I ignored any possible motive Knox might have—and there seemed to be plenty—and focused on the fact that she had a poor alibi at best and added the articles of clothing from at least one of the dead girls that I'd found in her desk, I might actually have something close to a viable suspect on my hands.

I stared at Deb Knox's name on my notepad and felt a wave of determination.

I need to get those trophy items so Adele can test them for DNA.

It might not be evidence.

But it was better than sitting here staring at a notepad.

51

I took in a long breath to steady my nerves. On the one hand, broad-day burglary of Knox's office at Le World School de Paris would give me a sense that I was actually doing something other than just drinking dry the city's vast inventory of coffee. But on the other hand, it made more sense to do it when I was sure all the school's personnel were gone.

That left a much bigger and possibly more important task for the next part of my day. The fact that I would probably not even get the chance to perform that task didn't deter me in the slightest.

I was at the point where I was starting to rank even the most hopeless tasks on my list as worth trying.

As long as Dezi's body didn't show up in the river.

One of the reasons Adele and I'd chosen to meet at Ladurée —aside from the macarons, of course—was the fact that it was on the Champs-Élysées, roughly halfway between my apartment and Adele's office in the eighth arrondissement.

It made getting to my next destination—the one with the task that I was almost certain to fail at—just a short Métro ride away across the river to the sixteenth arrondissement. And

since from Dezi's apartment—which was where I was heading
—it was an easy walk to the International school, I could
schedule my break-in for later in the afternoon when hopefully
all school personnel would be gone.

I am usually more organized than this as far as constructing
my cases. But I'm also usually doing skip tracing or employ-
ment backgrounds and not profiling serial killers. With my
usual jobs I don't ever need to even leave my apartment. I'm
often trying to find a runaway which, unless he or she is living
rough on the streets, is not that difficult. Everyone can be traced
fairly easily via their phone calls, ATM visits, credit card
purchases or—even more quickly—through clueless friends
and acquaintances.

But finding a lost girl who is deliberately being held from
you by a diabolical genius who has no limits to what he or she
will do is something else again.

I was way out of my depth. But I still couldn't stop.

On the train, I texted Laura for Dezi White's address. I
could do it myself, of course, much like how I tracked down
Beckie Kirkland, but I think a part of me wanted to make sure
somebody knew where I was going to be this morning.

And that's because of course, I hadn't at all taken Mark
White off my suspect's list. While it would be highly unusual—
not to mention horrific—if he were involved in the kidnapping
of his own daughter, I wouldn't be so stupid as to give him a
pass based on that.

Laura texted me the address as I was leaving the train
station.

<I rang Audrey to tell her you were coming>

I frowned when I read that since I do like to do things
without giving anyone advance warning, but by the time I
found myself standing in front of Dezi's apartment building I
was relieved that Laura had done it. It would give Dezi's parents

time to decide if they were going to slam the door in my face—probably—or let me in to try to help them.

Their degree of desperation would indicate which it would be.

There was a policeman standing at the double doors leading into Dezi White's apartment building. He too must have been alerted that I was coming because he simply nodded at me and opened the door.

"The lobby door is open. Second floor," he said as I stepped into the covered alcove that led to the courtyard and the lobby.

I thanked him and went through to the lobby and up the stairs to the second floor. There was only one apartment on this floor, confirming to me just how rich the Whites were. The door to the apartment was open. A uniformed policewomen stood at the open door and nodded at me to enter.

Audrey and Mark White's apartment was breathtaking. From what I could see from the foyer, the living room must have been the work of a major designing talent. A Queen Anne secretary anchored one wall and was surrounded by gilt-framed oil paintings, a vintage mantel clock, and a breathtaking collection of blue and white china.

On the other side of the secretary was a pair of Chinese lacquered straight-back dining chairs. They looked old. And expensive.

As I stepped into the foyer, a tall, well-dressed woman came to greet me. She wore a beautiful long-sleeve silk blouse that looked too warm for the season and held a steaming teacup in her hands. She made no move toward me, not to shake my hand or direct me to enter further or sit down. The look on her face was one of heartbreak and hopelessness.

I very nearly turned around and left. Using every bit of bravery I had, I stepped into the apartment.

"I'm Claire Baskerville," I said.

"I know," Audrey White said. Her accent was southern US, like mine. "Laura Murphy called."

"I'm afraid I can't promise anything," I said.

"I know," she repeated, her eyes glistening with unshed tears as she beckoned me inside.

52

D ezi's bedroom must have been every girl's fantasy—if that girl had any taste at all. The centerpiece of the room was a dramatic French Provincial four-poster bed draped in silk and linen. The walls were papered in toile in hushed tones of rose and cream.

Audrey White stood beside me in the doorway. I could hear the tremble of her china cup against its saucer in her hands. She took me straight to Dezi's bedroom and now we both stood staring at the artifacts of a teenage girl and her adolescent passions.

It was enough to break your heart.

Everything about the room let the visitor know who Dezi was and who she aspired to be. The room emphatically revealed that Dezi loved everything French. The posters of Edith Piaf, Vanessa Paradis and Josephine Baker on the walls painted Dezi as a hopeless romantic who aligned herself with the creative but tragic heroines of history.

Open shelving opposite the bed showcased a beret collec-tion in every color, as well as a vinyl record player, and an assortment of stuffed teddy bears each wearing the iconic Breton-striped sailor shirt.

"She wanted so much to be French," Audrey murmured.

I turned to her.

"What is it that her father does in Paris?"

"He is a sales supervisor," she said gazing around the room. "When his company transferred him here, it felt like a miracle for all of us."

Why all of us? I wondered. Had Audrey been trying to save her marriage? What had been wrong that she'd needed a miracle?

"This is killing Mark," Audrey said. "Both of us, of course. But Mark just adores Dezi."

I turned back to the picture-perfect room and spotted the laptop on her desk.

"Did the police not take Dezi's laptop?"

Audrey nodded. "Yes. They took it and returned it," she said. "They said they found nothing helpful."

I wondered if the cops had really looked. I wondered if there really was *nothing helpful* on it. I knew Jean-Marc was crazy busy what with canvassing half of Paris, desperate to find any clues. It was possible that going through Dezi's laptop had just been way down his priorities list.

"Do you mind if I look at it?" I asked, already moving into the room.

When I sat down at Dezi's desk I could see the Eiffel Tower in plain view from her bedroom window.

What a magical room for a young girl in love with Paris, I thought. *And parents rich enough and devoted enough to give it to her.*

"The password is *joie1221*," Audrey said. "Please excuse me."

She turned and hurried away.

I opened Dezi's laptop with the password and went to scan her history but it had been wiped. Then I went to Facebook and on a hunch used the same password to reactivate Dezi's Facebook account. It was the fastest way for me to see what she'd posted before the account had been shut down.

Dezi had not posted anything in more than a week which would have been around the time I'd first met her. That coincided with the timing of my number being blocked on her phone. Presumably her parents had concomitantly disabled her Facebook account at that time. I made a mental note to ask them.

I drilled down into her posts and saw that Dezi posted irregularly, sometimes every other day and sometimes going weeks without a post. That wasn't a surprise because of her overprotective parents, but I'd noticed of course that Ali wasn't on Facebook at all. Whether that was because she—or one of her parents—had disabled her account or because she'd never had one, I didn't know.

But I intended to find out in short order.

Further searching revealed a post of Dezi's that Ali's name was ghosted out—indicating that Ali *had* had a Facebook presence at one time but she was no longer Facebook friends with Dezi. I scrolled down to a photo that Dezi had posted that had tagged Ali. It was a selfie picture of the two of them smiling at the camera. I looked at the date of the photo. It was posted two weeks before Ali went missing.

I picked up my phone and texted Laura.

<Pls ask Jessica if she disabled Ali's FB account>

I looked at the photo that Dezi had posted before that. It was an extremely unflattering picture of Mikayla Macintre at a party, drunk, with the caption reading: "Skank!"

Laura's text came back to me. *<I'd rather not. Is important?>*

Annoyed, I texted her back. *<YES>*

I clicked on the photo to enlarge it and looked at the background. There were five other kids in the picture, none of whom, thanks to my face blindness, I was able to recognize. I tried to remember what Jackie looked like from when I'd met her in the park with Ben the other day, but it was hopeless. She was a pretty blonde girl with no striking features—basically what all blonde girls look like to me.

The major focus of the skank photo was two girls making out in the foreground whose faces were hidden by their long hair and one boy wearing green jeans trying to stick his tongue in a drunk Mikayla's ear.

There was little doubt who the "Skank!" caption referred to. I moved the cursor over the boy but he wasn't tagged. Neither were the two kissing girls. I went back to Dezi's home page and noted that she had over five hundred friends. I typed *Ali Burton* into the search window of those five hundred friends.

But nothing came up.

53

My skin tingled ominously at what I'd discovered.

Why wouldn't Ali show up as a friend on Dezi's Facebook page? According to both Dezi and Ben, Ali and Dezi were best friends.

I squinted again at the picture of Mikayla, clearly tagged—the ugly caption obviously meant for her—and wondered why Dezi had posted it.

I pushed back from the laptop and let my gaze drift around Dezi's room. It was heartbreaking to see all the things that revealed so clearly what she loved and who she was. The thought came to me that Dezi might never come back to this room again. My stomach clenched painfully and I reminded myself that thinking such things was not going to help anyone.

Not that anything I'd done up to now had been helpful but at least I could refrain from making it worse before time.

"Did you find anything?" Mark White said, his voice low and threatening from where he'd materialized in the doorway of the bedroom.

"Not really," I said calmly, turning to search his face for a hint of the man I'd seen last time—the one with the temper that had scared me enough to make me pull out my Taser.

That man was nowhere to be found.

Mark staggered to Dezi's bed and collapsed into a seated position on it, holding his face in his hands.

"The police haven't a clue," he said, his voice broken with wracked emotion.

I had to quickly determine if what I was witnessing was real or not. I know that should be obvious—a parent loses a child to kidnapping and waits to hear if she's been found dead—but there was nothing obvious about Mark White.

Authentic or not, Mark appeared vulnerable. I knew I needed to take advantage of that and hope I was talking to the real Mark White.

"I'm sorry for what you're going through," I said.

"I can't believe it," he said, his words muffled behind his hands. "I just can't believe it."

"Have the police narrowed down the time as to when she was taken?" I asked.

He looked at me, his face streaked with tears and I could see him reach for facts as a way to push away from his pain.

"They said it could've been any time between two and three o'clock."

"How did they get to that?"

He wiped his face and stared at his wet hands.

"Because Audrey and I came home at three," he said. "And Dez spoke to someone on her phone at two-thirty."

"Who did she speak to?"

He waved a hand as if it were unimportant. "One of her friends," he said.

I wondered who. It couldn't be Mikayla, Ben or Jackie or they would have volunteered that information. Wouldn't they? But the police knew. The police had a list of all the numbers that had come in and gone from Dezi's phone.

I texted Jean-Marc. *<Who did Dezi talk to on her phone the aft she was taken?>*

"I'm sorry I was such an a-hole when we met," Mark said.

"That's all right. I understand protective parenthood."

He looked at me and cocked his head.

"A daughter?" he said.

I nodded.

"They're the worst," he said, looking down at his hands and then quickly back up at me. "I mean they're the best but...you know."

"Yes, I know," I said.

He covered his face again with his hands, his shoulders quaking with the effort to hold himself together.

"I'd just give anything," he said, in a wrenching sob. "Just anything at all if only..."

There was no way he was faking this. This man was destroyed by what had happened...what might soon happen... to his only child.

I mentally crossed Mark White off my list.

And felt a vague shimmer of hope.

I was narrowing the list.

From five down to three.

Eric Watson. Deb Knox. Maurice Dubonnet.

54

B y the time I finally left Dezi White's house, the beautiful June day had turned into a gloomy grey day with low-hanging clouds fat with impending rain. I normally wore slacks but because the day had started out so pleasant I'd worn a mid-calf peasant skirt today. I was already feeling chilly in it.

Even so, the school wasn't five blocks from Dezi's house. I walked briskly away from the posh neighborhood in the sixteenth arrondissement until I came to the Pont Alexandre III over the river.

The Eiffel Tower loomed large in front of me as I walked and I was reminded of how it had looked from Dezi's bedroom window.

Such a magical bedroom for a romantic girl in love with Paris.

I shook off the feeling of mounting dread. I was doing everything I could.

I felt a vibration coming from my purse and pulled out my phone.

<A schoolmate called her> Jean-Marc had texted.

I felt a pinch of annoyance.

<*Who?*> I texted back.

I waited as I watched the bubbles form next to the text message and then stop. In frustration, I tossed my phone back in my bag and forged on.

I was tempted to text him back and ask if he'd ever done anything about the trophies in Deb Knox's desk, but I already knew the answer. No matter. I'd get the trophies myself and get Adele to test them. The items probably didn't mean anything but considering I had absolutely no other leads to go on, I thought it was worth my time.

Like yesterday, the school appeared deserted. I didn't bother scouting the area like I had last time but went straight to the back and let myself in through the play yard gate. Just to be safe, I put my phone on mute and slipped in through the unlocked building door on the far side of the playground.

The more I thought about it, the more I found myself believing that the so-called Lost and Found drawer was important. *One of the items—a wristband—had Haley Johnson's initials on it.* What if there were others? What if the items in that drawer were *only* items belonging to either Ali, Haley or Cecily?

Just the thought of that sent a shiver of excitement through me and I found myself practically running down the hall toward Deb Knox's office.

Once I reached her office, I hesitated, glad of the plate glass window that afforded me an unimpeded view inside. The room was empty. Listening to the silence of the school, I reached for the door handle.

It was locked.

I felt my jaw tighten.

And of course I'd left my lock-picking tools in Robbie's diaper bag.

I looked inside the office. I had not come all this way to stop now. Looking behind me, I saw a dumbbell on a bench in the hallway. Without thinking too much about it, I picked it up and brought it back to the office door. I spent a long moment trying to figure out exactly how I was going to do this without treating myself to a trip to the French emergency room. Then I remembered that I'd tucked a spare diaper in my tote bag a few days ago.

Quickly I dug it out, dropping my bag in the hallway, and wrapped the diaper around the dumbbell. My first tap against the window wasn't hard enough. It made a loud thunking sound but didn't break. Scolding myself for my weak effort, I hit the glass again more solidly.

This time the glass broke, sending a thrill of triumph through me at the sound.

Carefully, I dropped the glass-encrusted diaper on the floor and snaked my hand through the broken pane of glass to manage the lock on the inside. Within seconds I had the door open and I was inside.

By this time my heart was pounding so loudly the only thing I could hear was the sound of my own blood rushing in my ears.

I hurried to the front of Knox's desk and, fully expecting the drawer to be stuck again, wrenched it as hard as I could. The whole drawer came out in my hand.

I staggered backward, holding the drawer as pencils, pens and erasers bounced out onto the hardwood floor under my feet.

What I was looking for was not in the drawer.

I'm sure I stood there for several seconds staring at the empty drawer before my brain was able to catch up to what had happened.

Knox had moved the trophies!

How stupid did I think she was? She probably did it within seconds of my leaving her office two days ago!

I put the drawer back in its place and looked around as if refusing to accept my disappointment. There had to be some-place else she would have moved the trophies to! But clearly

Knox wasn't going to be that obvious, moving her trophies from the drawer only to stash them someplace equally as obvious.

Would she?

Pinching my lips together in frustration I sat down in the desk chair for a moment and let my mind go back over what I knew. I'd gone through too much to break in here to just tuck my tail and run.

One thing was for sure, if I'd had any doubt about whether or not the items in the drawer were really Lost and Found items, the mere fact that she'd moved them erased that doubt for good.

Why would she hide them unless they were evidence of her crime?

As I sat in the chair, my eyes went to the tall metal armoire in the corner of her office. It was painted the same drab gunmetal gray as the walls.

It was probably too obvious a place to look but wasn't it true what I'd read about psychopaths—that they all think they are so much smarter than everyone else? Wouldn't it be the height of arrogance for Deb to take the trophies and move them from the drawer to a shelf in the armoire? In the same room? Isn't that *exactly* what someone would do who considered the world her intellectual inferior?

My pulse racing with renewed excitement, I stepped over to the armoire. I pulled open the doors and saw four shelves of boxes and spare sports jerseys. I pulled the first box out and holding it in one hand, rummaged through it.

Ribbons, cheap medals, small plastic winners' trophies.

I tossed the box back in and grabbed the next one. With every move I knew I was right.

The trophies were here. I just knew it.

I pulled a second, larger box out and rested it on my hip while I went through it with my free hand. Pamphlets, score cards, tennis balls, a couple of beanbags.

It was the very moment when I was beginning to feel like perhaps I'd been wrong after all when I saw it.

The tip of a purple scrunchie was sticking out of a box in the very back of the armoire. Excited, and with my back to the door, I reached deep inside the recesses of the armoire.

I felt the cloth scrunchie in my fingers but before I could pull it out, I felt an iron-hard pressure abruptly encircle my windpipe.

55

I gasped and dropped the box. My hands went immediately to the arm around my throat, hard and unyielding.

I could smell him now, rank and noisome. His body, shoved hard against my back as he held me, felt wiry and compact.

He was speaking but the sound of my pounding heart obliterated his words.

I couldn't breathe. I desperately dug my nails into the forearm around my neck. When I did he yelled and flung me into the armoire. I hit my head on one of the shelves and felt myself start to go down.

I grappled for something to hold onto to stop my fall.

I could hear him now. He was cursing in French. And he was close.

I managed to stay on my feet and, leaning against the armoire, snatched up a handful of pencils from an open tray on one of the shelves and whirled around.

He was slim, his face unshaven. His hair was long and dirty. He looked at me with loathing.

Of course I didn't recognize him. All I knew was that he was French.

"Who are you?" I asked in French, holding the unsharpened pencils in my fist. Blunt pencils wouldn't kill him but they might take an eye out.

"*La pute!*" he swore. "You told them it was me!"

Could this be the school custodian? But that was impossible. Why would he attack me? I backed further into the armoire and watched him rub away the bloody marks my nails had made on his arm.

He locked his eyes on me, every bit as determined as before. He didn't want to call the police on me.

He wanted to hurt me.

"Why are you here?" I asked. "I am an American citizen. If you hurt me, my government will put you in jail for the rest of your life."

He spat. "You think that scares me? I just came from jail!"

My eyes went to my purse lying on the floor in the hallway.

That's when I remembered I hadn't brought my Taser. Even if I could get to my bag it was hopeless. I couldn't fight him. Escape was my only hope.

But how was I going to get past him?

In the next split second, he answered that question for me.

I wasn't.

He slapped the pencils out of my hands. I twisted away to try to maneuver from the armoire and put the desk between us. But he moved faster, grabbing a fistful of my hair and jerking me off my feet and into his arms.

I struggled but it was no use. He was too strong. He flipped me over on my back onto the desk, knocking off staplers, framed pictures and a coffee mug to the floor. I pulled my knees up between me and him and he let go of my hair long enough to pry my legs down.

And apart.

I lifted my head up and cracked my forehead hard into his nose. I felt the arms holding me loosen on impact. I squirmed off the desk, bringing the desk blotter and a stack of loose notebooks with me.

"I'll fix you for that, you bitch!" he screamed, his anger filling the room with a throbbing intensity.

I saw the field hockey stick on the shelf against the wall. Some part of my brain must have known running was never going to work. I grabbed the stick, my fingers too slick with sweat to get a proper grip on the handle as I turned and ran to the door.

When he grabbed my arm and whipped me around to face him, it gave my swing the momentum it needed.

I smashed the stick across his chin as hard as I could.

He fell backwards and I turned to the door. In my mind's eye I saw myself leaping over him and racing down the hall and through the outer door, across the playground and over the chain link fence.

Terror and adrenalin drove every sane thought out of my head except escape.

I made it as far as the door to the office.

He grabbed my hair again and jerked me back to him and then abruptly released me. I fell to the floor.

This was bad. Being on the floor was the one place you did not want to be in an attack.

"Just hold right there, bitch," he growled. "Because this is going to hurt."

He grabbed my skirt and began raking it up roughly, scratching my legs with his fingernails as he did. I blotted out his voice, his odor, his touch on my bare legs. I blotted it all out and only focused on my purse that I was now lying on top of.

I gouged my fingers deep inside my bag at the same moment he flipped me over on my back, my head bouncing hard on the floor. My vision blurred with the impact.

I looked into his face, his leering, furious face as he bent over me.

And then I jammed the nozzle of the pepper spray can up his nose.

And squeezed the trigger for all I was worth.

56

I called the police from a café down the street.

I'm sure I looked an absolute sight, my hair sticking straight up, my skirt ripped, all the buttons on my cardigan completely missing with streaks of blood down my arms and face.

I didn't stop to make the phone call until I was well and truly out of the school and safely with a crowd of people. I was fairly sure that my attacker would still be in the process of clawing at his face and howling when the police arrived but I couldn't take the chance that he might recover and try to find me.

I called Jean-Marc first but of course he didn't take my call. That was fine. Fifteen minutes later and I'd already had two whiskeys by the time I heard the iconic sound of a Paris police car racing to the international school. I'd stayed on the line with the dispatcher the whole time, so by the time a police cruiser drove up to my café looking for me, I had paid my bill and was nursing a cup of coffee to mitigate somewhat the effects of my three whiskeys.

"Madame Baskerville?" the very polite policeman asked as I stood up.

"Did you get him?" I asked.

"*Oui*. He is on his way downtown. You will come with me?"

Once at the *préfecture*, they escorted me to a very utilitarian office—something I would have assumed detectives might have if they rated their own office. They closed the door, asking first if I'd like more coffee which I declined. I wasn't sure how long I'd have to wait but as soon as I sat down, I felt a wave of exhaustion crash over me.

Like a lot of people, once committed to a goal, I can go forever on very little resources and fuel. But as soon as I rest for just a moment, I'm done. Then all the reasons why I'm too old and too tired to do this any more become painfully apparent.

I tried to ignore all my aching, throbbing joints and scratches, closed my eyes and allowed myself to rest.

"Well, you've had a nice little outing," Jean-Marc said as he entered the interrogation room where Maurice Dubonnet now sat chained to the table. "Too bad it's the last you'll get for a few years."

"You can't threaten me, LaRue," Dubonnet said. "I've got nothing left to lose."

"So why not tell me the truth, if that's so?"

Jean-Marc leaned on the table with both arms. Both Caron and Dartre were in the room with him.

Were they afraid I'd abuse the suspect otherwise?

It was true, Jean-Marc had to consciously tamp down the emotions he'd felt when he heard the dispatch report had been triggered by Claire's call. But he was calm now. He was almost completely calm now.

"Want to tell me why you left police custody and attacked a woman on school grounds at Le World School de Paris?"

"I deny it."

"CCTV cameras show you entering the school from the east side."

"Do they show *her* breaking in? Or am I the only one being charged with burglary?"

"You're not being charged with burglary, Maurice," Jean-Marc said evenly. "You're being charged with aggravated assault and attempted rape."

It was all he could do to get the words out without grinding his teeth or in some other way giving himself away.

"I deny it," Dubonnet said again. "It's her word against mine."

"Your word means much less than hers does," Jean-Marc said.

"That's prejudice!" Dubonnet said.

"Why did you follow her?"

"I didn't!"

"CCTV, Maurice," Jean-Marc reminded him.

"Okay, but I want a deal."

"What kind of deal?"

"A lighter sentence or something. Or drop the attempted rape charge. Can you do that?"

Rather than drop the charge Jean-Marc would prefer to hang the man by his *couilles* from the Eiffel Tower, but he also wanted information.

"Sure," Jean-Marc said. Out of the corner of his eye he caught Caron moving and assumed it was to register his opposition to the idea.

"A friend told me she fingered me to the *flic*," Dubonnet said.

"What friend?"

"I don't know his name."

"What kind of friend is he that you don't know his name?"

"He's someone who comes to the café. We got to talking. He knows I have a record."

"And he told you this woman..." Jean-Marc put a photo of Claire in front of him. "This woman reported you to the police?"

Dubonnet nodded.

"When did he tell you that?"

"About an hour after I left here today. I ran into him and he told me."

"You just happened to run into this guy when you left here?"

Dubonnet looked at Caron and Dartre.

"It's the truth," he said.

"How did you know the woman you attacked at the school was the same woman your friend told you about?"

Dubonnet seemed eager to talk now.

"That's easy," he said. "He showed me a picture of her on his phone."

I must have only been asleep for a few minutes but I felt much better when I awakened, except for the fact that like the Tin Man in the Wizard of Oz all my joints had frozen up with my brief rest. It took me forever to finally stand up and even then I wasn't completely straight.

This was a new situation where I was brought into a police station but not taken to an interview room to be interrogated. I decided to explore my environment a little more closely.

The wooden desk fit squarely in the room leaving hardly any room for much else. The top was bare except for a bottle of water. Either the person whose office this was had just moved in or they were chronically neat to a nearly pathological level.

I moved behind the desk where there was a narrow credenza. On it was a tray with a stapler, a tape dispenser and a box of paper clips. There was also a mug, clean with no evidence of ever having been used, and a cheaply framed photograph of a young Jean-Marc poised with his arm around a pretty if unsmiling brunette woman. They were standing together on a mountaintop.

She wasn't in a wheelchair so I suppose this had been happier days.

"I can get you a fingerprint dusting kit if that would make things easier for you," Jean-Marc said as he came into the office.

"I wasn't snooping. I was just curious." I stood up to face him. "It was Maurice Dubonnet who attacked me, wasn't it?"

Instantly, his face clouded over and while I knew it was probably because I must look a sight, I have to admit, the look of pain and fierce protectiveness on his face was almost worth what I went through.

Almost.

"*Mon Dieu, chérie,*" he said, taking my elbow and steering me to a chair by the desk. He sat in the only other chair. "You are hurt."

I had a huge lump in the middle of my forehead where I'd cracked Dubonnet in the nose but none of my other injuries were visible.

"No, I'm just a little bruised is all," I said. "It was Dubonnet, wasn't it?"

I'd come to the conclusion on my second whiskey that it had to be him although honestly it could just as easily be some random reprobate who happened to wander in off the street.

"*Oui,*" Jean-Marc said, his jaw tensing in barely suppressed anger. "He was released accidentally. A stupid clerical mistake."

Now that it was confirmed to me that it *was* in fact Dubonnet, I couldn't help but feel that what had happened in the school was a targeted attack. Dubonnet had probably overhead my name while he was in police custody. I told Jean-Marc as much.

"*Non, chérie.* That is not possible. My men would never allow a suspect to hear anything unintended."

I decided to let it go. It didn't matter. *However* it had happened, Dubonnet was now safely back in police custody.

Knowing Jean-Marc was seconds from asking me what the heck I was doing in the school in the first place, I spoke up quickly.

"Have you talked to Eric Watson yet? You have him in custody, right?"

"He is here. And no, I have not spoken to him yet."

"How long can you hold him without charging him?"

"Things are different in France," he said.

I figured that either meant Jean-Marc had gone off book with Watson or he was just telling me what he thought I wanted to hear.

"He's hiding something," I said. "Did you get a search warrant for his apartment?"

"You will allow me to conduct my own investigation in my own way, I hope?" Jean-Marc said sarcastically. "At present, Maurice Dubonnet is at the top of my list."

"You can't be serious," I said. "Dubonnet is not your killer. He doesn't exhibit any typical serial killer behavior."

"He tried to rape you, *chérie!*"

"Yes, but I'm not *this* serial killer's victim type. You know that's true, Jean-Marc. *This* serial killer would never toss in a rape of an older woman to get his jollies. Never. He's got very specific preferences."

Jean-Marc leaned over and touched my cheek. It was so gentle and so sad at the same time that I felt a welling up in my throat. I tried to remember the last time I'd seen him. And the last time we'd been alone.

"Why were you at the school, *chérie?*"

"You know why," I said. "I wanted those trophies."

Jean-Marc threw up his hands in an *I give up* gesture.

"They were moved," I said. "Isn't that evidence of guilt? Why would Knox move them if she didn't have something to hide?"

"The killer is not Deb Knox," he said firmly. "We confirmed her alibi for both abduction dates, the fifth and the seventh."

"That's interesting. Because I talked to her partner and she said the alibi was only good for the fifth."

"You must stop this, *chérie*. I know it is frustrating. But this is not helping."

"Jean-Marc, I'm telling you that Knox's alibi isn't good for the seventh of May. And did you check to see if she was really home sick on the eighth?"

"What difference does it make?"

"It makes a difference because it means she *lied*. Why would she lie?!"

"I am not looking at a woman for this," he said firmly.

"Well, you're wrong," I said in frustration. "Can you at least tell me the name of the school friend who called Dezi the afternoon she was taken?"

Sighing dramatically, Jean-Marc got up and went to his desk where he got on his computer.

"Mikayla Macintire," he said after looking at a file on his screen.

I felt a pinch of surprise. Why hadn't Mikayla mentioned she'd called Dezi the afternoon she disappeared?

"I find that very strange," I said.

Jean-Marc moved from behind the computer but didn't sit down again.

"Did you get DNA confirmation from Haley and Ali's fathers?" I asked.

"Yes. They are both cleared and both confirmed to have been in the US at the time. There is no doubt."

"What about Mark White? Dezi's father?"

"You think he would kidnap his own daughter?"

Unless that's exactly what he wants us to think.

"In any case, he refused to give us a sample," Jean-Marc said.

Alarm bells went off in my skull.

"Doesn't that sound suspicious to you?" I said.

"Unless we have reason to insist, it's within his legal right to refuse."

I felt suddenly exhausted and the few bruises that I'd discounted to him just a few minutes ago were suddenly feeling very achy and undeniable.

"Go home, *chérie*," Jean-Marc said. "You have been through a terrible ordeal. I will have one of my men take you."

Honestly I *was* feeling a little shaky so I was happy to take Jean-Marc up on his offer of a ride home. I wished our relationship could stand up to a comforting kiss on the mouth about now but we weren't there yet.

And very well might never be.

I thought back to the framed picture on his desk and felt a wave of sorrow.

As I got up to leave, it hit me that neither of us had mentioned that the thirty-hour period for Dezi had come and gone while we were talking in his office.

Now we just needed to pray.

While we waited for the body to show up.

57

I don't remember the ride to my apartment. I probably dozed off at some point. I'd texted Geneviève that I was on my way and she told me that Robbie was settled for the night and I should just go on to my apartment. I could pick up the baby and Izzy in the morning.

By the time I staggered upstairs I did spare a glance at Luc's door. I briefly wondered if Courtney had come back to my apartment today or if was she was still in there with him?

I was so tired and discouraged by that point that I took the elevator to my apartment—something I never do—my mind reverberating with the question, *How many hours were left for Dezi?*

There should be none. Her time had run out two hours ago. And still there was no body.

Did I dare hope?

I'm sure her parents were daring to hope. Even if it made the inevitable horror that much more painful.

As soon as I stepped into my apartment, I was struck by how quiet it was. Not just the absence of Courtney and Robbie but of Izzy too.

I took a handful of ibuprofen, washed it down with a large glass of water—I'd had way too much coffee today and absolutely no water—and fell into bed at seven in the evening where I fell immediately to sleep.

In the morning, I pried open one eye and was again hit by how peaceful everything was. I got up slowly and instantly felt as if I'd been thrown down a well and stomped on. My knees and hips were already purple and I moved as if I were eighty.

Correction. I didn't move as well as if I were eighty.

I looked at my phone, fully expecting to see the text that would tell me Dezi's body had been found. But there was nothing.

I hobbled to the bathroom and stood under a hot shower allowing the heat and the steam to do what magic they could for a sixty-year-old woman who'd been through what I'd been through the day before.

My only hope for today was to review what I'd discovered yesterday and try to get a hold of Adele to see if she had any new information from Ali's autopsy.

Just saying the words made me want to be ill, but I reminded myself that nobody had given up on Dezi yet and this was just one of the painful tasks that needed doing until we all admitted it was too late.

After I dressed I decided to restock Robbie's diaper bag. I didn't know what I was doing today but I was pretty sure I didn't want to be stuck in the apartment all day and I wanted to give Geneviève a break from babysitting.

I went to Courtney's bedroom, not surprised to see the unmade bed.

The thing that did surprise me was what I *didn't* see.

I didn't see any of Courtney's clothes.

Or her suitcase.

I stood for a moment and tried to put together in my befuddled mind what this meant. It seemed a bit over the top if Courtney was just going to spend a couple of nights with Luc who after all was just one floor below me. Dropping the diaper bag, I ran for the door and hurried down the two flights of stairs to Geneviève's door. I knocked on the door.

Would Courtney have taken Robbie with her? Did that make sense?

Did anything that whack job did make sense?

Geneviève opened the door, a look of surprise on her face. She wore her dressing gown. Robbie was in her arms.

Thank God. Although I couldn't tell you why. Maybe because now that I knew Courtney even a little bit, I knew that Robbie wasn't entirely safe with her. And maybe that's not fair. All I know is that wherever Courtney had gone, I thanked God she hadn't taken Robbie with her.

Izzy ran to me and jumped against my legs.

"Is everything all right, *chérie*?" Geneviève asked, frowning.

I'm sure she was looking at my bruises on my cheek and forehead from yesterday's throwdown with Maurice Dubonnet.

"Can you hold on just a sec?" I asked before turning and walking across the hall to Luc's door.

I didn't expect him to answer quickly and he didn't. I felt Geneviève's eyes on me from where she stood in her doorway watching and listening.

I counted to ten. I took a deep breath and knocked again. Finally the door opened.

Luc stood there, his hair rumpled, his eyes bleary. He wore only a pair of briefs.

If I had to guess I'd say he woke up angry.

I was pretty sure I knew why.

"What the hell do you want?" he asked and then glanced at Geneviève standing in her door. Propriety forced him to curb his natural inclination. He looked back at me. "She's not here."

"Her suitcase is missing," I said. "So if she's not with you...?"

"She left the dance club with someone else."

I waited. I knew this wasn't easy for him but I needed answers.

"Who?" I asked.

"How would I know who?"

"Where did she leave you?" I asked. "She's left a five-month-old baby behind is the reason I ask."

Again, Luc glanced at Geneviève holding the baby and he gave her a weak smile.

"At *Le Verdun*," he said. "After dinner. We were dancing. She danced with this guy and never came back to the table."

He was referring to *two* nights ago. Which meant that Courtney had been gone for forty-eight hours.

"You didn't know him?"

"Never seen him before." He turned as if to close the door and hesitated. "Claire," he said. "I am sorry."

I nodded and turned away. Whether he was sorry about my current situation of having a baby left on my hands or sorry for acting like the jerk he always managed to act like, it didn't matter.

I still had a lost girl to find.

I walked into Geneviève's apartment and pulled out my smartphone.

"The mother is gone?" Geneviève asked with incredulity. "But where? She knows no one in Paris."

"I have no idea," I said.

I had the number for the prepaid phone I'd given Courtney but before I called I decided to see in what part of the city she was hiding. This was easily done since when I'd given Courtney the phone I'd added a tracking app to it.

I came into Geneviève's living room and sat down.

Geneviève frowned. "She did not leave a note?" She closed the front door and handed me Robbie.

"Doesn't appear to be her style."

"Coffee, *chérie*?"

"That would be awesome," I said, lightly bouncing Robbie in my lap as I opened up the tracking app. I watched as Courtney's icon appeared on the map.

I actually laughed out loud when I saw where she was.

"*Chérie*?" Genevieve asked at the sound of my laugh.

"You're not going to believe this," I said, shaking my head in disbelief. "She's in Germany."

58

Heidelberg, to be specific.

I called her phone number.

"Hello?" Courtney answered, groggily.

"Want to tell me what you're doing?" I asked.

"Who is this?"

"Who do you think it is?"

"Oh, hey, Claire. God. It's a little early." She turned to talk to someone else with her. "What time is it in Germany?"

I felt my jaw tighten in frustration.

Courtney came back to the phone. "Gunther says it's the same time as France. Can you call back later? I'm just heading to bed."

Gunther?

"No, Courtney, I can't call back later. What the hell? What are you doing in Germany?"

"I'm in love. I found the one I'm meant to be with."

I honestly don't remember ever being at such a complete loss for words.

"I know, I know," she said with a giggle. "What are the odds, right?"

"What about Robbie?" I said. "Any thoughts?"

"Well, geez, I didn't just leave him, you know. Is that what you think?"

"Well, he's here and you're in Germany."

"For now, yes. I've got to nail this down, you know?" She lowered her voice conspiratorially. "I've got to secure my future —you know, mine and Robbie's."

"Does this man know Robbie exists?"

"Of course. In a way."

"What the hell does that mean?"

"Look, don't worry about it. I know what I'm doing, okay? Give Mister Schmuggums a kiss for me, kay? I gotta go."

She hung up.

I sat on Geneviève's couch and watched as Robbie giggled and grabbed for Izzy's collar, clapping his hands in delight whether he succeeded or failed.

I honestly had no idea what it meant that Robbie was mine now. I had no idea if I should call French social services—probably—or Abe Newsman back in Atlanta to see what my legal rights were.

Why would I do that? Was I thinking of adopting him?

Geneviève came in and sat down on the couch and held out her hands to Robbie who instantly reached for her.

"We will be fine, *chérie*," Geneviève said, her eyes on Robbie as if speaking only to him.

After finishing my coffee, I once more thanked Geneviève and gathered up my dog and my dead husband's love child and went back to my apartment.

As I maneuvered Robbie and his stroller up the stairs to my place, I thought about how things had been left with Jean-Marc last night and then quickly decided that that was a path more convoluted and exhausting then thinking about the murder case. So I would focus on what I knew. And that was a positive.

Dezi was still alive.

I had to believe that.

Or at least her body was as yet undiscovered.

It had been forty hours since her abduction.

I changed Robbie and put him on the floor, telling myself I'd keep an eye on him and any lamp plugs within his reach. I received a text from Jean-Marc.

<How are you feeling?>

I knew he was worried about me and that he cared. Our situation was complicated. It might very well always be complicated.

<Im good> I texted back. I was tempted to add *<any leads?>* In fact I'd actually typed that but erased it. He'd have told me if there were and it would only make him feel worse to have to tell me there weren't.

Even after my long sleep last night, I was exhausted. I put on some music and lit some candles—all designed to relax my conscious mind in order that I might be able to tease to the foreground any observations that I wasn't consciously aware of.

I thought of Maurice Dubonnet who was safely back in custody—for all that mattered as far as the case was concerned, since I was sure he was not the serial killer. He had none of the characteristics. From Jean-Marc's interview with him, Dubonnet was pathetically apologetic and only marginally intelligent—the total opposite of your typical psychopath's profile. Although I must say I'd feel better if I could interview him myself.

I turned my attention to Mark White. This was a tough one to rationalize. Dezi's father—even though he refused to take the DNA test—couldn't possibly kidnap his own daughter.

Right?

And with Cedric Potter largely in the clear—at least for Ali's murder—then that just left Eric Watson and Deb Knox.

Trying again to distract myself with something other than the case in order that an elusive clue might pop into my head, I opened up my laptop and ordered a playpen, a crib, a bouncy chair, and a highchair. When I was finished, I glanced at Robbie who'd fallen asleep on the carpeted floor in the salon.

I tried to imagine what Jean-Marc was going to think the next time he visited me in my beautiful Paris apartment to see all kinds of neon-colored baby stuff everywhere.

He'll think I've lost my mind. Like I'm trying to be thirty-five again.

Am I really thinking of keeping the child of my husband's lover? It is every bit as ridiculous as it sounds.

A horn honked outside which prompted Izzy to bark which woke up Robbie. He didn't wake up happily. After setting up Geneviève as my backup to receive Amazon parcels in case I wasn't home, I propped Robbie up against the pillows on the couch with his bottle and joined him with an iced tea and my laptop.

Izzy jumped onto the couch and squeezed between us.

Uh oh. Please don't let me have to deal with sibling rivalry on top of everything else.

The first thing I did was to search Eric Watson's social media pages. Watson had an Instagram account with some black and white photos of seminude women. Not porn but hardly tasteful either.

I did find a Facebook page for Deb Knox, but she'd never even put a profile pic up and it looked as if she'd never made a single post. I saw nothing else for her anywhere online.

I switched over to Ben Kent's Facebook page. I'd gotten the idea that the boy sticking his tongue in Mikayla's ear might be Ben but because of my inability to recognize faces I couldn't identify him by his looks alone, I took a screen snap of his profile picture and then went back to Dezi's Facebook page so I could find the Mikayla picture and compare Ben's picture to the boy in the photo with her.

But when I went to search for Dezi's Facebook page, I couldn't find it. In a few quick keystrokes I ascertained that it had been deactivated. *Again.*

I'd just reactivated it yesterday! This was so frustrating! Had her parents shut it down again? Why? I suppose it was possible that they were just feeling helpless and shutting down Dezi's social media accounts was *something* they could do.

I studied Ben's profile picture but there was no way I could determine if I'd seen this face before—even though of course I knew I had on two different occasions. Ben was handsome but it was a bland, non-distinct handsomeness—too insipid for me to recall.

Cursing the face blindness that made facial recognition so impossible for me I scrolled through Ben's Facebook posts to see if the Mikayla-tongue-in-ear picture might show up on his timeline. But he hadn't posted for months and then just a meme about French politics.

I leaned back into the couch in frustration. Even if Ben *was* the same boy licking Mikayla—what did that even mean? Kids did all kinds of crazy things and then recorded them for all eternity on social media. In their world, this was just business as usual.

I scoured Mikayla and Jackie's pages but there was no sign anywhere of the photo of Mikayla and the boy in the green jeans that Dezi had posted.

On impulse I sent a text to Ben.

<Was that you in the pic I saw on FB licking Mikayla's ear?>

Nothing like the direct approach. He responded immediately.

<R U serious?! No way. Ali was the #LOML.>

<Sorry. I'm bad with faces.>

I felt a surge of guilt. The poor kid was in mourning and here I was suggesting he'd screwed around on Ali. But I reminded myself that Dezi needed everything I could do for her right now—even if it meant stepping on toes and angering heartbroken teen boys.

<Any luck on finding Dez?> he texted.

<Not yet sorry>

<What about that creeper Maurice?>

<The cops have him>

<good>

I glanced back at my notebook list of suspects that I'd just reduced to two.

Eric Watson and Deb Knox.

Eric Watson was viable but I had no real evidence against him.

Deb Knox likewise. Viable but no evidence.

This process of looking at each of my suspects and running through the pros and cons was getting me nowhere. I needed to try a different approach.

I pulled out my phone and called up a photo montage that I'd made of the three dead girl's faces. I studied the faces. What was different about them? What was the same?

The commonalities were obvious. Cecily, Haley and Ali were all kidnapped on their way home from the school.

Dezi was snatched at her house because the school was closed down.

Okay, that was logical but it was still something different.

What else?

I stared at each of the three dead girls' faces. All three were killed within thirty-six hours.

Dezi was still missing after forty.

The three dead girls each had only a single parent—the mother.

Dezi had both parents.

Was I just grasping at straws? Or did there seem to be a lot of differences between Dezi and the three dead girls?

Telling myself not to get too excited, I looked back at my composite photo and was instantly struck by their physical similarities. It's true I see all blond attractive females as basically the same with no distinguishing characteristics. And this was especially true with the three schoolgirls. All three girls were blonde and slim. Virtually indistinguishable to me.

I scrolled to the picture of Dezi that I'd taken with my phone from her bulletin board when I was in her bedroom.

Dezi had brown hair and was curvy.

Serial killers stuck to a type.

Dezi was the thing that was not like the others.

That was the moment when the impossible notion dropped into my brain. And when it did, chills inched down my arms.

What if there were *two* killers?

59

O r more specifically, one killer and one who had not yet killed.

Hopefully.

One who was the serial killer and another one who was taking advantage of the murderous chaos to kill for his or her own reasons.

This put Mark White back in the picture.

Just because Mark White didn't kidnap his own daughter didn't mean he didn't grab and kill the others.

And Deb Knox was front and center for this now too. Because her being out of Paris during the critical time didn't matter. She was definitely in Paris when Dezi was taken.

I called Jean-Marc and miracles upon miracles, he took my call.

"Have you interviewed Eric Watson yet?" I asked.

"I am just about to."

"Okay, good. Listen, I have a theory."

"I am listening."

Those three words alone told me the depths to which Jean-Marc was currently plumbing. If he was willing to hear whatever crackpot idea I had, he officially had no leads and no other resources.

"What if there are two killers?" I said. "One who follows the code of psychopaths everywhere and one who kills with a motive."

He was silent and I imagined him mulling over my words.

"This puts Cedric Potter back in the picture," I said. "And also Mark White."

Jean-Marc groaned on his end of the line.

"Are you serious?" he said. "Mark White?'

"Yes, I'm serious," I said, only slightly offended by his tone. "Think about it. He's got a violent temper and he leers after Dezi's school friends—"

Jean-Marc snorted loudly.

"*Plus*," I said, "don't you think it's weird that we all assume Dezi was taken by the serial killer but White never even refers to him or seems angry at him? Some of the social media threads in the expat community rant and rave about wanting to get their hands on the *In-Seine Killer* and beat his face in. For someone as angry as Mark White is, doesn't that seem weird to you?"

This was the thing that had stuck in my brain with Mikayla told me how her father and his friends wanted to find and pound the *In-Seine Killer* into something resembling a mound of *foie gras*. Did it make sense that Mark White never even referred to the guy?

"Are you finished?" Jean-Marc said.

"Ask yourself why he won't give you his DNA to rule him out," I continued. "That is the behavior of someone with something to hide. Have you interviewed *him* yet?"

"He is not a suspect," Jean-Marc said. "He is a victim."

"See? That's just it! He's not on your radar because you see him as a distraught parent with a missing daughter."

"Which is what he is. He's not faking his emotion."

"He doesn't have to fake it," I said, feeling my excitement build as I talked my theory out loud. "His emotion is *real*. Especially since he wasn't the one who kidnapped Dezi."

"I see," Jean-Marc said with unabashed sarcasm. "And who kidnapped Dezi?"

"Honestly, my money's on Deb Knox," I said. "But you should probably still talk to Eric Watson."

"Oh? Do you think so?"

"But you'll need to bring in Mark White too."

The noise Jean-Marc made then was very difficult to describe. It was something between a snort and a laugh. A very unfunny kind of laugh.

"Are you suggesting I bring him in?" he said incredulously. "And question him on murders while we wait to see if his daughter's body turns up in the Seine?"

"Yes! First, he'll probably crack because he's already stretched to his limit by real emotion as a result of Dezi's kidnapping and second he'd never expect you to do it under the circumstances."

"Because it's a heinous thing to do. I would lose my career."

"You're exaggerating."

"Mark White is an American *and* he's perceived as a grieving father during an unimaginable crisis. For me to even *appear* to accuse him of being the *In-Seine Killer* would be the end of my career."

We were both silent for a moment.

"Only if you're wrong," I said.

"I have no evidence against him."

"Bring him in for questioning. Then get a DNA sample."

"I need a reason to get a warrant to obtain a sample from an unwilling witness," Jean-Marc said in frustration.

"Bring him in and give the coffee cup he drinks from to me."

"You are going to use Adele to confirm his DNA without his knowledge or permission? It won't stand up in court."

"It doesn't have to. As soon as you know he's our killer, you can target him to find the evidence you need. At the very least you'll watch him so closely he won't be able to take any more girls."

"It is illegal what you are suggesting, *chérie*."

"Oh, and one more thing," I said. "I heard about the homeless guy whose semen ended up inside Haley Johnson—"

"How did you—?"

"It doesn't matter. Anyway, I had this idea that since the first two bodies both had semen in them but you were only able to trace one of them—"

"Claire, I must go," Jean-Marc said firmly.

"Just *wait* a minute, please. My idea is what if you did a dragnet of all the homeless men in Paris? Bring them in and ask if any of them got any weird offers or were attacked recently. Maybe the reason Ali Burton didn't have some random guy's semen inside her was because the killer wasn't able to finish the job on her sperm donor."

"Do you know how many homeless people there are in Paris?" Jean-Marc said, with exasperation. "Twenty thousand, at least."

"You don't need to round them all up," I said, defensively. "Just the men."

"Good bye, *chérie*," he said. "I am glad you are feeling better."

He ended the call and I looked over at Robbie who'd fallen asleep next to Izzy on the couch. He looked so happy, so peaceful, so sweet. My first thought was that I really did look forward to Catherine meeting this little guy.

My second was, *God how did my life get so complicated?*

I eased off the couch without waking him and went to the guest room to find his diaper bag where I'd dropped it this morning. Then I went to the kitchen and packed his formula when there was a knock at the door.

I opened it to reveal Geneviève standing there with a bag of groceries and a sack from Eric Kayer's bakery.

"I was just coming down to see you," I said.

"I thought I would watch the baby from your apartment today," she said, coming inside.

I felt a rush of relief cascade over me. "This is the last time, I swear," I said.

She began to put her provisions on the counter, and looked over her shoulder at me.

"Take as much time as you need, *chérie*. Just be careful."

60

J ean-Marc entered the interrogation room with Caron. Eric Watson sat at the table, his limbs loose and relaxed.

Regardless of what Claire said, Jean-Marc knew that Watson was his only viable suspect. The next hour could make all the difference in solving this case and—if Watson hadn't killed her already—in getting Dezi home safely too.

Jean-Marc had kept the art teacher cooling his heels for a full night and two days—right up to the legal limit. Because of the man's nationality, if Watson were truly innocent, Jean-Marc would have political hell to pay. It had not escaped his notice, however, that Watson never asked to have his American Embassy contacted on his behalf.

That told Jean-Marc the man had something to hide.

It also hadn't escaped Jean-Marc's notice that with Dezi's body still undiscovered the killer was once more changing up his MO. And that could well be because the killer had been detained in police custody during the time he'd planned to dump the body.

Caron took his position by the wall and Jean-Marc sat opposite Watson at which point he noticed several things about him at once.

He was handsome. Even after two days in lock up, the man's clothes were relatively neat and orderly. Add to that the fact that he was smiling. If Watson wasn't their serial killer then he had the cold, heartless affect of a cyborg.

"Monsieur Watson," Jean-Marc said, tossing down his file folder with the photos of the four girls inside. "I hope you have not been made too uncomfortable."

"I'm going to bring charges against that crazy woman who barged her way into my apartment two nights ago. She had no right to come into my home making wild accusations."

"What accusations are those?" Jean-Marc said.

"You know which ones! That I supposedly slept with my students. That's a firing offense and I would never do it."

Jean-Marc glanced at his notes.

"Except for Ali Burton? I overheard you on the phone admit to Madame Baskerville that you slept with Ali Burton."

Watson made a face as if he'd tasted something nasty.

"She was willing," he said.

"She was underage. Even in France."

"Well, it never happened. You have no proof it did."

Watson crossed his arms and Jean-Marc fought the urge to slap the confident smirk from the bastard's face. He had no proof of the charge because Ali wasn't alive to say otherwise.

"So you deny it," Jean-Marc said.

"Yeah. I deny it."

"We are currently in the process of procuring a deposition from Ali Burton's friends. It seems she revealed to them that she did in face have sexual intercourse with you."

"She lied," Watson said with a shrug. "It's all hearsay."

It had been worth a shot.

"Where were you on May fifth?"

"I was giving an online Masterclass in textiles. I have the time and date stamped on the video to prove it."

"Video date-stamping can be altered," Jean-Marc observed.

"I gave it in front of a live Facebook audience. I can give you their names."

"And May seventh?"

"Same class, different topic. Acrylics, I think."

"May eighth?"

"What time?"

Watson was playing with him. He knew very well these dates corresponded with the dates each girl was snatched from a public street.

"Fourteen hundred hours."

"Ah, yes. I was meeting a student for after-hours help. I can give you her contact information."

The bastard was grinning now. Either he was telling the truth or he was confident of his charm and power over whatever student he'd conned into giving him an alibi for that day.

"May ninth?" Jean-Marc asked tightly.

"Back to my Masterclass. Acrylics again. It's very popular. I can send you the link if you're interested, Detective," he said, winking at him.

Jean-Marc watched as Dartre directed Eric Watson to the front desk so that he could be processed and released. A part of him was tempted to keep Watson another day but the interview had definitely illustrated that he had nothing on the man and no reason to hold him. Since Watson pretty obviously knew it too, he probably *would* call his embassy.

Caron joined him in the hall.

"We've still got time to toss his apartment before he gets home," the sergeant said.

Jean-Marc thought about it. He had no legal right to do it. The fact that Watson was an American national made things trickier. Jean-Marc wasn't above bending the rules or even planting evidence if he had to—enough to at least allow a search warrant. He'd done it many times before.

"No," Jean-Marc said. "Let him go."

He turned back to the murder room and went to the murder board. With the lack of anything concrete, it helped to look at it. He felt in a way almost as if it might speak to him, or as if the lines connecting the four girls might somehow magically appear.

He stared at the three black and white suspect photos on the board.

Dubonnet. Potter. Watson.

Jean-Marc had scrawled a huge question mark on the picture of Maurice Dubonnet. He didn't feel like he could take the photo down but neither did he believe Dubonnet was involved in the murders.

The fact that someone had shown Dubonnet a picture of Claire in order to target her meant there was another larger piece of the puzzle where Dubonnet fit but Jean-Marc couldn't see where. For that reason he would keep Dubonnet's photo on the board. But he wouldn't tell Claire that she'd been deliberately targeted—not so much by Dubonnet as the mysterious "friend" who'd shown the angry con her photo on his phone.

Jean-Marc did take Potter's picture down and tossed it on his desk.

Which just left Eric Watson.

For a moment Jean-Marc thought of what Claire had said on the phone and debated putting Mark White's picture on the board. But thinking how he'd explain that to Caron who was watching him closely made him reconsider.

He looked at Eric Watson's photo again, someone he couldn't even call a suspect.

A man with four iron-clad alibis.

But wouldn't the guilty party make sure he had his alibis lined up?

Watson was smart enough. He was sleazy enough. He had opportunity and access to all the girls. And Jean-Marc had detected a coldness in him, a deadness behind his eyes that marked him as a classic psychopath.

But there were those four alibies.

Jean-Marc walked to the window and gazed out.

From here he could see a shadow of what he knew was Notre-Dame Cathedral. He saw the streets below crammed with tourists and office workers going home or to their favorite bars and restaurants. The Pont de l'Archevêché was clearly visible from his vantage point.

Did this maniac look at that beautiful bridge and see it as a good staging ground for another of his gruesome kills?

Time had run out for Dezi White ten hours ago. It was now a full forty-two hours since she'd been taken. This wasn't a search and rescue any more regardless of what he wanted to believe.

It was a search and recovery.

Why hadn't the body turned up? Had there been a problem in dumping it?

Like, had the killer been sitting in a police holding cell for the past twenty-four hours?

It made sense but it still didn't lead Jean-Marc any closer to the path he needed to find evidence against Watson.

If Watson was the *In-Seine Killer*.

He turned to Dartre who was watching him from his desk.

"Did you check out Watson's alibis?"

"So far they check out. I'm having our IT department confirm that the time stamps haven't been altered but they said from the face of it, they look authentic."

Jean-Marc gritted his teeth and turned back to the window.

There were thirty-seven bridges on the Seine. The killer had already used Pont Des Arts, Pont Alexandre III, and Pont d'Alma. Would he reuse a bridge?

He rubbed a hand over his face.

Take a stand! he told himself.

Okay. So that left thirty-four bridges.

He went to the map and carefully drew a circle around the bridges surrounding the Île de la Cité. There were ten but he didn't have the resources to cover all ten. He took a breath and turned to both his sergeants.

"Set up covert stakeouts of two men each at Pont Neuf, Pont Notre-Dame and Pont Saint-Michel bridges," Jean-Marc said.

"We're giving up?" Dartre said.

"If we can't find the girl," Jean-Marc said, "we can at least grab the bastard as he's dumping her body. I'm not saying give up looking, but..." He felt the weight of the three dead girls press relentlessly onto his shoulders.

"Also stake out Watson's apartment," he said. "Caron, you take the first six hours. I'll spell you."

He couldn't stop this bastard from killing again.

But he could at least catch him in the act of trying to get rid of the evidence of his crime.

Which did absolutely nothing to relieve the feel of the leaden ball in the pit of his stomach.

He turned to Dartre.

"And bring Mark White in for further questioning," he said.

"White? What for?" Dartre said, turning to give a look to Caron as if to brazenly express his belief that Jean-Marc had lost his mind.

Jean-Marc turned away so as not to see Caron's return look. He stared unseeing at the scene out the window.

"I believe in America it's called a Hail Mary," he said bitterly.

61

Eric Watson slipped the key into the lock and entered his apartment. He didn't have to look far to realize that the police had not searched his place in his absence. His shoulders sagged with relief.

Idiots, he thought immediately with growing glee.

He tossed his keys on the hall table and paused in the corridor outside his bedroom door. The hall's window blinds were half up, affording him a good view of the street below. Instantly, he saw the man—so conspicuous if you knew what to look for—confirming to him that the police were watching him.

He grinned.

Knock yourselves out. Your only chance was finding what's inside this apartment.

He turned and went to the door of the second bedroom, his hand resting on the handle for a moment to calm himself.

If the cops had given him a lie detector test while he'd been in custody he wasn't at all sure he could've passed it. Just the thought that they were back here rifling through his things— his *special room*—had nearly been enough to drive him mad.

If this had been the US, the bastards would've turned his

flat upside down. He'd have gone straight from the holding cell to a pretrial detention facility.

Vive la difference!

But the Paris cops had no evidence against him. And they couldn't search his premises until they did. He considered for a moment about whether or not he needed to dismantle his *special room*. There might be no necessity. And it would take so much time and effort to recreate it.

He unlocked the door and entered, holding his breath for the sounds he knew were coming.

At first there was only silence. The room was dark except for a flickering of light in the furthest corner by the bed.

And then he heard it. A prolonged, exquisite whimper that told him all was as it should be.

"Did you miss me?" he said softly as he closed the door behind him.

And moved relentlessly toward the sounds of pain and despair.

62

One thing I knew if I knew anything: I didn't have time to play games. Dezi, if she was still alive, needed me to do something *now*.

Having a plan is always half the battle. And I was ready for battle.

My new set of facts made it very clear that I had to confront Deb Knox. Jean-Marc never would. That was also clear.

From my apartment I took the train to Le Marais, disembarking at the Hôtel de Ville station where I walked to rue de Rivoli and on to rue Moussy where I located Deb Knox's apartment building.

Le Marais is a melting pot neighborhood in Paris with a fascinating history. In the middle ages it had been marshy and considered an undesirable place to live. Eventually it was developed and became a wealthy and diverse neighborhood. In the last twenty years it filled up with hip boutiques, galleries and gay bars, not to mention the largest number of kosher restaurants in the city.

Deb Knox's neighborhood was upscale. Her apartment building might be in the heart of trendy shopping and five-star dining choices near Rue des Frances-Bourgeois. I assumed this was a reflection of Knox's partner's income, because I knew what Miss Knox made as a gym teacher at Le World School de Paris. I gazed up at the strikingly fashionable Haussmann building. There was no way Deb Knox could afford to live here on her salary.

My plan was to confront Knox in her apartment. I had my Taser with me and I was fully prepared to use it if that's what I needed to do to get the answers I wanted.

Correction. To get the *confession* I wanted.

As I strode across the street to her apartment building, I saw Deb Knox exit through the double front doors. This threw me for a few seconds. I'd grown attached to the idea of controlling the environment by trapping Knox in her apartment, and now that option wasn't possible.

No matter. She was going to talk to me whether in her apartment or a public street. I slipped my hand into my bag and felt the reassuring touch of the Taser. As she crossed the street, Knox looked up and recognized me.

Bizarrely, her face cleared when she saw me as if she were not only *not* sorry to see me but even happy about it. I reminded myself to stay out of the minds of psychopaths. They didn't think like normal people. I needed to stop comparing them to how I might behave.

"Fancy meeting you here," she said although she kept walking to the far side of the street.

I hurried to catch up with her.

"I would like a word, please, Miss Knox," I said breathlessly.

"Do we need to stop somewhere, Grandma?" she said as she quickened her pace. "Only you sound like you're about to have a heart attack."

I glanced around and saw that the street was relatively deserted. An elderly man walked twenty feet ahead of us and further down the block a few other people were milling about.

It would have to do.

I pulled my Taser out and jammed the snout of it into Knox's formidable side as we came upon a small alley.

"In there," I commanded, pressing the weapon's nozzle firmly into her flesh.

"Ouch, watch it, Granny," Knox said, moving away from the Taser's nose by stepping into the alley.

I allowed her to move away from me. After all, I didn't need contact to render her helpless with the Taser. I pointed it at her and watched her look at it as if it were a baffling but fascinating specimen of some kind. Then she burst out laughing.

"You are wicked, Grandma!" she said with a grin. "I wish I'd met someone like you when you were younger. Do you even know how to work that thing?"

"It's not all that tricky," I said. "I'm here to talk to you about your alibi for Haley Johnson's abduction. It appears you don't have one."

"Yeah, I heard," she said with a sigh, looking not at all bothered by the fact that I was pointing a fully charged electroshock weapon at her. "But it doesn't matter. The cops can't imagine a woman for these crimes."

"But you and I both know you are definitely capable of them, don't we?" I said.

She placed her hands on her thick hips, confronting me directly. I tightened my grip on the Taser.

"You think that toy will stop me?" she said. "I'm pretty tough."

"Trust me, one zap from this and you'll wake up straight."

Knox threw back her head and howled with laughter.

"I love your generation. Boomers just say what's on their minds. No BS about it." She nodded at the Taser. "Those things are practically illegal in France, you know, Gran."

I knew. The effort I'd gone to to buy it and have it mailed to me by my lawyer in Atlanta had been considerable. If I did have to shoot her, I'm not sure I wouldn't be in more trouble than if I'd used real bullets.

"Where is Dezi?" I asked.

"Oh, God is that what this is about? You're a regular pit bull, aren't you? I have no idea."

"You kidnapped her."

"I really didn't."

"You hated her."

"No more than I did her bratty friends."

Listening to Knox it was hard to decide if I was talking to a sociopath. It was true her disdain and disrespect fit the definition if she were the serial killer. On the other hand if she was just your garden-variety horrible person taking advantage of all the confusion with the serial killings—that would fit too.

The third option was that she'd had nothing to do with Dezi's disappearance at all.

I couldn't accept that. If I did, I was left with nothing.

Could there really be *two* serial killers in one French school district? What were the odds of that? My research had indicated that *one* was unlikely.

I recalibrated my approach with her.

"You're telling me you didn't kidnap Dezi," I said, feeling the awful taste of the words in my mouth.

"Now you're getting the message, Granny."

"Quit calling me that. I can still shoot you with this."

"I'm getting hot, believe me."

"I saw that you removed your trophies from your desk drawer."

"My what?"

"The headbands and things. Your Lost and Found drawer."

As soon as I said it, I knew I was wrong about that drawer. They were exactly what she said they were. A Lost and Found drawer. They couldn't be trophies because she couldn't be the serial killer. She wasn't even in town for the first killing.

"Oh!" she said with a shrug. "Well, you seemed to think they meant I was involved in Danvers and Johnson's murders so I got rid of them."

As any sane person would.

I'd been wrong. The only hope I'd had was the theory that Knox had taken Dezi. But the woman facing me—although unpleasant in many aspects—did not come close to resembling the kind of true deviant you'd have to be to kidnap and hide the body of a young girl.

My shoulders slumped in realization.

Knox hadn't taken Dezi. Or killed the other girls.

She must have seen me arrive at this conclusion because she grinned at me.

"I'm not mad at you," she said. "I won't report you. You're badass. Would you consider coming and doing a guest talk next semester for my Fitness Fundamentals class? You're exactly who I'm trying to make these girls into."

My Taser arm was getting awfully heavy. I let it sag to my side.

"I'm serious, Granny. You're a real pistol, you know that?"

I swear I came *that* close to nailing her right in her smart-alecky va-jay-jay.

ark White sat in the interview room while Jean-Marc and Caron watched from the other side of the one-way mirror. A thorough forensic sweep had already been performed on White's apartment as soon as Dezi had been reported missing. It had turned up nothing of any use or relevance.

"You think he has more to tell us about his daughter's disappearance?" Caron asked.

Jean-Marc appreciated his diffidence. His sergeant was clearly confused as to why Jean-Marc would ask the father of their missing girl to come in to add to his statement.

"Do we have a statement from him on where he was during the disappearance of the other girls?" Jean-Marc asked.

Caron turned to look at him.

"You know we don't," Caron said. "To what end? He was never a suspect. Is he now?"

Jean-Marc refused to meet Caron's indicting gaze. He focused instead on White where he sat in the room. He was a big man and he had rank in his job. He wasn't used to being

SUSAN KIERNAN-LEWIS

kept waiting. He wasn't used to being escorted into a police interrogation room.

White drummed his fingers on the metal table he sat at and fiddled with the cuffs on his shirt. He tilted his head at the ceiling and twisted his body around to face the door every few seconds.

"He might be," Jean-Marc said.

Caron huffed out a snort.

"Based on what?" he asked scornfully. "The fact that we don't have anyone else? Why not the concierge in my building?"

Jean-Marc wouldn't allow himself to rise to the bait. Besides, Caron was absolutely right. This was idiotic, desperate, and futile.

He'd done so much to work his way back up the ladder of respect not only with Caron and Dartre but with the whole department.

And he was about to throw away all that with both hands.

"Based on the fact that he is connected to the school and his daughter is connected to the murdered girls," Jean-Marc said.

"So you think he kidnapped his own daughter." The contempt in Caron's tone was like a knife between Jean-Marc's ribs.

"I'm not sure that's the only crime he could be guilty of," Jean-Marc said. He turned to Caron. "Do you want me to have Dartre in there instead?"

Caron blushed angrily and turned away. Allowing a junior sergeant in on the interrogation would be a slap in the face and while he might deserve it for his insubordination to a superior officer, he wouldn't accept the demotion.

"No, I'll do it," he said.

Of all the things Jean-Marc knew he'd lost with this case— status, respect, and credibility as a detective—he was surprised to realize that losing Pierre Caron's good opinion of him actually hurt worse than all the rest.

As soon as Jean-Marc and Caron stepped into the interrogation room, Mark White stood up and faced them.

"Sit down, please, Monsieur White," Jean-Marc said.

"I was brought here under false pretenses," White said, not sitting. "I demand to speak with my solicitor."

"Of course," Jean-Marc said. "Sergeant Caron will take your attorney's contact information and you may call him after we meet."

"I'll call him *now*, Detective," White said, his hands on his hips. "Or I'll have your badge."

"Trust me, you wouldn't want it," Jean-Marc said, seating himself. "This is France, Monsieur. I have the authority to hold you for twenty-four hours without cause and another seventy-two after that if I feel I have the hint of a reason. Please, take a seat."

Jean-Marc flipped through the folder on the metal table and waited. After a few seconds, White sat back down.

"You'll be sorry for this," White said.

Jean-Marc turned on the recording device in the room.

"This is Jean-Marc LaRue," he said into it. "Interviewing Mark White who has just threatened me. Monsieur? Will you repeat the threat for the recorder? It wasn't running when you originally made it."

Jean-Marc looked into White's eyes and saw the hatred, frustration and finally defeat in them.

"Monsieur White has indicated," Jean-Marc said, "his desire not to repeat his threat. *Bon.*"

Jean-Marc pulled the three photographs of the three dead

girls from his folder and carefully arranged them in front of White.

"I don't even believe this," White said under his breath as he looked at the photographs.

"Monsieur, can you identify any of these girls?" Jean-Marc said.

"Everyone knows who they are," White said sullenly.

"Yes. But how do you know them?"

"They've been in the paper. They're the victims of the serial killer."

"Do you know them in any other way?" Caron asked from where he stood by the wall.

His speaking surprised Jean-Marc and boosted his spirit. Even if he didn't believe that Mark White should be here, he would support Jean-Marc. That wasn't nothing.

Even if it eventually led to nothing.

"They were schoolmates of my daughter's," White said, glowering at the photos as if the girls were to blame for his presence in the police interrogation room.

Jean-Marc paused dramatically and then got up and went to the counter in the back of the room where he poured a cup of water and brought it back to the table for White. White eyed it suspiciously and didn't touch it.

Jean-Marc tapped his finger on the first picture, the one of Cecily Danvers. She was blonde with big blue eyes and a toothy smile.

"Cecily Danvers," he said, "was taken from rue St-Charles on her way home from school on May fifth at around fourteen hundred hours."

White merely grunted.

"Where were you on May fifth around fourteen hundred hours, Monsieur?"

"You can't be serious."

"Answer the question, Monsieur," Caron said.

"I was at work," White said.

Jean-Marc looked at a piece of paper in the folder.

"We have spoken to your office for that day," Jean-Marc said. "You took the afternoon off."

"What? You contacted my office?" The cords on his neck vibrated and he pulled back his lips, baring his teeth. "This is character assassination! How dare you?"

"We dare," Jean-Marc said coolly, "because three girls have died." He tapped the second picture with a pen. "Haley Johnson. May seventh, also at fourteen hundred hours."

"I'll have your job for this," White snarled. He leaned across the desk toward Jean-Marc, his face red with fury, and jabbed a finger in the air before his face.

"And I don't care how many recordings you make of me saying it. I'll go to the damn newspapers! My daughter is missing! Someone you can't find and so you're doing what you can to distract attention! This is heinous! My embassy will hear of this! I demand to speak to your superior immediately!"

Jean-Marc gathered up the photos and put them back in the folder on the desk. He was very clearly going to get nothing of substance from the man in the way of an alibi or anything that might be possibly used as a lead.

He'd done exactly what he knew he'd do in this interview—he'd attacked an emotionally-vulnerable man with useless, torturing questions—and destroyed his police career in the bargain.

And oh, yes, he'd wasted another precious hour when Dezi White might be counting down the seconds left in her life.

Jean-Marc glanced at Caron to see his appraisal of White's tantrum but Caron wasn't looking at White. He was looking at Jean-Marc.

64

After my little contretemps with Deb Knox, I ended up walking from Le Marais to the Île de la Cîté. I think I just needed to walk and not think about what I was doing or where I was going.

I don't know about you, but whenever that happens to me, I always end up—unerringly—somewhere in the vicinity of Notre-Dame Cathedral.

I should be grateful—or embarrassed to be so pretentious —that I'm able to even say something like that but it's true. When I'm not thinking or allowing my brain to lead the way, my feet will always head to the Latin Quarter. And specifically this church.

I found a bench in the nearly deserted garden behind the church. Granted there wasn't much of a view of the actual church from this vantage point, but there were almost no people to contend with so I considered it an acceptable trade-off.

I sat in the relative quiet, listening to the primal hum of traffic on the Quai de Saint-Michel and the ongoing restoration noise on the Cathedral itself. A few sparrows came over to my bench to inquire after me until they realized I had no crumbs to throw their way.

I eased back into the hard bench and looked skyward. Even without a clear view of its two iconic towers, Notre-Dame always succeeded in giving me peace, even half-burned the way it was now.

How could you not marvel when you looked at this amazing church, knowing that Henry VI was crowned King of France here in 1431? Or that the very garden where I now sat was where the Third Crusade began in 1185?

Like most Americans, I could barely process the idea of 1185, let alone sitting in a site that was virtually unchanged since that time.

There was something so eternal and irrepressible about Notre-Dame's familiar outline against a Paris sky that never failed to buoy me.

Except today.

I cannot ever remember feeling so despondent. Taking Deb Knox off the table left me with Mark White and Eric Watson as suspects. One of them was in police custody as far as I knew, and the other hopefully soon would be.

As I sat there wondering what I was going to do next, I got a text from Jean-Marc.

<M White brought in to make a statement>

I felt a shiver of hope and quickly called him. I expected him to be spending the next hour or two sweating a confession out of Mark White so I was surprised to have him take my call.

"Why aren't you still interrogating Mark White?" I asked.

"I have already questioned him."

"Really? That was fast. What were his alibis? Where did he say he was?"

"It was a mistake bringing him in."

"What about his DNA? Were you able to get a sample?"

"Stop!" Jean-Marc said heatedly. "I got *nothing* except

possibly a one-way ticket to becoming a traffic cop in Dijon. I had nothing to trip him up with, nothing to ask him. Indeed *I* never even believed he had anything to do with the killings."

I groaned. "Did you have to let him go?"

"He wasn't here as a suspect! Do you not understand that? I cannot believe I listened to you."

It's testimony to how desperate you are, I thought but didn't say.

"What about Watson?" I asked.

"We are watching his apartment. If he leaves we'll follow him."

I felt a headache forming.

"Which is all well and good," I said, "unless it's his apartment where he's keeping Dezi!"

"Enough, Claire. These are all just guesses—"

"What about Maurice Dubonnet? Did you ever find out how he knew to go after me? That can't have been a coincidence."

"Claire, enough! I need real leads, not personal biases and guesses. Stop calling me."

He hung up.

Because I knew that Jean-Marc was every bit as frustrated as I was, I wasn't going to hold that against him.

Then I realized if the police were watching Eric Watson's apartment, it meant that they had let him go.

And the fact that Dezi hadn't shown up dead anywhere? Was it really a coincidence that Watson was in police custody during the time she would've been dumped in the river? Surely Jean-Marc saw that? I debated texting him but decided he'd come to that conclusion himself and pointing it out would just make him madder and less open to taking my calls.

Besides, our last contretemps was because I'd told him I was sure Mark White was the In-Seine Killer. I wasn't sure how open Jean-Marc would be to me pivoting to Eric Watson now.

The fact was I wasn't sure which of the two it was. But I did know that it was infuriating that Mark White had come and gone from the police station. I thought about calling one of the cops sitting with the family at the White apartment to ask if they would keep track of Mark's comings and goings since it was clear Jean-Marc wasn't going to do it.

But they were hardly going to listen to me. They took their orders from Jean-Marc.

And he definitely wasn't listening to me.

Not yet sure of my next step, I put a call in to Geneviève to see how she was doing.

"We are fine, *chérie*. It is you I am worried about. What happened to you last night?"

"I was exhausted," I said. "I fell asleep early. Sorry I didn't collect Robbie from—"

"No, I was referring to your bruises. You looked as if you'd been attacked."

I sighed. "I had a run-in with someone."

"Someone?" she prompted.

"Someone the cops were questioning. And I guess they let my name slip and he thought I'd fingered him to the cops or something."

As I said the words, I remembered Jean-Marc insisting it couldn't have been any of his men. At the time it hadn't felt that important, but now that I thought of it, it really didn't sound plausible that his men could have made such a mistake.

But how else would Dubonnet have known to follow me? And why else would he attack me?

My brain was buzzing. There was something right on the edge of my thoughts but I couldn't seem to see it.

"*Chérie?*"

"Oh, I'm sorry, Geneviève," I said. A ding on my phone gave me an excuse to get away. "I've got to take this. I'll call you later, okay? I'm fine. Really."

It turned out that the phone chime was an alert that told me that Catherine had posted something on Facebook. It had been so long since I'd even thought of her and what she was wrestling with about Robbie and her dad that I felt instantly guilty.

Another ding made me look again at my phone to see that Catherine had posted a photo of Cameron on Facebook. I thought how nice it was that I can be sitting here on a bench four thousand miles away and my daughter can reach out and poke me without even—

And then it hit me.

I quickly typed in Dezi's name in the search window of my open Facebook page. I knew I couldn't access her page since it was closed down, but that shouldn't stop people from being able to tag her on their pages. Upon typing in Dezi's name, Ben's Facebook page came up. He still hadn't posted anything since I checked last *but the fact that Facebook called up his page when I searched for Dezi's name* was significant.

It meant I could find evidence of Dezi's presence through her Likes and Comments on Ben or Mikayla or Jackie's Facebook pages even if I couldn't find Dezi's page anymore.

And the same went for Ali.

I scrolled through Ben's timeline until I found a post that had been shared to his page by Ali and *Liked* by Dezi. It was a meme with white sans serif type reversed out of a black background that read: *A snake doesn't know he's a snake.*

I stared at the meme.

This was a message about Ben.

Why would Ali do that?

I looked at the date. It was posted two months ago. I tried to remember the date of the kissing photo with Mikayla and the unidentified boy. Could this meme have been posted *after* that one? Frustrated that I didn't have Dezi's page to refer to I continued to scroll through Ben's timeline to try to find the photo until I was nearly two years in the past. Way too far back to be of any help.

Just when I was about to give up I saw a different photo.

This was a photograph of a teen boy standing with his arm around the waist of a pretty blonde girl. They were both facing the camera and smiling. I tapped on the photo of the girl's face and a little box popped up identifying her as Ali Burton.

I looked at the boy. I'd never seen him before—*that I could remember*. But this was on Ben's Facebook page so there was every reason to believe that this was Ben. Sure enough, when I tapped on the boy's face another little box popped up identifying him as Benjamin Kent.

And none of that would be reason for me to drop my jaw in astonishment except for the fact that the boy in the photo was wearing green jeans.

65

Ben was the boy trying to stick his tongue in Mikayla's ear in the deleted Facebook picture.

Without the original photo for comparison, my deduction was based on the fact that both boys in each of the two photos were wearing green jeans. I am fairly sure there couldn't be two teen boys in the modern universe wearing green jeans.

Was the fact that Dezi posted the incriminating picture to Facebook enough for Ben to want to get revenge on her?

I didn't know.

All I knew was that I was now positive there was only one serial killer but two psychopaths.

As I stood up from the bench, I realized that if Jean-Marc was right and Dubonnet hadn't heard my name through one of his detectives, he could have heard it through Ben—the very person who put me onto Dubonnet in the first place.

I texted Jean-Marc.

<*Please confirm how Dubonnet knew I was at the school yesterday. I think Ben Kent told him.*>

Then I turned and ran for the train station, my light rain

jacket unzipped and flapping behind me as I dodged slow-moving tourists and startled pigeons.

I had no time but Dezi had even less.

I knew it couldn't be Mark White holding Dezi. That made no sense at all.

I also didn't believe it was Deb Knox and the timeline for snatching Dezi didn't work for Cedric Potter.

Eric Watson and Ben Kent were now the only possible suspects who could have kidnapped Dezi. And since I now believed that her kidnapper *wasn't* also the serial killer, that meant there needed to be a motive for taking her.

Watson wouldn't be mad enough to kidnap Dezi in the midst of a serial killer manhunt. For what possible reason? Again, he had no obvious motive. I'm not saying he might not have one I didn't know about but I can only go with the facts I have.

And the facts that I had said that only Ben had a motive for taking Dezi. *And* if he used Mikayla's phone to call Dezi that day—the opportunity too.

In the midst of this exultant revelation, my skin crawled ominously.

Because if it *was* Ben holding her, he could not just let her walk away.

Which is probably why, unlike the kills from the serial killer, Dezi had been missing now for more than two full days.

I pulled out my phone and called Ali's mom, Jessica. I hated to. I knew her grief was raw and all-consuming right now but she was the only one I could think of who might know where her daughter's ex-boyfriend lived.

It was five in the afternoon by the time I found Ben's apartment building in a less than affluent suburb in the fourteenth arrondissement. It took me nearly forty minutes and two train line changes from Le Marais to get there. I figured it must take him close to an hour to get to the international school from this section of town.

Unlike the classic Haussmann buildings in which so many of his classmates—and myself—lived, Ben's apartment building was modern and ugly. Probably built in the nineteen seventies, it was devoid of any element of architectural charm or enhancement. The front door keypad was long since broken and the small green space that would be surrounded by flowers in a better neighborhood was crowded with weeds and trash.

I had no real evidence against Ben. I was running purely on intuition and a whole lot of hope. At this point and with the clock ticking down on Dezi, it was all I had left.

Five minutes later and I'd gone upstairs, knocked repeatedly on his door and finally returned to the street. Nobody home.

I stood on the street and pulled out my phone and made a call.

"Yeah?" Mikayla answered.

"Why didn't you tell me you called Dezi the day she was kidnapped?" I asked.

Mikayla snorted. "What are you talking about?"

"The cops have her phone records. You called her just before she was snatched."

"Well, I didn't. Dezi and I weren't even friends! Why would I call her?"

It was as I'd suspected. If Mikayla hadn't called Dezi then somebody had used her phone to call her. Somebody who didn't want the cops—or Dezi—to know it was him calling. Someone who would have had easy access to Mikayla's phone.

Ben.

"I'm looking for Ben," I said. "Nobody's home in his family's apartment. Any idea where he is?"

"I don't hang with Ben."

"Really? Isn't there a picture of you on the Internet with Ben's tongue in your ear?"

Mikayla gasped.

So it was Ben in the picture.

"We were drunk!" she said.

"Did that excuse hold water with Ali?"

"Hold *what*?"

God I'm starting to hate Generation Zers.

"How did Ali take it?" I asked.

"Well, not good. And she would never have known anything if that bitch Dezi hadn't posted the picture."

"Why did she?"

"Dezi hated Ben. She was always telling Ali what a jerk he was."

The pieces of the picture were falling together faster and faster.

"I need to talk to him," I said. "Where does he go, Mikayla? It's important."

"He skateboards at Ledoux Park sometimes."

"Thank you. And Mikayla, one last question. Can you tell me what happened when Ali saw the picture of you and Ben?"

"What do you think? She dumped his ass."

I didn't need to ask her how Ben took that.

66

S quare Claude-Nicolas Ledoux is located off the Place Denfert-Rochereau. It's a beautiful park, laid out like an English garden.

Mikayla said Ben came here to skateboard the curving pathways around the fountains and statues. She said he never went home until dark.

"His home life is not the best, you know?" she said.

I didn't. But an unstable homelife would be just one more explanation for why Ben might be unstable himself.

I walked to the park from Ben's neighborhood—which was a good six-block hike. It was now closer to *apéro* time and the clouds overhead bunched together to drop Paris further into a cold, dark shadow.

I wore linen slacks today with a sleeveless shell under my light rain jacket. Even though it was June, I actually shivered as I hurried down the wide avenues toward the park.

It wasn't hard to imagine how angry Ben must have been at Dezi for posting the picture which resulted in him getting dumped by Ali. He must have held in his fury and his resentment for weeks until it finally exploded because of Ali's disappearance—which someone like Ben might well be inclined to see as the ultimate rejection by his beloved.

After that, all he had to do was wait until there was so much media noise over the *In-Seine Killer* before making his move against the one person he felt had wronged him.

In any case, Ben knew that a fourth kidnapping would surely be placed at the feet of the *In-Seine Killer*, leaving the stage wide open for him to do whatever he wanted.

As I crested the hill and got my first sight of the park I reminded myself *that I needed evidence. Or failing that, a confession.*

That meant I needed to talk to Ben. I wasn't so naive as to think I could bully a confession out of him. But I was going to try. I didn't even need to record him. All I had to do was get the truth and pass it along to the cops. When Jean-Marc learned what Ben had done, he'd get it out of him again for the record.

Square Claude-Nicolas Ledoux was designed as an English-style garden with cherry, honey locust and hazel trees against an abundance of unfettered flowerbeds and meandering path-ways—so unlike the French gardening style with its typically formal, straight lines and tidy beds as seen in the nearby Jardin du Luxembourg.

As soon as I entered the park, it began to rain. I was grateful for this on two counts. One, it meant that Ben would have to stop skateboarding and therefore couldn't glide away from me so easily. And two, since it was still light out and too early to go home, he would be forced to find somewhere out of the rain.

I was counting on that *somewhere* being where he was holding Dezi.

I had to believe that Ben hadn't killed her yet. Hating someone and wanting them dead were vastly different from being able to hold a knife to their throat.

Ben had already taken more time to complete his deadly task than he'd planned. He was way past the timeline of the original serial killer he'd been trying to copy. But it couldn't last much longer. If he was trying to make this look like the *In-Seine Killer's* work he had to get Dezi in the water soon or the cops would begin to suspect a copycat killing. And a sloppy one at that.

The thought crossed my mind to tell Jean-Marc what I was doing but only briefly. First, I wasn't afraid of Ben—mostly because I remembered to pack my Taser this morning. And second, I had serious doubts Jean-Marc would even hear me out on my reasons for thinking Ben was Dezi's kidnapper.

The rain beat down on my shoulders and I was beginning to feel the full brunt of my injuries from yesterday. My legs and back throbbed painfully.

The park was empty. Not even a dog walker which was not surprising in this weather.

I stuck close to the perimeter of the garden walking behind the park benches and moving as slowly as I dared. In the dimming light and in the rain, it was very possible I could be camouflaged enough to avoid detection by someone who wasn't expecting to see anyone else in the park.

Up ahead of me I saw a figure in the rain and knew immediately it was Ben. Not that I recognized him, of course. But his posture looked vaguely familiar to me—the way he stood with his head bowed, a skateboard tucked under one arm. It had to be him. I stopped and prayed he wouldn't turn toward me on his way out of the park.

I needed not to confront him. Not yet anyway. I needed to follow him so he could lead me to Dezi. I knew he was desperate. He had to kill her soon. If he'd already done it then he needed to dispose of the body.

One way or the other I knew in my bones that tonight was the night.

Suddenly, without looking back, the figure ahead turned and walked purposefully down the path. I was close enough that even over the sound of the rainfall I could hear the gravel path crunch beneath his feet. My heart began to beat in double time.

67

As soon as Ben left the park, it would get trickier keeping him in sight without being seen myself. I let him stay a good thirty feet ahead of me. I turned my phone on its vibrate setting and picked my steps carefully in the deepening shadows around me. The last thing I needed to do now was catch my foot in a hole or grassy divot and fall.

I shivered and glanced over my shoulder. A shadow wobbled in the distance. Was it the breeze moving a tree limb? Or just the light shifting?

While I still didn't absolutely recognize Ben, I did recognize the skull outlined in white on his red skateboard which was partially visible under his arm. I worried that he'd actually get on the board—which would put an end to my following him. But thankfully the sidewalks were just congested enough to make that impossible.

I hesitated by a large trash bin as Ben turned a corner. I followed but slowed my pace. If he had picked up that he was being followed, this turn onto a narrow street would be a perfect place to ambush me.

On the other hand, if he *hadn't* seen me, then the more I

delayed the further ahead of me he'd get. I had no choice but to hurry to the corner and hope he wasn't waiting around it ready to slam his skateboard into my head.

I turned the corner and saw his back moving from me, now easily fifty feet ahead of me. I slowed, knowing that a careless footfall or knocking into a garbage bin would immediately give me away. I touched a hand to the wall to force myself to slow down and steady myself at the same time.

Smells seemed to pour off both buildings and pool into the space between them, roiling up from the wet stone floor beneath my feet.

It was quiet on this narrow street. It felt as if the two buildings had essentially cut off all sound at the same time they dimmed the lights. As Ben moved steadily away from me, I instinctively quickened my pace.

All of a sudden I saw Ben stop and my heart flew to my throat. Instead of turning around which I really thought he was about to do, he seemed to disappear before my eyes.

I blinked as if I'd imagined what I saw, then pushed off from the wall and ran down the alley looking around to see if I could spot a possible access out of the narrow street. I slowed when I came to the spot where I thought Ben had disappeared. There was a window near to the ground that appeared to be half open.

I stopped and let my heart rate steady itself as I stared at the window. There was nothing about it to suggest that someone had just used it to climb inside but there was no other way for Ben to have disappeared like he did except through the window. I took a step back, and looked up at the building. My hands were damp with perspiration and rain as I realized that Ben must have entered this building. The walls of the building were old, its facade dark with grit and centuries of grime.

Was Dezi in here?

I went to the window and stood there hesitating before

finally lowering myself to a squatting position in order to peer inside. It was too dark to see anything. I fumbled for my phone in my purse and turned on its flashlight function. I hesitated only a moment before shining the light on the interior of the room.

The rain coming down on my shoulders felt like a gentle nudge. I tucked my phone under one arm and grabbed the edge of the window frame and eased it up, grateful that it made no noise. I sat on the sill and swung both legs over the windowsill and eased myself down into the room, my heart thundering in my head.

There on the floor was Ben's skateboard.

I scanned the room with my cellphone light.

The room appeared to be more of a basement than a room where anyone might live. The walls and floor were made of dark stone. The room was empty except for a few pieces of broken wooden furniture.

I felt a wave of determination sweep over me. I didn't know what this place was but the fact that Ben had come here had to mean that Dezi was here too.

It crossed my mind for just the barest of seconds to call Jean-Marc. But not only was it still unconfirmed that Dezi was here, I was only too aware that even now Ben might be attempting to murder her.

I didn't have time to waste because Dezi didn't.

Across the room was a door and I began moving toward it, picking my way through the room's trash and debris. When I reached the door I saw that while closed, the latch hadn't caught. I pulled the door open onto a darkened hallway.

Instantly my nose told me the corridor was made of damp dirt and organic rot. The ground beneath my feet slanted downward and I went with it. Tree roots poked through the dirt walls and water dripped from the ceiling.

A scratching sound like little mouse feet scrambling out of

my path made my hands go instantly damp. As I walked, my breath coming in stuttered hitches of mounting fear, I dug my hand into my purse and wrapped my fingers around my Taser, pulling it free.

The moment I did the light from my phone caught the glow of a ball on the ground. Two steps closer and I realized with sickening horror that I was looking at a human skull.

It couldn't be her, I told myself.

It was then that I realized where I must be. This had to be one of the few still-secret entrances into the Paris Catacombs. Everyone knew there wasn't just one way into the Catacombs. There were several secret and illegal ways. Like where I was standing right now.

I forced myself to walk past the skull.

Ahead in the phone's flashlight beam I saw another door at the end of the dirt conduit. This one was wooden and half the size of a normal door.

The hand holding the Taser shook as I pulled open the door.

A feeling of dread and foreboding crawled over my skin as I shined the light inside the room—its beam bouncing erratically with my shaking hand..

It was then that I saw the luminescent objects built into the walls all around me.

Bones. Stacks and stacks of human bones.

They were everywhere, lying crisscrossed into tumbled mounds on the ground and formed into towering piles. Skulls with leering grins—some with teeth, others with them broken out—lined the walls in haphazard stacks around the border of the room.

Two lanterns were lit and provided a wavering, haunting light to the room which told me that there must be a breeze coming from somewhere. I stepped nearer to the lamps.

That's when I saw the body in the center of the room.

It was on its side, its hands tied in front, a wide band of metallic duct tape covering half the face.

The body moved, its eyes wide as they looked at me in terror.

It was Dezi White.

68

I fought my impulse to run to her.

I stepped closer and saw the knife on the ground beside her. I couldn't tell if she'd been stabbed. She looked at me with desperate hope. I saw no blood.

She was bait. Ben was here somewhere.

"Show yourself, Ben," I said in a clear voice. "It's over now."

Dezi whimpered and I fought not to look at her. I needed to stay alert. I had no idea from what direction he would attack.

Only the sounds of my breathing and Dezi's moans filled the small close space.

"I followed you, Ben. So I know it's you. You can't hide. And the cops are on their way. You might as well give—"

Before I'd finished my sentence, he materialized from behind a mound of bones, his face ghostly white.

"I can't believe you found me," he said.

I aimed the Taser at his chest. If it weren't for the fact that the knife was right there by Dezi—clearly evidence that I'd interrupted him just before he was about to kill her—I would have forced him to untie her. But with the knife right there, I didn't want him anywhere near her.

I might be able to kick the knife away but there was no way I could lean down and pick it up without him attacking. Just stepping any closer to Dezi might trigger a charge by him.

I was holding my phone in one hand and the Taser in the other. If I tried to call the cops I was sure he would attack. He must be thinking if he could disarm me, he could kill both me and Dezi. It was the only way he would walk out of here unscathed.

My hands and arms felt itchy and hot.

"Put your hands up," I said. He complied, but a small smile etched across his face.

"I need you to go outside and wait for the police in the alley," I said, praying my command would resonate with his lifelong habit of obeying adults. I honestly didn't care if he took the opportunity to run away. We could always catch him later. I just needed to remove the threat of here right now in this cave.

No such luck.

"No," he said.

"Well, your other option is that I can shoot you, Ben," I said. "And leave you writhing in agony with a fifty thousand volt electrical discharge up your butt. Your call."

"I don't think you'll shoot me. I'm a kid."

"Not from where I'm standing," I said.

Out of the corner of my eye I saw Dezi struggle to sit up and it heartened me to think she had the strength after two days to do even that much. If I could get us both out of this room with our lives, she stood a chance of only being scarred for life for what she'd endured at Ben's hands.

I made a point not to look at her. Taking my eyes off Ben even for a second was exactly what he was hoping for. There would be plenty of time to question her if I could get her—*get us*—out of this room alive.

Even though I was holding a weapon, I knew that was not at all guaranteed.

"You did all this over a Facebook post?" I said, stalling for time.

"You saw it?" Ben said, his breath catching in surprise. Then his eyes went to Dezi and the knife beside her. "She posted that picture of me and Mikayla knowing how much it would upset Ali."

He moved a few steps closer to Dezi and the knife.

"Please stay where you are," I said. "So you decided to kidnap her, kill her, and dump her in the river? Bit of an overreaction, wouldn't you say?"

"You didn't know Ali!" Ben said, turning to me, his eyes blazing with anger. "She was a goddess! She loved me and that...that bitch ruined it all." He turned and took another step toward Dezi.

"Wasn't it *you* who ruined it all, Ben?" I said quickly. "Didn't you do that when you stuck your tongue in Mikayla's ear?"

He turned on me, taking two steps toward me.

"Shut up!" he said. "I was drunk! It didn't mean anything!"

"Is that what you told Ali?" I said, holding the Taser up higher wondering if I could continue doing this long enough to wear one of us out.

And unfortunately having no doubt which one that would be.

"Ali didn't believe me because that bitch poisoned her against me!" Ben said as he launched himself at me without warning.

I was so startled I didn't even have time to find the trigger with my finger. He hit me full force, knocking the Taser out of my hand. My head smacked hard against the rock wall behind me.

Stars crawled across my brain as my head exploded in pain. I felt Ben's hands on my rain jacket as he jerked me off the ground and flung me into the nearest pyramid of bones and skulls across the room.

Somewhere in the back of my mind I heard him ranting like a soundtrack that was malfunctioning. It came and went, far away and then louder. It was all I could do to register it at all, let alone follow the plot.

"....ruined everything for me and Ali!...made sure....never would have died if not for you!...You killed her! No one will blame me....I'm going to kill you...kill you...kill you!"

The words swam in my brain as I tried to make sense of them until they were all finally, mercifully extinguished in one relieving black fog.

69

I t was the sounds of wailing that brought me out of my oblivion.

I don't know how long I was out but the fact that there was crying made me realize that whatever was happening was not over.

I struggled to move from where Ben had flung me. Groaning loudly, I turned, setting off a cascade of splintered bones skidding to the ground around me.

"Help me!" Dezi screamed.

I woke up quickly, fighting through sharp shards of pain as I tried to orient myself. The lighting from the lanterns shot irregular bursts of lamplight across the room. There was a body at the base of the far wall twenty feet away.

The body convulsed and then settled. Dezi screamed again.

I rubbed a hand across my eyes to try to see better in the gloom. My vision was cloudy and I felt a blaze of white agony stitch across my shoulder and down my side that took my breath away.

"Help me," Dezi said again, her voice laced with desperation and panic.

I turned my head and saw her in the flickering lamplight, the Taser in her hand still pointed at Ben—his body was the one on the floor. He groaned and jerked and let out a long moan.

Dezi must have been able to pick up the Taser when I dropped it.

Thank God for major miracles.

Except she was now out of ammunition. I had another cartridge in my shoulder bag which I was still wearing. I sat up painfully and gingerly reached for the buckle on my bag and nearly screamed.

"Dezi," I said, panting against the pain through gritted teeth. "I need you to come to me."

She collapsed to her knees, her shoulders shaking with sobs.

Ben lay only inches from her. His convulsions had stopped.

"Dezi!" I said firmly.

Just speaking shot daggers of agony into my side and shoulder. "Bring me the Taser. Do it now before he recovers!"

She ignored me, her sobs fading into tortured hiccoughs.

Cursing through the pain, I forced myself onto my knees. I spotted my phone on the floor by the door but I forced myself not to go for it.

Keeping Ben disabled was the first priority.

"Get away from him," I said as I tried again to open my purse with my good hand. The pain sliced up my arm, forcing me to stop.

Suddenly Ben's hand shot out and grabbed Dezi by the foot. She screamed and tried to shoot him again with the Taser. It clicked and clicked impotently.

"Bitch," he snarled. "I'll kill you for that."

I watched as he fumbled for the knife on the ground.

This was a nightmare coming to life in front of me. I was

about to see him stab Dezi to death and there was nothing I could do to stop it.

"Dezi!" I shouted. "Slide the Taser to me!"

She still had her hands tied in front of her and she dropped the Taser when he twisted around, pulling himself to his knees and grabbing her by the throat. He stood up slowly, his body taut with his violent fury as he pulled Dezi up onto her toes.

"Ali never would have dumped me," he said harshly into her face. "If not for you."

I felt the Taser hit my knee.

But it was too late.

Ben brought the hand with the knife to her neck. Dezi gave a small whimper as he pressed the blade to her throat.

I watched in horror as the relentless question of whether Dezi would survive was finally and at long last out of my hands.

70

T he only thing I could hope for now was to save my own life and make sure Ben paid the price for taking Dezi's.

With pain eclipsing my world, I slammed the cartridge into the Taser, my arm now numb as shock claimed my body. I raised and aimed the weapon and pulled the trigger. I saw the electrodes hit Ben's body, followed immediately by the fifty thousand volt pulse. His back arched violently as he convulsed in a ludicrous dance of lurching spasms.

The knife fell first, bouncing away, and then Dezi herself, who fell in a deadweight at his feet.

And finally Ben, his thrashing body lunging for the ground where he jerked and writhed in terrible spasms, the sounds coming from him nearly inhuman.

I dragged myself to Dezi first. The blood from where Ben had punctured her neck flowed freely but when her eyes flew open, I could see the wound was shallow.

"Put your hand on your throat to stop the blood," I said.

She raised both her hands, still bound, and felt for her throat.

"Listen to me, Dezi," I said. "I have no more cartridges. I need you to find my phone."

She nodded as if in a daze and crawled away from where Ben continued to seize and rock on the ground, his bladder emptying out on the cold pavers beneath him.

I forced myself to get to my feet, the effort prompting a sheen of sweat to develop on my cheeks in the ice-cold room. Dezi came back to me, my phone in her hands. It looked as if her neck wound had already stopped bleeding.

"Good girl," I said, huffing out a strained breath. "Let's do this outside. Can you walk?"

Her face flushed with emotion she turned to hobble through the small door of the bone-lined underground conduit to the room above and freedom.

Once outside, I called the police and then Dezi's mother before we made our way down the street to the nearest café opposite rue Froidevaux near the Claude-Nicolas Ledoux park. The idea briefly passed through my mind to wait in the alley for the police in case Ben recovered and tried to escape. But I was pretty sure I'd done enough for one sixty-year-old woman for one day.

If he escaped, the French police could bloody well track him down.

I was convinced my arm was broken—the pain was just too severe to be anything else. But once I got past the adrenalin rush of the past ten minutes and was sitting in a public café, I was able to move my arm without screaming.

By the time Jean-Marc made it onto the scene—literally minutes after the first wave of police cars and French SWAT team—Dezi was having a sobbing conversation with her mother on my cellphone. The proprietor of the café found a blanket to drape over her shoulders and brought both of us whiskies and cocoa.

When he arrived Jean-Marc sent his men to join the other police personnel outside the basement window in the alleyway and to the hidden room which I found out later really was a forgotten entrance to the Catacombs. He came over to the table where Dezi and I sat but I shooed him away.

"You can take our statements later," I said. "An ambulance is coming and I'm fine."

"You do not look fine," he said to me, but he was already walking toward the alleyway.

After that, Dezi was bundled into the back of an ambulance and a bossy but kind policewoman put me in the back of a police cruiser where I was able to watch them bring Ben out of the alley on a stretcher.

So at least I hadn't killed him.

Ben was young and strong. Although I don't know what kind of damage I might have done to his nervous system with a combined hit of one hundred thousand volts in less than five minutes it appeared that at least for now his heart was beating and his lungs were continuing to push air in and out.

After that, the policewoman took me to the police station. I'd have loved to have gone home to shower and change clothes first but I went along with the protocol.

Once at the station I was taken again to Jean-Marc's office where I promptly curled up on his sofa and napped on and off. I was presented with *palmiers, pâte à choux* and cappuccinos every half hour until Jean-Marc finally showed up.

He was tired but his face was wreathed in smiles.

Well, that's an exaggeration. This was Jean-Marc after all. But I could tell he was happy.

"The boy will live," he said.

"How's Dezi?" I asked.

"A strong girl. She has told us how Ben Kent came to her

house and said he knew where Ali was and then he took her to his secret hiding place."

"He was trying to get up his nerve to kill her, wasn't he?" I asked.

"I have every confidence he would've gotten there in the end," he said. "It was a miracle you found him."

"What about Mark White?" I asked. "Is he still in custody? Because Ben didn't kill those other girls."

"I'm afraid White is denying everything and we have nothing to hold him on."

I felt a tingle of frustration. I was very tired and I ached everywhere there was to ache. After everything I'd been through, I was in no mood for roadblocks. My shoulder hurt worse by the minute and I wondered if I'd rushed that clinical diagnosis of no broken arm.

"Did you at least get my coffee cup of DNA from him for Adele?" I asked him.

"He was very careful not to touch anything."

"That just proves he's who we think he is!" I said, wincing as I raised my voice which somehow seemed to connect with all the nerve centers in my shoulder.

"I agree with you. His being so careful reeks of guilt. But it is not proof. You are in pain, Claire."

"So you just let him go?"

"We will watch him." He stood next to me and lifted my hand gently.

I sucked in a sharp intake of breath.

"But this means he won't pay for what he did to Haley and Ali and Cecily," I said, feeling deflated and exhausted. With the exhaustion had clearly come the cold hard truth of my injuries.

"Come, *chérie*," Jean-Marc said. "You are going to the hospital."

71

It wasn't a bad fracture but just like you can't be a little bit pregnant, even a little fracture is still a broken bone. After Jean-Marc took me to the hospital to have the bones in my radius and ulna set, he drove me home.

The man literally put me to bed that night–not for the first time I might add—and active crime scene or not, he stayed with me until I fell asleep. I remember hearing his low voice as he explained to Geneviève what had happened tonight.

The next morning, I woke up to the fragrance of coffee in my kitchen and the feel of Izzy next to me in bed. I felt such an overwhelming sensation of being loved and cared for that tears pricked my eyes.

And then I tried to sit up and tears pricked my eyes for real.

"Ouch," I said as I carefully eased myself into a sitting position in bed. In seconds, Geneviève was in my bedroom, a steaming cup of coffee in her hands.

"How are you, *chérie*?"

"We found her in time," I said as I reached for the coffee mug with my good hand.

"Detective LaRue told me," she said with a smile. "*You*

found her in time."

I took a deep sip of the aromatic brew and felt a sense of well-being infuse me.

"How is your arm?" she asked.

"Hurts a little," I said. "Where's the baby?"

Geneviève nodded toward the dining room.

"Your parcels came from Amazon," she said. "Luc helped me put together the highchair."

"Luc?" I asked. "*Luc* was in my apartment?"

"He did not come into your bedroom, *chérie*. He just put together the baby's chair. Do you need help dressing or will you stay in bed today?"

I put the coffee mug on the nightstand and swung my legs out of bed. Instantly I felt the moment of impact when my feet hit the floor, my hips and legs screaming in unison. My head began to throb from where it had hit the stone wall when Ben had grabbed me, and my forearms protested where they'd been abraded and scraped when I'd been tossed into the bone pile.

Gingerly, I eased back into bed and closed my eyes.

"*Chérie?*"

"I'll need to get back to you on that," I said hoarsely, my entire body tingling in discomfort and outright pain. "Did Jean-Marc happen to leave a prescription for a painkiller before he left?"

Later that evening I sat in the living room with Geneviève and with little Robbie nestled in the crook of my good arm. Luc had dropped by with a bag of macarons and while he didn't come in to visit, I got the idea that he felt bad about how he'd acted this week.

Courtney called twice to reiterate to me that she was too young for her life to be over and she would be back soon for

Robbie. The next time I saw a call coming in from her, I let it go to voice mail, although a part of me did wonder, if she was having such a great time with Gunther in Heidelberg why she was calling so much?

Jean-Marc called too of course in his usual brief and no-nonsense style. I also got a call from Catherine but by then I was wearing out with all the virtual visits and so cut it short pleading weariness. My daughter didn't know much about my life in Paris and certainly nothing about this last case. As far as she was concerned, her sixty-year-old mother saying she was too tired to talk was absolutely believable.

I even got a thank-you call from Dezi and her mother. Dezi was polite but formal in her thanks and once she left the line, Audrey tried to apologize for her.

"She's still upset," she said.

"Of course she is," I said. "She went through a life-changing experience."

"I don't know everything that happened in that horrible cave," Audrey said to me on the phone, "but I know you were the one who found her. And for that I will be eternally grateful to you."

"I'm just sorry it took so long."

"I know her recovery will take a long time too," she said. "But I believe in time she'll be able to put it behind her."

I agreed because that's what a parent needs to hear but there was no way Dezi would ever be able to put what happened to her behind her. Those two days being held in a cave full of bones waiting to be murdered would define her for the rest of her life. I don't know who she would've become if it hadn't happened, but she was never going to be that person now.

"Mark and I have decided to help Dezi reframe her Paris experience," Audrey said. "We're moving back to the States at the end of the month."

I nearly dropped the phone when she said that. First of all, there was no way to *reframe* what had happened to Dezi even if you blew Paris off the world map.

And secondly, and maybe I should have led with this—because it's really the key takeaway to the news-bomb she'd just dropped—it meant a serial killer was moving to fresh territory.

I didn't know if Audrey was aware that I was the reason her husband had been brought in for questioning during Jean-Marc's search for Dezi—with regards to his involvement with the three dead girls. Probably not or she wouldn't have called me. I literally couldn't process the frustration and horror I felt at the thought of Mark White moving back to the States and continuing his reign of killing back there.

In any event, I wished Audrey well and we ended the conversation. I sat on the couch and thought of that family and what they were going through. Dezi would overcome this terrible experience or she wouldn't. I mentally wished her the best and prayed she'd find the kinds of therapy that would help her. Same with Audrey. The two days she'd endured believing her child was in the hands of a serial killer would scar her for life. But those were stories with a process and an end date. Nothing for me to do but pray for them.

Not so with Mark White.

I hate loose ends. Especially when one of those loose ends is a murdering psychopath.

The fact that Mark White was free after what he'd done bothered me incessantly. I'm not sure what doesn't bother me more is the fact that while Jean-Marc gives good lip service to feeling frustrated about that situation too, I don't think he really believes White is his serial killer.

I've asked him countless times: How do you account for the fact that no more girls have been snatched and murdered during the time you've had Mark White under tight scrutiny?

Jean-Marc won't answer that question but not, I think,

because he doesn't have an answer—I'm sure he thinks the real killer just moved onto somewhere else—but because he doesn't want to have this same, relentless conversation with me about it.

Besides, without evidence against White, what else can he or anybody do? It's a dead end. A sickening, frustrating dead-end with no way forward.

I shifted the baby's weight on my good arm and rearranged the sling on my broken one.

"Shall I take him, *chérie*?" Geneviève asked.

"No. You've already done more than anyone has a right to ask. And I knew you weren't thrilled with Robbie to begin with."

"What do you mean?"

"I mean, before you got recruited as a full-time daycare service, you didn't seem to want to be around him at all. I thought maybe he brought back bad memories for you or something."

"Oh, *chérie*. No. My memories of my boys as babies are all good, all sweet." She looked at Robbie and I saw her eyes were wet. "It is just sad to look backward sometimes," she said.

I reached out with my good hand and squeezed hers.

"And loving Robbie isn't looking backward," I said.

"*Exactement*," she said with a doting smile at him sleeping soundly in my arm.

When the next phone call came, I groaned before I saw who it was from.

"Let it go to voicemail," Geneviève urged me. "You have been through enough. It is time to rest."

But I'd seen the caller ID and knew I had to take the call.

I shifted Robbie gently onto the couch and cradled the phone to my ear.

"Hey, Jessica," I said. "I'm so glad you called."

72

A few days later things had calmed down enough that Geneviève didn't feel as if she needed to practically live with me. Mind you, she did need to take Robbie with her most of the time and only left him with me when she needed a break.

I hated that, except I did see how much she enjoyed the little guy. We both did. Even Izzy.

As for his mother, Courtney had recently gone radio dark which worried me. The prepaid cellphone had run out of minutes so I couldn't track or reach her through it.

And she'd stopped calling.

I cursed myself for not thinking to get Gunther's last name. I could've found him in fifteen minutes. But because Courtney had no credit cards of her own and with only Gunther's first name to go on and the fact that there were only about fifty thousand Gunthers living in Heidelberg—if the two of them were even still in Heidelberg—my chances of tracking her were practically nil.

I would just have to wait for her to resurface and hope for the best in the meantime.

Even after just a few days, my broken arm was considerably better and I very quickly found myself bored and restless. I'd broken my wrist the spring before and so was familiar with handling Izzy's leash with one hand while maneuvering myself downstairs without killing myself. Getting out for brief walks around the block with Izzy helped but I was soon ready to get back to work.

Jean-Marc clearly believed I didn't need regular appearances from him and so I had to be satisfied with his daily phone calls. I know our few meetings face to face couldn't have been as much fun for him as they were for me, since I tended to question him exhaustively about any new evidence there might be against Mark White.

Jean-Marc was being feted and lauded internally in the department for solving the Dezi White case. But it was still a blot on his record not to mention his reputation that he hadn't been able to close the *In-Seine Killer* case. I'd told him about my phone conversation with Audrey and how they were thinking of moving back Stateside and Jean-Marc assured me that a record of the Paris homicide department's suspicions would follow White and be transferred to the relevant law enforcement agency in the US.

Even so, it galled me no end to have done so much hard work to unmask this ruthless predator, only to see him walk away unpunished. I comforted myself with the knowledge that if Mark White did manage to somehow slip the chain and abduct another girl, with the heavy Paris surveillance he was under this time he'd have to use magic and time travel to do it.

At least until the end of the month when he would be free to kill again.

∽

One afternoon about a week after Dezi White had been

returned to her family, I was curled up on the couch trying to manage my TV remote control, a cup of tea, and keeping Robbie's bouncy chair going with my foot when a call came through from Jean-Marc.

"Hey, there," I said, answering the phone. He'd already called to check in on me this morning so the call was unexpected and instantly told me something was up.

"How's the arm?" he asked.

He always asked after my arm when he called and while on the one hand I of course appreciated it on the other I couldn't help but think that a small part of his asking was to remind me that I'd gotten hurt though my foolhardy actions.

"I'm good," I said. "How's everything on your end?"

"We have a break in the *In-Seine Killer* murders," he said casually.

I sat bolt upright.

"What's happened?" I asked breathlessly.

"A homeless man reported he was attacked two weeks ago at knifepoint," Jean-Marc said. "It seems he made an arrangement with an American to sell his semen and after completing his end of the bargain, he was attacked and barely escaped with his life."

"Oh my gosh!" I shouted, scaring the baby and prompting him to burst into tears. "Jean-Marc, you got him!"

I unbelted Robbie from his bouncy chair with one hand and picked him up while pressing the phone to my ear.

"It appears we do," Jean-Marc said. "We brought White in very early this morning and were able to demand a DNA sample. Within the hour, we had a match for the DNA found under both Ali Burton and Haley Johnson's fingernails."

Tears stung my eyes. I couldn't believe it. After all this.

"Did you get a confession?" I asked breathlessly.

"We did," Jean-Marc said. "To all three girls."

The sheer pleasure of his words crashed over me in a wave of joy and vindication.

We got him!

"...is even now in the process of attempting to work out a deal with our prosecutor."

"Wait. What?" I said. My throat constricted. "Why?"

"White says there are more locations of more bodies."

My shoulders sagged under the news and my arm began to hurt when it had been pain-free all morning.

I knew how valuable that sort of information was to relatives who were agonizing over their missing loved ones. And I would never deny them that relief no matter how meager. But it was still painful to think of Mark White getting a softer sentence for his crimes.

"Oh," I said, giving Robbie a kiss as he settled down in my good arm. "That's good, I guess."

"Unfortunately," Jean-Marc said, "we don't have any missing persons that fit the victim profile. But we are in communications with other areas of France."

"So do you think he's making it up?" I asked, trying not to get my hopes up.

"I think there's a certain amount of desperation involved," Jean-Marc said. "After all, if they have nothing tangible to offer to make a deal, she will go to prison for life."

I nearly dropped the baby.

"What did you say?"

"Oh, chérie, did I not make it clear? Both DNA matches and the homeless man's identification are for Audrey White."

It took me a while to digest that little bombshell, but once I did so much made sense to me. Audrey's weird long-sleeve blouse in the heat of summer when everyone else was wearing sleeveless or short sleeve outfits for one. She was probably hiding scratches from her attack on poor Ali. And of course Deb Knox aside I'd definitely been working against my own bias that a woman was capable of this kind of serial killing.

I would have to work on that in future.

"Any idea why she did it?" I asked.

"Early psychiatric reports we were able to access suggest she had an abusive mother," Jean-Marc said.

"Don't tell me," I said. "One who was blonde and pretty?"

"How did you guess?"

"I'm absolutely flabbergasted, Jean-Marc."

"She also confessed that after killing Ali she was so frustrated at screwing up her own MO that she had decided to take two girls next time."

"That's horrible. What stopped her?"

"Dezi was taken."

"Ah, I guess a kidnapped daughter will at least temporarily trump even the most sinister of murder plans."

"*Évidemment.*"

"So just to clarify, are you saying this homeless guy just wandered in off the street and made a complaint to the cops about being assaulted?"

"Ah, *non*," Jean-Marc said, a smile in his voice. "I might have taken your suggestion to bring in a few homeless men from around the Latin Quarter for questioning."

"It takes a big man to give credit where it's due," I said with a laugh.

"If I have not said it before now," Jean-Marc said, suddenly very serious, "thank you for your help. We wouldn't have found Dezi without you and we would likely not have found the *In-Seine Killer* without you either."

Whoa. When Jean-Marc finally lays it on, he does it with both barrels.

"We did it as a team," I said, a little breathless with embarrassment. "Anyway, please keep me informed. Nothing in this life would be more satisfying than to hear she goes away for life."

"You know I will, *chérie*."

"Oh, before you hang up, did you ever find out what Potter was hiding on his computer?"

"He had videos he'd taken of some of the girls from a peephole in the girl's locker room."

"That does not surprise me. Did he ever wake up?"

"He did. He's being moved to a long-term care facility outside Paris."

"Not as good as prison."

"Not to worry. It is a public health facility and I'm afraid it's not very nice."

"Karma, baby."

"Just so. And speaking of karma, Eric Watson was charged today with disturbing the peace."

"What was he doing? Partying too hard with one of his underage girlfriends?"

"He had a series of torture videos playing on a constant loop in his spare bedroom."

"What a sicko. And that's all you were able to charge him with? Disturbing the peace?"

"Unfortunately watching snuff movies or torture videos is not illegal. But the charge against him was *accidentally* leaked to his place of work and I understand he is now unemployed and returning to the U.S. with what is substantively a sexual-deviant footnote to his record."

"Well done, Jean-Marc! That's great! How did you catch him?"

"Neighbors complained about hearing what they said sounded like 'unusual lovemaking' coming from his apartment."

"Wow. You've really been busy in the tying-up-loose-ends department. Any news on Ben?"

I'd heard that Ben had survived the trauma of our encounter in the anteroom of the catacombs and was being held in juvenile detention before his trial for kidnapping, attempted murder and aggravated assault.

"He admitted to tipping Maurice Dubonnet off that you were the one who set the cops on him even going so far as to show him a photo of you. When Dubonnet saw you when you were on your way to break into the school, he decided to exact a little retribution."

"Wow," I said. "That Ben is a little stinker."

"For what it's worth, he seems contrite," Jean-Marc said.

"Anybody sitting where he's sitting would be."

"I take back what I said about you being too soft."

"When did you ever say that?"

"How's the baby?"

"Oh, good one, Jean-Marc. *Touché* as you people say. Don't you have work to do?"

He laughed. "As it happens, I do. But before I go, I've been meaning to ask you, do you have a permit for that Taser?"

73

Two weeks after Dezi had been found and a week after Audrey White had been taken into custody and charged with three homicides, life had lapsed into a version of normalcy for me. Luc had taken to coming by to drop off a bag of macarons for me most afternoons. I'm not sure whether it was the experience of dating Courtney that reminded him that he could do a lot worse than me or if he was genuinely sorry for his appalling behavior last spring. In any case, I like macarons.

There was still no word from Courtney and I was now officially worried. I'd done some preliminary searching online but had much less to work with than I usually did. Because Courtney was recently arrived in Europe she had no contacts that I could follow up on. And because she had no money and no credit cards, and now no phone, it was like she'd vanished off the face of the earth.

There wasn't a time when I picked up Robbie, changed him, fed him, or tucked him into his stroller for a spin around the block that I didn't wonder if he would ever see his mother again.

Because of my arm, Geneviève and I had taken to having most of our meals together and I found it a very pleasant ritual. Tonight I went downstairs to her place for a light supper.

A *light supper* means something different to French people. We had a rich cheese soufflé that was offset with a simple but exquisite green salad. And of course bread. And wine. And cheese afterward. With coffee. And a slice of raspberry tart.

In addition to Geneviève doing all the cooking almost all of Robbie's care was on her shoulders at the moment too. It was all very good to talk about *should I keep him?* when I wasn't doing any of the heavy lifting.

After dinner this evening Geneviève and I sat in her living room and watched an old mystery on television. Robbie was asleep in his baby bed in her bedroom—I'd ordered two beds for him last week so he could have one at her place—and Izzy was curled up between us on the couch.

"So the *In-Seine Killer* is unmasked, yes?" Geneviève said as the show we were watching went to commercial.

The news about Audrey White had been all over the media for days now. I felt a bit guilty for what Mark and Dezi must be going through—after they'd already gone through so much—but I hadn't reached out to them. Although I wasn't named in the media reports, there had been references to an American private investigator who'd assisted the Paris police in appre-hending Audrey White. And while it's true Dezi's mother had made her own bed, I didn't imagine Dezi or her father would welcome a call from me about how I had helped make her lie in it.

"Yes, finally," I said. "She tried to make a deal but couldn't come up with anything the prosecutors wanted. So she'll go to prison for life."

"Well done, *chérie*."

"It was a miracle," I said. "I had literally nothing to go on except guesses and instinct."

"As usual, you sell yourself short."

"What are we going to do with this baby?" I asked her suddenly.

"You think his mother will not return?"

"I don't know. You think we should just go forward and hope she does?"

"What other choice do we have?"

Oh, we had choices. But I appreciated the fact that Geneviève didn't seriously consider any of them. It made me feel like I wasn't totally alone in deciding Robbie's future.

Although, of course I was.

"I wonder what your sons would think of you raising another child at your age?" I said in as nonchalant a manner as I could muster.

"I am sure they would not be surprised," she said. "I made no secret of my desire to be a grandmother."

"But you're not?" I asked.

"*Non*. My boys did not marry."

I tried to do the math on how old her sons must be—probably in their fifties if not older. I was sorry that Geneviève didn't give me a reason for why her sons didn't marry but she didn't offer one and I felt I'd encroached on her memories enough. At least for tonight.

If she'd been an American, I'd have dug until I'd found out everything there was to know. But the French held their cards closer to the vest than we do in America. I'd known Geneviève a full year and considered her to be my very dearest of friends. But in her mind, I was a recent addition on her emotional landscape. As much as I knew she cared about me, I was too new a friend to trust completely.

I was more tired than usual tonight—doing nothing for hours on end will do that to you—and so made my excuses as soon as our show ended. Geneviève wouldn't hear of me trying to help with the dishes, and with my sling it would've been noisier and taken longer for her to do it anyway. So I kissed her goodnight and took Izzy and my broken arm upstairs to our apartment.

Once home, I showered and got in my pajamas and went to bed with a good book, a final glass of wine, and some pleasant music on the Home Pod until I was ready to turn the lights out.

I was just about to close my book and shut down for the night when I heard my phone ring. Because of the time difference, a late night call could always be Catherine. I glanced at the clock on the fireplace mantel. Eleven-thirty Paris time was five-thirty Atlanta time.

But when I picked up my phone the screen read UNKNOWN CALLER.

Frowning, I answered anyway.

"This is Claire."

"Hello, Claire," a warm male voice poured out onto the phone line. "I thought it was time we finally talked."

It was him.

I knew it for sure and I knew instantly. I knew it as if I'd heard his voice every day of my childhood which I certainly never had.

My father.

To follow more of Claire's sleuthing and adventures, watch for the release of *Ménage à Murder, Book 4 of An American in Paris Mysteries!*

AUTHOR'S NOTES

Paris Catacombs

The Catacombs of Paris hold the remains of more than six million people in an underground network built to consolidate Paris' ancient stone quarries. Extending south from the Barrière d'Enfer, the former city gate, this ossuary was created as part of the effort to eliminate the city's overflowing cemeteries.

The ossuary remained largely forgotten until it became a place for concerts and parties in the early 19th century. After renovations and the creation of accesses around Place Denfert-Rochereau in 1874 the ossuary was open to the public. Today, the Catacombs is considered a popular tourist destination, especially around Halloween, and of course a wonderful setting for any murder mystery.

Bois de Boulogne

At over two thousand acres and the second-largest park in Paris and located along the western edge of the 16th arrondissement of Paris, the land for the Bois de Boulogne was given to the city of Paris by the Emperor Napoleon III in 1852 for a public park. The park features an English landscape garden with several lakes and a cascade; two smaller botanical and landscape gardens, a zoo and amusement park, two horse race tracks, and a tennis stadium where the French Open tennis tournament is held each year. It is not very good for skateboarding.

The River Seine

The Seine flows right through the heart of Paris bordering 10 of the 20 arrondissements and is still the chief commercial waterway and the source of half of the water used in Paris.

There are thirty-seven bridges on the river in Paris, some of them more impressive than others. The Oldest bridge is the Pont Neuf (New Bridge). In the spring or summer there are many spots along the Seine to hang out under the willow trees or sunbathe on the stone embankments. Naturally, the Seine is a perfect place to dump dead bodies should that become necessary.

Notre Dame Cathedral

Notre-Dame de Paris or "Our Lady of Paris" is a medieval Catholic cathedral situated on the Île de la Cité in the 4th arrondissement. The most visited monument in Paris with roughly 12 million visitors a year Notre-Dame is definitely one of the most widely recognized symbols of the city of Paris.

Construction on Notre-Dame began in 1160 and was completed by 1260, although it has been renovated and repaired many times over the centuries. Considered one of the finest examples of French Gothic architecture, the cathedral is famous for its flying buttress, and its enormous rose windows.

On April 15, 2019 a structure fire broke out beneath the roof, destroying the roof and spire and damaging its windows and vaulted ceilings.

ABOUT THE AUTHOR

USA TODAY Bestselling Author Susan Kiernan-Lewis is the author of *The Maggie Newberry Mysteries,* the post-apocalyptic thriller series *The Irish End Games, The Mia Kazmaroff Mysteries, The Stranded in Provence Mysteries,* and *An American in Paris Mysteries.*

Visit www.susankiernanlewis.com or follow Author Susan Kiernan-Lewis on Facebook.

Made in the USA
Middletown, DE
19 September 2022

10805283R00201